Cow Across America

COW

ACROSS AMERICA

DALE NEAL

NOVELLO festival PRESS

CHARLOTTE,
NORTH CAROLINA
2009

Published in the United States by
Novello Festival Press, Charlotte, North Carolina

Design and composition by Jacky Woolsey,
Paper Moon Graphics, Inc.

Printed in the United States of America

Library of Congress Cataloging-in-Publication Data
Neal, Dale.
    Cow across America / by Dale Neal.
        p. cm.
    ISBN 978-0-9815192-3-4
        1. Storytelling—Fiction. 2. Grandparent and child—Fiction.
3. Fathers and sons—Fiction.   I. Title.
PS3614.E236C69 2009
813'.6—dc22
                                        2009026136

For my grandfathers,
    Raymond Eller *and* Beckum Neal

And my father who made me his namesake.

WHISTLE

Two weeks shy of turning ten, Dwight Martin wrote his first novel. It took most of the morning, far longer than he would have believed, and his finger hurt where the pencil had pressed a saddle-shaped callous against the knuckle, but he kept writing, filling the blue-ruled pages of a wire-bound notebook, nodding slowly as his sentences raced toward the red margins. He wrote about Africa, how the brave Brits of the Zanzibar Rifles battled seven-foot Zulu warriors in ostrich plumes and leopard skin loincloths. On the notebook's cover, Dwight had written NOVEL in monumental letters then drew besieged British snipers who aimed at hostile tribesmen swarming the sides of the *N* and the *L*. Inside the notebook, the battle raged back and forth, page after page, bullets and spears flying, with heroes and cowards, and even a minor love interest in the daughter of the regimental commander. His saga had reached seventeen pages when the unspeakable happened.

The No. 2 Black Warrior pencil broke.

Dwight tried to scrape away the wood with his thumbnail, succeeding only in getting a splinter in the quick. He sucked at his stinging thumb and his eyes watered. The words on the eighteenth page of his novel ended in a smudge and a rip in the paper itself, the work ruined.

Decades later as a grown man, Dwight Martin would still wince at the memory of this childish moment, a tiny foretaste of all the failures, disappointments, regrets, rejections that follow through any life. It always happened with the slightest slip, the smallest tear in the story he was trying to tell himself was his true life, the hero he wanted to imagine himself.

Dwight would grit his teeth and shake his head doggedly until he felt like his neck would snap, as if trying to throw those terrible doubts clear of his suddenly too-small skull. And as an almost ten-year-old, just as later when he was grown, it always felt the same, like the end of the world or at least the world where he wanted to be.

Now in that summer long ago, he was stuck at his grandparents' farm, far from home and any hope of fun. The snow-capped Kilimanjaro that towered over his novel turned here to dumpy mottled hills. No herds of grazing giraffe, zebra and wildebeest roamed this end of North Carolina, only a brown cow poking its broad head through the barnyard fence. No British colonel or Zulu chieftain, only his grandfather in a rocker at the end of the porch.

The old man didn't bother to rock, but slunk deep in his seat, heavy boots splayed. His jawbones were always working in his wrinkled face, back teeth and tongue going over the remnants of his last meal, ruminating much as the cow munching her cud by the fence line.

Dwight hopped off the porch swing where he had been writing, embarrassed any time he had to ask for help from a relative stranger like his grandfather.

"You got a pencil sharpener?"

He couldn't bring himself to say "Pop," at least not to the old man's wrinkled face. Dwight thought it sounded too childish for someone approaching ten. "You" was about as personal as Dwight wanted to get.

"Say what?" Pop cupped his jug ear where a thick plastic hearing aid whined on the earpiece of his spectacles.

His mother accused Dwight of mumbling, always urging him to speak up, enunciate, no baby talk since he was turning ten. So he was almost yelling. "See? My pencil. It broke!"

"So it did." Pop nodded, finally getting his bifocals fixed on the boy's dilemma. Lifting a thin haunch and digging deep in a hip pocket, Pop produced a folding knife with a bone handle. With a snap of his skinny wrist, he flicked open the blade and went to work on Dwight's pencil.

"Here you go."

Dwight stared at the mutilated pencil the old man handed back. The once perfect conical point had been hacked into uneven facets, exposing the graphite core. When he tried to write with it, the uneven tip broke when Dwight bore down. Now page eighteen had two smudges. It was all ruined.

What he was writing was stupid anyway, since all he knew about Africa came from Tarzan and Jungle Jim movies. He'd never been there, and he'd never go, not in a million years. His mother would never allow it. "Mom, I'm off to Africa," Dwight could say and she would reply, "No, you're not," and make him go to the mountains.

There was nothing in these mountains but old rocks and old people. No playgrounds here, no swing sets or sliding boards, let alone anyone his age to play with, only the hunkering hills, the brown creek and the brown cow, which terrified him. And at night, he had to lay under so many quilts and blankets that his grandmother spread over the lumpy mattress—in case he got cold, never mind it was the height of summer—so much cover that he could barely breathe. He lay awake and listened to the creek, which flowed all day by the house and even more through the night, and he thought he heard voices in the water, like the midnight murmurings of his mother and father through the bedroom wall . . . *Can't you take some time off? Not for two weeks this time, not with this project, besides it's your family . . . But you work all the time now . . . Overtime, it's adding up for us. . . .*

But Dwight couldn't be sure of what he heard and what he didn't. Even his teachers asked in exasperation if he couldn't understand plain English. "Dwight, didn't you hear me tell the class to put up your paper and take out your math books? What are you doing?"

When he surrendered his paper, a story he'd made up about a lost kingdom, the class tittered. And his teacher frowned at what he done. When she ripped the paper in half, Dwight felt that tearing go through him. Dwight understood he must be on guard. He had learned to write very small with his left arm hooked around the top of the notebook, ready to cover his tales of empires, ancient warriors and beautiful princesses.

His grandfather clasped his blade and pocketed the knife. "Never seen a boy so keen on his letters. What have you been writing?"

"Nothing." Dwight shut the suspect notebook.

"School work, huh?"

"No. Just a story."

"Why, that's something. Stories are always something."

The old man fell quiet. The brown creek rolled down by the house. A car came by. He waved. High over the back of Buckeye Mountain, a hawk whistled in the air. A breeze slid down the mountain, rustling the sides of the hemlocks like an invisible giant running his hand through the fur of the world. It might have been fifteen minutes or forever when the old man spoke again.

"So, you got some favorite stories?"

"I dunno. Adventures, I guess."

"True or made up or maybe a little of both?"

Dwight wasn't sure how to answer. It was okay to make up stories on paper so long as you didn't tell anyone. Stories you told people had to be true, especially your teacher or your father, or you could get in big trouble. But before the boy could come up with the right answer, the old man asked a different question.

"See that road there? Know where it heads?"

Dwight squinted at the narrow two lanes that ran from the sunshine into the shadows between the mountain and the creek. "Home," he wanted to say, since it was the way his mother had driven him for two hours.

"That very road," announced the old man, "that goes all the way west if you keep walking and don't stop."

He pointed in the opposite direction across the yard, toward the barnyard. "See that cow? When I was a boy about your age—wait, how old are you anyhow, boy?"

"Ten in two weeks."

"Well, maybe I was a little older than you, but I had me a buddy then who took a notion to take this cow," he nodded at the bovine in the barnyard, "well, not that very cow, but one looked just like her, and we would go down that road a spell."

"So?" the boy said, uncertain where all this was going.

"Bet you didn't know my buddy's name was Dwight." Pop slyly smiled.

"That's my name!"

"Yes, and it belonged to Dwight Sparks before you. Matter of fact, your mother might never have told you this, but you were named after him."

Dwight had always been under the impression that he had been named for the recent president of the United States. In the baby pictures, he possessed a passing resemblance to the famous Ike everyone liked, given the mutual lack of hair.

"You know how far me and Dwight went down that road with that cow?"

"How far?"

"California. You heard tell of it?"

Of course, he'd heard of California. That was where his father flew off to work now, and where Disneyland was. On Sunday nights, he watched the show on their black-and-white television where Tinkerbell always tapped her wand on the turrets of the magic Castle, and Disneyland exploded with what would be colorful fireworks in real life.

"Yessir, all the way to California, two boys and a cow." The old man gazed down the road. "You'd be interested in a story like that?"

"Sure."

"How much money you got?"

Dwight dug into the pocket of his shorts. Just that morning, Gram had given him a dime and a hug, and a promise of more bright coins if he would give her some sugar every night. Dwight didn't like to kiss his grandmother. Her skin was wrinkled and sour-smelling beneath the sweet honeysuckle scented powder she wore. Her breath was stale too, from the teeth she could take in and out of her mouth. Dwight's mother warned him never to say anything about Gram's teeth and not to wrinkle his nose when he pecked her cheek.

"That's all? Guess it'll have to do." The old man plucked the coin from his small palm, and slipped it into one of the bib pockets of his overalls. "Don't look so hurt. A dime's cheap for this story. How much you pay, two bits, to see one of them motion pictures?"

"Fifty cents for the matinee," Dwight corrected his grandfather.

"Well, this story cost me a bit more than a dime to learn it since I had to live through it. Everything comes at some cost and if you can get off paying no more than the money in your pocket, count yourself a lucky fellow."

The old man scratched at his chin where he never shaved on Saturday, a rasping sound that the boy could hear. Pop started rocking, as if to find the momentum to launch his tale.

———

I probably knowed Dwight Sparks all my life and most of his, except for the two years he was born ahead of me. He lived up the next holler, came to church some and school about as often, but I can't say that I paid him much mind, nor he, to me. He had no daddy nor mama, but lived with a pair of maiden aunts on a rundown farm in an unpainted house. I'm not sure they did much farming except for a garden. Mostly, they went and gathered 'sang and herbs, traded in chicken and eggs, and lived off wild game. By the time he turned twelve, he'd already brought down bucks, bear and turkey. They never went without, living back of the holler, though they were thin folk.

Like I said, I paid him no mind, until one day I was walking home after school let out. Dwight leapt off a rock at the bend with an Indian whoop and down I went.

"Hey Wylie," said Dwight, sitting pretty as you please on my spine.

"Hey Dwight." I spat grit and gravel from the road.

"You like rasslin', Wylie?"

"Only when I win."

I squirmed but he had me pinned good. Dwight was two years older than me, a head taller, and even thin as he was, had more muscle than me. I couldn't budge him from my back.

"Okay, 'Uncle.' I said it. We rassled. You win."

But Dwight wasn't ready to let me up yet. "Been meaning to compliment you on your cow. That's one fine heifer you got."

"Thank you." I was having a hard time getting air with no room for my ribs to move. I ate me a little more dirt as he propped his elbow on the back of my neck.

"Give me that cow, I might let you up."

"Ivy ain't for sale."

My Ivy was fully grown now, clean-limbed and as calm a cow as a body might meet. I could see me a blue ribbon and cash prize at the county fair come fall. Dwight Sparks wasn't going to steal that, no way.

"I don't care how long you sit on top of me. I ain't giving you my cow." I struggled mightily, but he took his leisure on my backbone like it was my mama's parlor sofa.

"Thinking of making a little trip out west," Dwight allowed. "Could use me some provisions. Wasn't sure what I could eat on the way. Then I thought why not take the farm with me, or at least a milk cow. I could be drinking milk across the Mississippi, Missouri, milk all the way down into Mexico. Throw a sack of milk over her back, walk her a ways, and then I'd have soft cheese churned. Then about the time I got to the desert, might get a little tired of milk and cheese, might like me a little beefsteak."

Eat Ivy? The thought so shocked me, it sent a jolt through my body, big enough to spring Dwight from my spine. I rolled away quick so he couldn't climb back on.

"You ain't gonna eat my cow, ever!"

And I ran home.

You better believe I had my eye on Dwight Sparks after that. I kept looking over my shoulder, making sure he wasn't going to jump me again. Course, Dwight was crafty. Next morning, on the way to school, around the same bend, I passed by a hickory tree, and stepped over its roots as I always did, when suddenly the tree seemed to grow an extra high root. Too late I saw it was a dungaree leg and down I went. But this time, Dwight didn't descend upon me. Instead, he jerked me up and brushed me off. "Best watch where you're going, Wylie."

He slung his arm around my shoulder. I didn't want his sympathy, but his grip was so tight I couldn't shrug him off either. "For a little guy, you're a pretty good wrassler. I didn't want a repeat of yesterday."

The cove's children were streaming into the open doors of the Beaverdam schoolhouse. Any moment now the schoolmarm, Miss Eller, was going to hoist her cowbell and clang her class to commence.

"I got a better idea than the one yesterday. Why don't you and the cow go west with me?"

"Why west?"

Dwight Sparks looked like I should know better than ask. "You heard tell of Pelham Humphries? How he went west after he killed a man?"

That was a fact well known at this late date around Beaverdam. I'd seen Pelham's place once when I was cutting winter wood with my daddy. The horse pulled the sledge into a clearing over the mountain. We came across a rock chimney holding up one end of a collapsed cabin. My daddy kicked away the leaves and the dirt with the edge of his boot, and there was a plank door like it led down to the devil's own house. The letters GTT were carved in the wood. Gone to Texas, was what my daddy said it meant.

"He fled west in the dark," Dwight was saying. "Went down to Texas and struck oil is what I heard tell. Killed himself a couple of Comanche, consorted with loose ladies and drank up whiskey like water. We could head for Texas too. Think about it, Wylie. You, me, the cow. Texas." He went off whistling, pleased as could be.

I listened to that whistle, from the back of the classroom all the school day, soft and faint like bird-song, what birds sounded like out west, I bet. The teacher heard it as well, lifting her head, but she never could quite determine if the whistle was made by one of her flighty students, or one of the winged creatures flocking out the open window. It was nearing spring, and the weather was warming. Beaverdam Creek was running high with thaw of the snow patches on the ridge tops, the woods were wet, the roads were mud. Soon we'd be shed of rough shoes and running barefoot through new grass.

I kept hearing that whistle in the back of the room, and in the back of my mind, Dwight's proposition. Why not west? My mind wandered off my multiplication tables and soon I was figuring how many miles it would be out to Texas, and how many days until the end of school.

"Wylie Rominger!"

I shook my head, I knew my own name, particularly when it got called a couple of times out loud.

"Wylie, pay some mind when I'm talking to you."

"Yes'm." I stood by my desk, the whistle in the back of the room now replaced by titters from the girls.

"What is the answer, if you please?"

"True," I guessed.

"What?"

"Two?"

"Wylie Rominger, come up here."

I went up and didn't yell or nothing to give her the satisfaction, but returned to my seat, with the stinging in my palm where she gave me the swat of her ruler.

After the clock struck the last hour on her desk, she yelled at us to behave and exit like ladies and gentlemen, and everyone ran whooping from the schoolroom, raising a cloud of dust from the plank floors in the afternoon light.

I went looking for Dwight by the same hickory tree where he'd tripped me this morning, this time, careful not to let him catch me off guard. I'd heard the whistle coming from the tree. I peered around the big trunk, then felt a nut hit my noggin hard.

Dang squirrels, I thought. Then I heard that whistle once more. I jumped with my back to the trunk, lest Dwight tackle me from behind. Then another nut crowned me.

"Oww!"

"Up here." Dwight slowly skinned the cat from the branch overhanging my aching head. "You're getting a bit better, Wylie. But you best get even better. Indians would steal your scalp out west."

I punched his belly and he dropped to the ground, doubled over with more laughter than pain from my half-hearted blow.

"There ain't no trees out west for the Indians to hide in," I argued.

"Oh, and just how far west have you been, Wylie?" he fired back.

Only to Boone, but never beyond. A morning's walk into town, and driving the wagon back with provisions, salt and needles, bananas and such, anything we didn't raise or make for ourselves back of Beaverdam.

"Far enough," I lied.

You would have thought I punched Dwight's belly once more the way he bent over double, laughing and wiping his eyes again. "That's rich, Wylie. You're going to be good for laughs along the way."

Still, I had my doubts. "What if we get lost? How do you know the way west?"

"Follow the sun." He poked his finger toward the horizon where Buckeye Bald sloped down to George's Gap and the River Ridge. A few hours and the sun would drop right snug into that notch and the night begin.

"And if it clouds up?"

"Wylie, didn't you know I got me a built-in compass? Watch this." He closed his eyes and his arm, like a whirligig, pointed out all the cardinal points of the compass: east, west, north, south and points in between.

"You can do that standing here in the place where you grew up, but what about when we get somewhere we ain't ever seen before?"

"Blindfold me then." Dwight handed me a bandanna from his hip pocket and wadded it into my palm. The rag was cruddy and probably smelled bad, but I wasn't putting it on my face. I tied it about his eyes.

"Hang on." I wiped my hands on my britches leg. I grabbed his shoulders and gave him a few good spins until he was unsteady on his feet. "Now which way's north?"

He righted himself and got his bearings. His tongue wet his lips. He seemed to sniff the air, as if north had a different smell to it. The wind wasn't from anywhere I could tell, but then he raised his arm and pointed true. "O.K., southwest." Again he seemed to sniff the air, and then his finger told the right direction. Too easy. I spun him again, and stepped back. "So, show me south."

Maybe he could feel the weight of the sun on his face, finding east and west that way. So I kept spinning him, and started calling off all the between points, south southwest, east northeast, and everything else I could think of. He just kept smiling and sniffing and pointing every which way right as far as I could tell.

Finally I run out of all the directions I knew, except one. "Due west."

Dwight grinned, then he pointed straight at me, and took the bandanna from his eyes. "You and me, bud, and let's not forget that milk cow of yours. What say, Wylie?"

"I'll study on it." I started for home, hearing that whistling in my ears.

I had my chores to do before supper and plenty of time to think while I refilled the kindling box by the back door for the cookstove, scattered the feed to the hens, slopped the hog, then settled down to milk Ivy. She was a good heifer who never kicked or backed a hoof in the milk and she knew the feel of my hands on her teats. I set my stool and positioned the pail. Leaning my forehead against her flank, I could hear the workings of her four stomachs as the warm milk squirted and sang against the tin sides of the pail slowly filling to the brim.

I closed my eyes and thought of miners, cowboys and Indians, fur trappers and buffalo hunters, all the folks who lived and roamed the west. I had a cow and was but a boy, but I wasn't a cowboy. You had to have a horse and a big hat for that line of work. What if we went on past Texas and through the desert, struck gold in California? Imagine coming home to Beaverdam with a big hat and horses and pockets full of gold. Seashells too, since the Pacific Ocean ran right up on the shores of the U.S. and I'd never seen salt water before. You couldn't drink it, but still I wondered what it would taste like. And I never seen a desert where nothing grew and I heard tell the mountains were even bigger out west than in Beaverdam, and wouldn't that be a sight to see once in your life?

"Well, girl, what do you think?"

And Ivy shifted her weight and lowed.

The bucket was about to run over and she must have been getting sore—I'd about milked her dry I'd been thinking so long and hard. I put Ivy in her stall for the night and closed the barnyard gate behind me and headed for the house. The last light glowed in the wavering windows of the house and a sliver of moon no bigger than your fingernail hung high over the Frozenhead Mountain. The sky turned as white as what I carried slopping in the pail, the light all milked out of the day. And I had to stop in the yard and remember how to breathe. I was so filled with love for this place, this house I knew and the family who raised me, brothers and sisters, mama and father, every tree and every rock that had watched me through so many years right down to this moment. I had to gasp and even as I did, I knew I had to go west with Dwight.

The next day at school, we didn't trade a word before the bell rang, but before long I heard that whistle, soft from the back of the class, the three notes of a whippoorwill. And I pursed my lips and repeated the three notes.

I grinned over my shoulder. Dwight cocked his forefinger at me and pulled the trigger, blew imaginary smoke off the barrel, and holstered his fancied firearm. Desperadoes, me and him.

"Are there birds in this room or children trying to learn better?" Miss Eller demanded and we bent to our school learning, but not for long. I kept the whistling all inside.

—

The old man pursed his lips and suddenly the three notes of a bird-song flew through the air, fifty years later, right over his grandson's head.

"You can whistle, can't you?" Pop asked.

Dwight pursed his lips and blew but nothing came out except blubbering breath.

"No, like this." The old man opened his mouth and showed how to roll the tongue.

Dwight stuck his finger in his mouth and tried to get his tongue to roll. Then he pressed it against the back of his teeth, but maybe his tongue was too fat or his teeth too small. He couldn't get much more than the whistle that the wind makes and not a bird.

"We'll have work on that," Pop suggested.

"Supper," sang Gram through the screen door.

The old man rose with a loud creak of his knees. "You hungry?"

His stomach growled, but he wanted to know more about this Wylie who was his grandfather when he was younger and about this other Dwight who shared his name but seemed more heroic and knowing and grown-up than the boy could ever imagine himself. If that was really his namesake, Dwight sounded more interesting and more fun than the President of the United States. And how did you get west? Did you really have to walk the whole way? No cars, he guessed, back then, but didn't they have covered wagons? Could you have a covered wagon with a cow, he wondered? And weren't they afraid of Indians and how long did it take back in olden days to get anywhere?

All during supper, Dwight chewed over these questions with a mouthful of mashed potatoes.

His mother and grandmother kept up their constant conversation, which never seemed to have ended since the car pulled over the bridge. Dwight tuned out this talk of people. Gram was catching his mother up to date on all her classmates and her kin and everyone she had ever met in her youth. Whenever she posed a question about Dwight's father, his mother gently deflected the thrust. "Oh, Gary's been working hard. A lot of overtime."

So this must be undertime, Dwight thought, submerged in hours, minutes dripping slowly, the slow flood of summer days. He stirred the food on his plate into a map of the West. Here in the mountains of mashed potatoes, they crossed a river of gravy and through the forest of green beans, traveled the plains of creamed corn, and over to the fat fried California of spare-rib.

"Quit playing with your food and eat it, please."

Dwight started shoveling, and after he cleared his plate, he asked to be excused.

"What, don't you want any cake, no banana pudding?" Gram asked.

Dwight thought of a Pacific Ocean of meringue, but he was full and shook his head, said no ma'am, and pushed his chair under the table, demonstrating his good manners.

He ran to the porch and waited for Pop to appear. He sat on the swing, flying through the air, practicing his whistle. He could make a sound, a shrill little note, but he couldn't figure out how to change his tune.

He made strange contortions of his face trying to get his tongue tamed against the back of his teeth. When was Pop going to come and finish his story? How long did it take him to chew and swallow?

Dwight heard the continuing murmur of his mother's and grandmother's voices, and now the clatter of china and silver being stacked and collected and carried into the kitchen. Then another voice.

Dwight jumped down and went to the door. Through the screen he could peer into the parlor where the TV showed a man reading the evening news. The announcer had hang-dog jowls and a fierce frown. His hair was cut in a severe flat-top and his eyes looked pained behind his heavy horn-rimmed glasses. Behind the constant snow and static on the screen, he shuffled his papers and cleared his throat. He spoke as if he were sorry he had to share all this bad news with his audience.

His grandfather sat in his usual chair, his hand cupped around his ear, straining to hear all that the sad man said on the TV. Dwight waited for his grandfather to come out and finish his story of walking west. He tried to whistle, but he couldn't get more than the one note out of his pursed lips. He started idly opening the screen door and letting the long coiled spring slap the door back to the threshold. Creak, slap, creak, slap. Until his grandfather shuffled in his easy chair and glared over his shoulder. "Coming or going? Boy, make up your mind!"

Dwight retreated to the swing, sadly, slowly letting his legs kick out, sailing up, then letting his feet dangle on the downward arc. Soon the shadows would spread from the hemlocks across the road where he knew all sorts of monsters and bears and Indian ghosts lived. And the long night would begin, and not end soon enough, and tomorrow he would still be here, stuck in this dull place. He understood "homesick" now. His belly ached, he wanted so bad to go home.

The screen door opened. It wasn't Pop as he'd hoped, but his mother. She had a sweater draped over her shoulders, and she was rubbing her hands with cream, the way she did every night after doing the dishes.

"You've got room for one more? Not too fast. That's right." She made him swing slower, like an adult, he supposed.

Dwight liked to see how high he could made the glider go, hurling himself off the back of the porch and across the tobacco plants or perhaps smashing up through the ceiling of the porch and into the bedroom where he would sleep tonight.

"When are we going home?"

She sighed, all the tired breath she held within her. "You promised to be good about this. Your grandparents don't get to see you all that often."

They had driven up yesterday. They would stay for a week this time, while his father was working hard. If he pestered her enough, maybe they would only stay three days and then they would get in the car and drive back down the mountain and they would be home again, but Dwight's dad still wouldn't be there, but away on business.

"There's nothing to do."

"I used to have all kind of fun when I was your age. When I was a little girl, your Pop built me a playhouse on top of that big rock by the barn. He'd tell me all these stories about princesses and castles, and knights who would rescue the princess on the rock."

"A playhouse?" Dwight peered into the dusk and in disbelief at the rock she spoke of. About the size of two cars parked side by side, the granite outcropping was draped with honeysuckle and briars. Nothing stood on top except for the TV antenna lashed with baling wire around a weathered fence post. "What happened to it?"

"Oh, it got old and I grew up. Pop tore it down a long time ago."

Which explained the loose planks shoved under a crevice in the rock.

And as if reading his mind beneath her hand, his mother warned, "Now don't you go poking around out there. There's no telling what snakes are in there."

His mother had told him a true story from her own childhood, how one of her playmates, a little girl, had gone to the henhouse to gather eggs for her mama, and reaching in the straw had grabbed hold, not of a warm pullet's egg, but a copperhead. But the moral of his mother's story was that the girl had told no one about the snake bite, the twin punctures on the back of her hand, until it was too late.

"If you ever see a snake, you come tell me or Gram or Pop right away, you hear? Don't you be like that little girl and be afraid to say something."

But something about the story about the playhouse troubled him, not just the snakes. It was hard to imagine his mom at his age, feeling perhaps as small and worried as he did in the course of so many days now. And why would Pop just tear down a playhouse where his mama was so happy and let snakes and briars take over the rock?

So she wouldn't see his face and know he was afraid, Dwight lay with his head in her lap. Her hand stroked his hair as he thought about all these things he didn't want to think about.

"I saw you out here before listening to one of Pop's tall tales."

"Yes," Dwight said, "but he didn't finish it."

"He's busy watching the news right now. Maybe you could ask him tomorrow."

"So Pop, he makes up stuff or is it real?"

"They're just stories, Dwight. You take things so seriously."

Seriously.

That night was the first he could recall his mother passing this verdict upon him, but it certainly wasn't the last, a refrain he would remember through his childhood, and the anxieties of adolescence, and even entering the drudgery of adulthood. The story of his life, he heard it from his parents, his teachers, his classmates, his professors, his colleagues, his girlfriends and later his wife. He couldn't help it, that was how Dwight Martin always took things.

How else do you face up to your life, but seriously?

And shouldn't stories be true somehow, if they are to be of any use?

But that night in the summer mountains, the chains creaked overhead as they swung through the air, back and forth. He didn't worry, but lay with his knees tight against his chest, his head on his mother's warm lap, her hand in his hair. He watched the screen door, how the blue glow of the TV inside appeared and disappeared with the back-and-forth swaying of the swing. The boy and his mother sailed toward the light, then slipped again into the shadows, sailed and slipped.

WHITTLING

Growing up, Dwight Martin always heard his mother saying that he had 20/20 hearing, that his ears must be always burning. It was a complaint rather than a compliment his mother was making, that he could hear so well, but never listen.

Starting about the age of ten and well into his middle age, Dwight had a habit of tugging at his earlobe, as if straining to catch the tiniest stir, the most minute buzz, a passing whir, but mostly it was a telltale sign that he was lost in his own thoughts, minding some secret story of his own telling.

He heard most acutely in the dark of night when everything was still and he could hear the dripping decibels of the leaky tap in the bathroom, the car carrying rock radio through the midnight street, the sirens in the distance, the mournful train on the outskirts of town. He heard his eyes blinking in his insomnia. He could hear his bank balances dropping, his stock portfolio deflating, his cholesterol climbing, his arteries narrowing.

Dwight blamed that night in Beaverdam as starting it all. He could piece together his insomnia from the shards of the glass that shattered in the darkness downstairs and the dreams in his head. His earlobe ached where his sleeping fingers had yanked him wide awake. Water was all he could hear, running downstairs in the springhouse built off the back of the kitchen. Each evening, his grandparents secured that back door with a ten-penny nail slid through the hasp to lock in the heat, lock out the damp. But Pop and Gram were getting old. What if they had forgotten to lock up last night?

He imagined the door nosed open by a wild beast down from the mountain, some animal sniffing through the kitchen, then through the parlor, scratching at the door of his grandparents, deaf as posts and toothlessly snoring in their beds. Tossing its horned head, the intruder clicked its claws up the stairs, following the scent of a scared boy, a tempting morsel.

Still holding his breath, hoping the blood would quit beating so hard in his head, Dwight stared at the ceiling. The faint outline of the light bulb hung overhead, useless as a dead and distant moon. The unseen twine cord was within reach if he sat up and waved his hand. But if he turned on the fatal light, the monster he was sure was inside the house would know where to find him.

There were twelve steps to the top of the landing, then two to the left, another landing, then three more. He tried counting slowly, the seventeen steps, wondering why it was taking so long for the intruder to come after him. One, two, three . . .

Dwight's dad had recently read in the newspaper about a burglary in their neighborhood and had started checking the locks on the door each night before going to bed. Now on the verge of turning ten, the added weight of those double digits, the upcoming fifth grade this fall where his father had warned him about the fractions, where two plus two equaled four wouldn't be the only answer, Dwight found himself terrified at nighttime, like a baby, afraid not just of the dark, but of all the darker things he saw when he closed his eyes.

It had been years since he'd had a nightlight; now when he needed such low-watt reassurance, he was too old. Instead, he cracked his bedroom door wider, gathering more of the lamplight from the living room, lulled by his parents' conversation, the pages turning quietly in the Life magazines and the Reader's Digest condensed books they read. He only pretended to be asleep when his mother came to check on him, but she was never fooled. "Why are you still awake, sweetheart?"

"I am sleeping. My eyes are closed."

"People don't sleep with their eyes squinched shut. What's the matter?"

So close to turning ten, he was too old to speak the childish truth—that he was afraid.

"Nothing," he said, hoping she would keep rubbing his back.

She stooped to kiss his head. "Good night. Go to sleep."

His mother joined his father, yawning by his door, and they went arm in arm down the hall to their bedroom. The last light beneath their door disappeared, and he was left alone in the darkness.

But Dwight figured no one could murder him in his bed if he wasn't to be found lying there. So he waited trembling until he thought his parents might be asleep. Taking his pillow, he slipped from beneath the covers and tiptoed into the linen closet to fetch the small blue fleece throw, actually a baby blanket his mother kept folded in the linen closet. He stole down the carpeted hall and lay by their door, his feet sticking out from beneath the too-short blanket, napping a little before sneaking back into his room.

Dwight knew he was nothing but a big baby.

But now he lay in mortal danger in a strange bed in the upstairs of an old creaky house far from home. Gram had sealed his fate, piling so many quilts against the cool mountain night, he couldn't move. There was no carpet to muffle his tiptoes, only the creaking floorboards that betrayed his every step or the steady creep of whatever was climbing the stairs.

He thought about calling out in the night for his mother, wondering how loud he would have to cry out before she would come. But what if the monster stopped to eat his mother before heading down the hall for him? This made terrible sense, since the seventeen steps he had counted over and over, first passed by the room where his mother was sleeping, by herself, without her father to protect her.

His mother didn't have good ears, asleep or awake. Childhood ear-aches had punched holes in her eardrums and left her hard of hearing. When she had been Dwight's age, unimaginable as it was, she'd slept in this very room, where she played with dolls, dreamed of growing up and marrying a handsome prince who would take her far from these mountains. Her room was overly warm in the winter, heat rising from the cast-iron woodstove downstairs through a metal grate in the floor, but when she went out into the hall, she could see her breath in the icy passage. She took sick one winter, and at night she lay in her bed, this same bed, with the pillow over her head, trying to blot out the terrible pain drumming in her ears, counting the steps of a giant coming to get her, one, two, three, four, five, six . . .

. . .Fourteen, fifteen, sixteen, seventeen. As he slowly chanted the numbers, Dwight stared wide-eyed into the darkness. The bedroom showed no signs of her childhood, only the looming shapes of the ancient furniture that inhabited the whole house. The closets were filled with the clothes of old people, and their smells, and the walls were covered with the pictures of people he didn't know, but he knew they were dead, and they were looking down on him even in the darkness.

The old house creaked on the most peaceful of nights, its timbers settling into the foundations, but whenever the wind blew down the mountain, sashes bumped all night against window frames. The wind whistled around the house, pressing all the panes of glass, trying to find its way in.

He lay so long in the dark, holding his breath, he felt dizzy, and after a while, he began to wonder if he had dreamed the sound of glass breaking. So, the slow hours passed, counted out seventeen by seventeen by seventeen into the night, but nothing stirred in the house, nothing creaked or groaned, and exhausted with listening so hard, sick with the fear, first for himself, then for himself unable to protect his mother from harm, his eyes closed again . . .

—

Dwight woke with a start, the sun glaring through the window where the wind had tried to get in last night. He remembered the broken glass from last night, but all the windows were intact.

Downstairs, the house was deserted. The butter sat on the table, the jars of preserves, the salt and pepper shakers, the countertop wiped down, the pots and pans from breakfast put away. He checked the oven and found a few hard biscuits. Snacking on one, he crossed into the parlor, ducked his head into his grandparents' deserted bedroom, then outside into the bright morning.

He found his mother out on the porch, with the dishrag still wet in her hand. Her other hand held the porch trellis as she stared down the road, lost in thought, longing perhaps for something around the bend. Dwight scurried to her side, wormed his way under her raised arm, against her hip. He was getting taller and his head crooked nicely beneath her warm arm, the ready-made hug.

"Look who decided to finally get up? I see you found your break-fast."

He yawned and nibbled his biscuit.

"Such as a sleepyhead." Mom mussed his sleep-mashed hair. "Look at the size of this cowlick. Your father needs to get you a haircut when you get home."

She felt his forehead. He liked her cool hand against his skin. He pulled her hand over his tired eyes, but she tipped his chin up to look at her.

"You sleep well? You didn't get scared last night?"

"Umm," Dwight mumbled, chewing the dried biscuit.

"You heard that breaking glass?" She looked at him, narrowing her eyes like she didn't believe him. "That was just Pop up getting a drink of water in the middle of the night. He dropped it in the dark. You heard that?"

"Yeah." Dwight swallowed hard, the crumbs sticking in his throat.

"And you stayed in your bed, didn't cry out. You went right back to sleep, didn't you?"

"Yeah." He looked down. Did she know about him getting up at night? "Where's Pop and Gram?" he asked to change the uncomfortable subject.

"They went off to church. So it's you and me this morning, sport. We've got some chores to do before they get back."

He frowned. "Sport" was something his father would call him, to cheer him up, to bring him up short when Dwight was not acting his age. His mother calling him "sport" didn't seem fair.

"Let me go finish cleaning the kitchen. You go up and make your bed and get dressed. Scoot."

Dwight trudged up the stairs. He hated making his bed. And the bed here was even bigger than his at home. He pulled up the sheets and smoothed out the corners. The quilts were so heavy he could barely heave them back toward the headboard.

After he had smoothed out half the wrinkles in the bedspread, enough to say he'd done all the work a boy should do on a summer Sunday, he went to his suitcase. After his mother had packed his clothes, he'd slipped in his father's pack of cards.

He shuffled the deck. He hadn't mastered a true shuffle yet, that flipping of cards with the pleasing sound it made, then politely shoved together. Dwight mashed the cards in his right hand into the cards in his left. Dwight brought the deck downstairs and out on the porch where he knelt, dealing out cards one by one, making up stories about each card he turned over: seven of clubs, how many times they club you over the head; the four of spades, spade was like a shovel his father told him, they could beat you with a club, as well as a shovel, then bury your body. If they were green they would have been shamrocks, but they were black clubs. Up came the suicide King with the sovereign running the sword into his temple; the one-eyed Jack with his dandy beard, the Queen of Spades, dark-haired like his mother, yet imperious and cruel. He kept looking for the Joker, but the evil clown kept hiding from him.

His mother came out of the kitchen and onto the porch. She flapped her dishrag in the air, and collapsed in mid-air, falling into the rocker. "Law me."

He laughed. "That's what she says."

"Who?"

"Gram. She always goes, 'Law me,' when she sits down."

"She does, doesn't she?" His mother shook her head, then she did something Gram never did. She reached into her apron pocket and drew out her cigarettes, an ashtray and opened her paperback romance.

Dwight liked watching his mother smoke. His mother smoked only as a private celebration, when she had women friends over in the kitchen or when couples came over to play cards with his parents at night. He admired the practiced flip of the cigarette between her lips, held primly between two first fingers, then aiming the match at the right end of the cigarette, puffing just so, knowing when to tamp the ash away, another adult skill he might have to master someday. Although the smoke itself made him sneeze sometimes, and sometimes the drinks that she and his father made didn't taste that good.

"You finished all your chores?" she asked, still slowly turning the pages of her paperback. "What happened to that book you were writing yesterday?"

Dwight gave her a pained look. He was past that. His novel was an embarrassment to him today. Besides the pencil was broken.

"It's a pretty day. You ought to put those cards up and go out and play."

He shook his head. The dew didn't dry on the grass until late in the morning. If he went out to play now, his sneakers would be soaked for the rest of the day. Besides, once the grass was dried out and the sun was up high, that was when the snakes came out. His father had patiently explained that snakes were cold-blooded and had to lie in the sun to warm their clammy scales.

Dwight liked to trail his Dad about the farm, sticking close to him in case of snakes. His father strolled about the premises, his hands grasped behind his back to keep him from throwing them up in the air when he got exasperated. The farm itself was a hundred years old. While anything that old awed Dwight, it only seemed to anger his father. Old meant useless. The fields on the upper slopes were fallow, the pastures gone to seed, fences falling down, the barn and woodshed leaning toward collapse. Even the apple tree was so far gone, unpruned, that the fruit was small and bitter. The futility of the place frustrated his father, probably why he had refused to come this time.

"What do you think Dad's doing right now?" Dwight wondered.

"I don't know," his mother said. "He might be working. He works really hard, you know."

She looked up for once from her book.

"You miss your dad, don't you honey?" His mother sighed. "So do I."

"Do you think he went to church today?"

"I don't think so."

"Why don't we go to church?" he asked.

"I forgot to pack any church clothes. You need to dress up to go to church."

"No, I mean at home."

"We do," his mother insisted.

They didn't, except on occasions like Christmas, when they sang a lot, or like the wedding of his Aunt Muriel, his father's sister down east, but most Sundays, his family slept in, then his parents read the newspaper while he lay on the floor with the comics spread before him.

He was curious about his grandparents' church, which they had passed, a whitewashed building with a gravel parking lot. His mother had grown up there, but he'd never been inside. A brick marquee with white removable letters against the black background announced this week's sermon: "Where will you spend eternity?"

"What's eternity?" He had wondered when they drove by.

"Sitting in the Beaverdam Baptist on a Sunday morning." His mother had laughed, but he couldn't see her eyes behind her sunglasses. It didn't sound like she was making a joke.

"What do people do in church every Sunday?" Dwight still wanted to know.

His mother ignored him, turning the page of her book. Dwight stared at the cover with its picture of a sad looking woman in a long dress standing in the wind before a castle. There were no archers on the turrets or knights or nothing. At least his African novel had some action on the cover.

"Why can't I go to church?"

His mother finally put the paperback on her lap and sighed out her mentholated smoke. "Honey, listen to me. You know you get scared sometimes. The reason I didn't want to take you to that church is the sermon. I thought it might scare you. I know it scared me when I was a little girl."

"Scary how?"

"Well, there's a lot of yelling and talking about burning in fire for the bad things you do sometimes, and sometimes for things that aren't even bad."

"Like what?"

"Mama will have a hissy fit if she sees you playing cards, me smoking a cig, reading like this on Sunday."

"Why? It's just playing."

"They think playing cards is like gambling, like drinking, and dancing or reading what you want to. They don't approve. People aren't supposed to have fun on Sundays, when everybody's supposed to be in church."

There they were again, back to that mysterious question of church. "Why?"

"That's just the way your grandmother was raised. The way she tried to raise me. I just didn't want you growing up, feeling the way I did sometimes when I was your age." He saw her shifting uncomfortably in the swing. "That's enough questions. Let's put up the cards, Dwight."

"Wait, I know a game we can play."

Donna Bright, a girl in the neighborhood had showed him the game he never heard of before. Fifty-two card pick-up. "How do you play?" He stupidly asked, and Donna Bright flung the deck of cards, jacks, kings and queens flying in his face. It was mean when the girl laughed at him, and now he wanted to throw the cards at his mother, who seemed to be angry with him for no reason.

But his mother was in no mood to play. "No back-talk, Dwight. Just do what I say."

Back-talk was an ugly word she only used when she meant business.

"It's not fair," he wailed. "I never have any fun."

—

"Law me." Gram sighed heavily as she finally sat down to the dinner table, signaling everyone to begin.

"Pass the potatoes," Pop said. He plopped a spoonful of spuds onto Dwight's plate.

"You missed some fine preaching this morning, June," Gram said, handing the plate of sliced tomatoes around.

"Maybe next time. I promise, Momma."

"Evangelist from over in Blowing Rock, he dealt directly with some hearts this morning. Two or three of them Baker boys came forward at the altar call, made their decision for eternity."

That word again. "What's eternity?" Dwight needed to know.

"What's what?" Pop reached for his hearing aid that began to whine.

"You need to go to church and find out," Gram said. "Maybe your mother can take you some time."

"Good singing," said Pop. "Sang my favorite hymn this morning. *Amazing Grace*, all five verses and the first and the last again, when the preacher was hoping for some stragglers."

"Dwight, please sit up and quit playing with your food." His mother said.

He had his chin cupped in his hand, forlorn as he drew his fork through his food, stirring a mishmash on his plate. "Not hungry," he mumbled.

"I fixed all your favorites, macaroni and cheese, there's pork roast, and peas and potatoes," Gram said.

"I want ravioli."

"Ravioli? I don't know what that is, honey." The word sounded funny when she repeated it. "Ravioli. Is it like macaroni? Maybe there's something I can do to the macaroni and we'll call it ravioli."

"No, you can't make it. It comes in a can. It's good."

"Dwight!" His mother chided.

But he couldn't keep quiet, the unfairness of not getting his favorite food. "I eat it at school, I eat it at home. I eat it everywhere but here."

"You wouldn't be acting this way if your father were here," she said.

"But he's not. He hates this place."

Their mouths fell open, all the shoveling of food, clinking of glasses, scraping of forks on china and the constant chewing of artificial teeth on overcooked food, ceased. Their faces were white, and Dwight could see the welling in his mother's dark eyes.

He slid from his chair, never minding his manners, or asking permission or scooting his chair back under the table. He ran from the room and upstairs and into his mother's old bedroom, latching the door behind him.

"Dwight." The doorknob rattled. The door caught against the hook he'd latched. His mother's eye peered through the crack. "You better open this door. Now."

At home, he would be headed for a whipping, his father's thin leather belt like a snake about his wrist, undone and doubled up in his fist. Sometimes, he left the belt coiled on the doorknob of Dwight's bedroom, a threat of what was to come if he didn't mind. But here, in his grandparents' house, Dwight would not be punished. He could flaunt his disappointment, his boredom. He could sulk and mumble and pout and still win nickels from Gram, winks from his Pop.

"O.K., if that's what you want." The knob quit rattling as her hand fell away. "When you decide to act your age, let me know. You can come down stairs, mister, when you're good and ready to apologize to everyone."

If his father were here, Dwight would act differently. He would be older, and not acting like a baby. Acting his age, almost ten. Almost ten. Two weeks away. Another week they would be home. His lip curled and trembled, but he refused to cry.

———

When Dwight descended the stairs, the house seemed deserted. The clock chided him from the parlor mantel. Motes of dust hovered in the hazy shafts of light hanging in the parlor. Dwight felt small and insignificant like the bug trapped in the honeycomb he found once in a jar of his grandmother's honey.

He drew a dipper of water from the trough in the springwater and drank until his throat ached with the cold. He found another old biscuit in the pan in the cold oven. He deserved nothing more than bread and water, what he read prisoners were given in dungeons in olden days. He was a prisoner here in his grandparents' house, sentenced to an impossible life or at least another week, probably, solitary confinement with nothing to do and no one to play with. But secretly, Dwight knew as bad as he had been acting, he deserved his punishment.

He could hear women's voices out on the porch. He crept through the parlor and close to the screen door to hear what they were saying.

Ever since they had arrived, his mother and grandmother had been talking, a steady feminine stream of conversation that ran just out of his hearing, a murmuring like the creek in front of the house. Whether in the kitchen, or on the porch, or in the parlor after he had gone to bed, whenever he left the room, he could hear their voices change. His grandmother dropped her cooing singsong for a flatter, accusatory tone. His mother's soft sighs became high, pinched explanations. She was being called to task, failing some question-and-answer test, a true-or-false examination. Why wasn't he eating better? Why wasn't he taller? Was he smart or too smart, or dumb? Why didn't he do better in school? How come he acted so badly, so like a baby at times?

But as he edged toward these answers, his shadow caught in the mesh screen, their voices changed again. They had been waiting for him all along. "Here he is now. Don't you be hiding. Come on out where we can see you?"

He stepped out on the porch where the two of them sat snapping green beans into a colander.

"Ready to apologize?" Mom asked.

"I'm sorry."

"Speak up so people can hear you when you apologize."

"I'm sorry, Gram."

"Now, that didn't kill you, did it?" Mom asked.

"Of course, not. He's a big boy now," Gram said. "Look what we're having for dinner tonight. You like green beans?"

He wrinkled his nose at them. He liked the tender white bean part, but not particularly the green outsides.

"Dwight is almost ten now. He can eat all sorts of grown up foods," his mother announced, a handful of green beans spread in her lap.

He knew she hated green beans as much as he did, or at least, the fixing of them. She had helped her mother can countless quarts, so many beans out of the gardens of years past, that some were never eaten, moldy jars lining the pantry. Mom said there were beans back there older than Dwight.

"Tell you what, Dwight. If you eat all your beans tonight, I'll give you a nickel. Fetch me my purse."

Dwight ran into the house. He heard the fierce whispers sieved through the screen door. "You don't need to bribe him, Mama!"

"I can spoil my only grandbaby, can't I?"

He found the purse on the dresser of his grandparents' bedroom, a shiny plastic purse with gold painted hasps. He had been through his mother's purse before, and it was much like this, full of wadded up kerchiefs, the faint smell of powder and makeup, but not lipstick and ointments. He reached in his arm halfway up to his elbow. He felt brush bristles and the prick of hairpins, soft tissues and power-puffs, and all sorts of different papers and leathery covers, and there at the bottom, the round cold coins.

In the mirror, he saw himself, up to his elbow in the open purse, a look of larceny on his face, and then over his shoulder, reflected in the glass, he saw a secret he'd never seen before.

A gun hung over the door on two big nails, one through the trigger guard, the other beneath the long barrel.

He went to the threshold, gazing up at the dark stock of walnut, the blued barrel. If he had a chair, he could touch the gun. He'd seen them in movies, of course, and on television, cowboys shooting bad guys and Indians who fell down with their hands clutched to their hearts. A gun solved most dramas he'd seen at the movies or on TV.

"Dwight?" his mother was calling. He grabbed a quarter and pocketed it before he ran with the purse to the porch.

"What took you so long, honey? Now let me see." Gram rummaged through the purse. "I'll bet there's something for a bright little boy."

"Mama, please."

"Hush now, just a little something won't hurt the boy."

Dwight smirked at his mother as he held out his hand for his reward.

Fair play. She got hushed, she got hushed. He wanted to gloat, but the frown warned him against any overt glee.

"Here we go." Gram produced a bright dime. "And a peppermint to go with it."

"What do you say, Dwight?" his mother prompted

"Thank you, Gram," he said in his most insincere whine.

"Good, give me some sugar now."

What he had to do for a little loot. He closed his eyes and held his breath and pressed his lips against her funny feeling, wrinkly skin.

Dwight stepped off the porch, then stopped. Even with the money in his pocket, there was no place to spend it. No 7-Eleven up the street like at home where he rode his bike to buy comics and Slurpees and bubble gum. Several miles away over the gap, they passed a dimly lit, crossroads store with rusted signs advertising hardware and feed. They never stopped there, but drove by under the watch of the strange men on the sagging front porch. Unlike Pop, those men never waved at the passing cars.

He felt guilty for stealing his Gram's money. Back on the porch, he couldn't help but whine. "There's nothing to do."

"I believe your Pop's out there in the shed," Gram said.

"So?"

"He might have a surprise for you," his mother said.

He walked across the grass, going out of his way to stomp a few of the soft apples that had dropped from the apple tree that seemed to hold up the leaning woodshed. At the door, he scraped the yellow apple mush from the suctioned craters and ridges of the rubber soles. He admired the threshold, a single block of ancient wood that over the long years had assumed a pleasant bowed shape, worn down by the crossing of his grandfather's brogans each morning and each evening, to gather more wood for his fires.

Inside, the air was ripe with fresh-cut wood and dried tobacco. Wood chips and shavings littered the dirt floor and the brown shriveled ghosts of last year's burley hung from the rafters. Dwight's eyes adjusted to the shady coolness. The walls were filled with all sorts of neat stuff, iron implements of mysterious purpose and mildewed leather straps hung from corroded ten-penny nails, even a horseshoe half-eaten with red rust. That would look good in his room at home, but Pop would probably get mad like his father whenever Dwight took tools from the basement workshop.

"I see you ain't sick now, are you?" Pop was sitting on his chopping block, rubbing the back of his creased neck with a red bandanna. "It' so hot I don't blame you for losing your appetite."

The mountains were much cooler than the humid heat of the town where he lived, but his grandparents seemed obsessed with the temperature. Thus, Gram's desire to always pile more quilts and comforters atop his bed at night, and Pop's passion for stoking the wood stove, and keeping a full box of kindling by the back door. Then they complained about the heat on a day like this when Dwight wore shorts.

"Still, it ain't a good idea to go without your dinner, especially on a Sunday." Pop pocketed the bandanna and took up his Barlow knife and the stick he was whittling.

"Believe me, I learned that the hard way when me and Dwight Sparks wandered out west. I got so hungry I swore I'd never miss a home-cooked meal again if I ever made it back to Beaverdam. I recollect there were times wandering out west when me and Dwight Sparks had no supper for a while, ate a root or two, or even boiled up some grass and called it supper."

"You ate grass?"

"Well, only that once. Wouldn't recommend it. But a body can't be picky when you're pioneering your way west. We had to eat whatever we could forage or shoot along the way."

"You had a gun, a real gun like the one in your room?"

Dwight hadn't meant to blurt this out, but he couldn't get the gun out of his mind since he'd seen the weapon hung over the door of his grandfather's bedroom. Too bad his grandparents weren't going off to church again for a couple of hours, so he could pull a chair over and get a closer look, maybe even touch it, maybe if it wasn't too heavy and wouldn't fall, take it down and hold it, a real gun in his two almost ten-year-old hands.

"That old scattergun?" The old man lowered his knife and his stick of wood but not his eyes, giving the boy a look that seemed more knowing than usual, daring Dwight to come clean.

"No, not that gun in my room," Pop said slowly. He cleared his throat, the prologue of phlegm. He resumed his whittling and his story.

———

Dwight Sparks and me had a week of school left and then there was the long summer ahead to head west.

We had us a hiding place where we hooked up every day after school, the Rendezvous Rock. It was back off the road and across the creek and through a lot of laurel up to this cliff face back of Buckeye Mountain. I'd be whistling down the road, then look around, making sure no one had seen me, and I'd take off up the side of the hill, twenty minutes of twists and turns and it was easy to get turned around before you reached the rock face. Each day, we'd bring something new for our trek, coils of rope, sacks of salt and beads to trade to passing Indian tribes, lye soap in a can, and sprigs of wintergreen for brushing our teeth, strips of cloth for tourniquets and bandages, and a pair of pliers to pull out splinters and any bad teeth. Pots and pans, and griddles and grills, extra straps of leather for shoes, two hats, heavy coats in case it got cold, a couple changes of underwear, even a cane bottom chair for easy setting by the campfire.

"Who's going to carry all this stuff?"

"What about your cow?"

"She's a cow, not a pack horse. I never heard tell of a pack-cow."

"Right as rain, Wylie." Dwight was pulling at his one whisker, a new habit of his since he'd discovered a whisker rooted just south of his dimple, evidence of his advanced manhood.

"And what we going to eat?" I asked.

"Miles ahead of you, Wylie. We'll have to live off the land. I've got this." From behind a tree, Dwight pulled out a long shotgun, pointed the barrel toward the holler, and mouthed "Kapow."

Now, let me explain that we were farmers, and Beaverdam was pretty much hunted out as far as wild game. The guns my family kept were for executing hogs for slaughter or warding off occasional varmints. Weren't none of us what I'd call sharpshooters.

"Here, you try."

The gun was heavy, but I knew enough to steady it against my shoulder and hold it still. I closed one eye and sighted down the barrel in the general direction of a beech tree quivering its leaves down by the creek.

"No, fool, it's a shotgun. Keep both eyes open," Dwight directed. "Move your face or it'll knock your nose off."

I closed my eyes anyway, held my breath, and squeezed.

The noise I felt more than heard, like someone had hit me upside the head. Dwight was saying something, his mouth was moving but the world was full of so much noise and commotion right then that I couldn't hear at first. Then the words filtered through my ears like they were stuffed with cotton.

"Are you crazy? You weren't supposed to shoot it. We've got to save our shells for game."

I looked at the tree where I was aiming; the leaves stood absolutely still like I'd scared them stiff on the branches. Then I saw a good ten feet away from the beech, a pine torn in two. I looked at the gun in my hands. Either I was the world's worst shot or the barrel of this gun was bent bad. . . .

———

"Now here's the part I want you to pay attention to." Pop stopped his story and his whittling. "That gun over the door? Listen to me, it ain't a toy. A gun's serious business as me and Dwight Sparks learned to our great regret out west."

"What happened?" Dwight was dying now to know.

"What do you think the rest of the story is worth?"

"A nickel?"

"Speak up, boy. My ears are too old for such a young voice." He snapped his fingers and held out his hand.

"A quarter," Dwight conceded.

Rustling deep in Dwight's pocket were the coins, both the one his grandmother had given him in good faith and the illicit one he'd taken from her purse. He couldn't tell which was the guilty coin, but held both out flat in his palm. The old man was quick when it came to money. He pocketed the loot as usual. The whittling resumed, and the story. . . .

———

'Course we didn't take a tenth of all that gear we stashed under the Rendezvous Rock, but we carried that blasted gun, and I wish that was the one thing we might have left behind. Looking back, I'm not sure we shot a thing with the sights all off, like that. And by the time we reached the high plains of Nebraska, I'm talking about two right hungry boys and the cow's ribs, you could count.

Dwight kept looking over his bony shoulder at Ivy and kind of licking his tongue around his lips.

"Don't even think it," I warned.

We stumbled on a ways, and he looked back again. "No sir," I said. Though by this time, I was kind of walking with one arm looped around the heifer's neck. When he looked back a third time, I pulled out the shotgun to make my point.

"Dwight Sparks. You promised me and I tend to hold you to your word."

Weak as I was, the gun was heavy, and I rested the barrel in the dirt. "So where are we?" I tried to change the course of our conversation.

"We'll make it Meat Camp."

Dwight stepped closer, and I snapped the breech closed.

"Don't."

"Sirloin," he chanted. "Rump roast, shoulder, flank."

"Dwight, don't make me."

By then, I had the gun raised and the hammer cocked. But Dwight kept coming, no longer aimed west, his eyes glazed over so he couldn't see the gun he was walking right into, like he was going to crawl down the barrel if need be to get to some beef.

Too late I remembered that old cuss of a blunderbuss was so warped, that pointing it well past Dwight's shoulder, I was probably targeting his very heart. But I forgot the hair trigger and I must have twitched my finger.

The noise was louder than I believed possible on this earth. There was fire in my face and smoke in my eyes. And not only had I killed my best friend, I'd slain myself. When my eyes finally uncrossed themselves, I was looking up at Dwight, already descended up above and looking all warm and soft and concerned, an angel, and I thought all woozy to myself, if Dwight made it to heaven without going to church, well, God Almighty has a sense of humor. And then I figured, oops, I must be in the other place, for having gone and murdered him like that.

"Are we dead yet?"

"Not yet, fool. You had the barrel all stopped with dirt and it misfired."

"So who got hit?" I hollered.

"Ouch!" The first bird pelted Dwight's back, then another, and soon a whole flock of migrating pigeons were raining down on our heads, sprayed with the birdshot from the gun I must have fired a little high.

Dwight marveled. "I don't know who taught you to shoot, Wylie."

"You did, friend." I grinned.

We had plenty to eat that evening. The gun laying off to the side had kind of caught fire and was burning up its own stock so we plucked a few pigeons, spitted them and roasted them over the flames. We weren't hungry no more, but I still hear the blast of that gun all these many years later. . . .

—————

The hearing aid was whining in the old man's ear and his hand went up like he was about to swat away a pesky insect, but lighted to adjust the device behind his ear.

"So let that be a lesson to you," Pop said. "A gun is not always a good thing, at least not an old gun like the one hanging in an old man's bedroom that a certain little boy ought to know better than to play with. A gun can hurt you."

All the while the old man had shaped his story, his blade had been whittling away on the wood. What had been an apple branch was now a long ramrod with a curved stock at one end. Pop sighted down its length.

"Yep, don't think this one's warped."

The boy watched as the old man took a stalk of rough looking wood and a piece of wire. The tough fingers fed the wire into one end and a cottony white pith suddenly appeared at the other end.

"Alder," the old man explained. "Soft in the middle."

Pop worked the wire all the way through, then blew through it a perfectly round hole in a smoothbore muzzle. Next he spit on the ramrod once and then fed the applewood into the alder, making sure it fit snugly, but could slide freely to and fro.

Then the old man took a bit of dried newspaper, and tore a chunk off in his mouth, chewed some and then pulled from the tip of his tongue a spit-wad that boys in Dwight's fourth-grade class would have been proud to produce. He wadded the wet paper into one end of the barrel, then inserted the ramrod at the other end.

"Now what did Dwight and me learn out west about guns?"

The boy went over all the details, trying to remember what must have been meant as the moral. "Guns are for grown-ups?" he finally guessed.

"Don't point the business end of anything at anyone you don't aim to hurt."

To make his point, Pop turned the bark barrel to the shed wall. With a quick jerk, he pushed the ramrod and the spit-wad flew out with a loud pleasing *pop* and pasted itself against a plank.

"Here, you try."

Dwight tore a piece of dirty newspaper and put in his mouth, ink and dirt taste on his tongue, then stuck his fingers in his mouth and retrieved the spit-wad, and loaded the gun as he had seen his grandfather do. He took careful aim at the same shadow on the wall where Pop's spit-wad was plastered, then he snapped alder barrel and apple ramrod together. *Pop* went the weapon in a puff of trapped air, and a white bullet sailed though the air.

"Not a bad deal?" The old man winked. "Two bits for a good story and a gun at the end. Now you go see if you can shoot some villains."

———

That night, Dwight sat in the high bed of his mother's childhood room, unafraid for the first time in weeks. He made soft explosions inside his mouth as he aimed his gun at the shadows in the corner. He flopped upside-down and raked a fusillade beneath the bedsprings, massacring the monsters that lay waiting for him to fall asleep. He was far too old, of course, for the pop-gun, and he would never show anybody back home, not when there were plastic ray guns to play with. But he had watched his Pop make it personally. Dwight had never seen anyone so clever with his hands, not even his own dad.

His mother came in and took the gun from his hands, placed it on the dresser. "O.K., that's enough. You've had a long day once you got over your fit. Let's get some sleep."

She tucked the covers under his chin, and brushed the hair back from his head, and pressed her lips there, sealing the thought deep within his head. *She loves me. She won't ever leave me.*

"Goodnight, Dwight."

He heard the snap of the twine pull to the overhead light. The room was dark and his mother was a silhouette at the door.

"Mama?"

"What, sweetie?"

He wanted to know so many things he didn't know how to say. Not the monsters under the bed or creeping down the hall, but those uncertainties about the future. Would his father come home? Would he learn how to whistle, to drive a car, make change from a twenty? Would he do well in school? Would he be good enough for college? Would he find a career, something he could be decent at doing? Would he find someone to love, to marry, someone to be good to?

The flutters he felt in his tummy at ten would gnaw at his gut when he was twenty and thirty and more. Would everything be all right? How would the story turn out?

"What's wrong now?" His mother was getting impatient, her hand on the knob ready to close the door on this particular day.

"Nothing," he mumbled, knowing himself a coward. "'Night."

"G'night honey." The door shut behind her.

He allowed himself one childish gesture. He slipped out of bed, found the gun on the dresser and burrowed under the quilts once more. The gun he tucked under the feather pillow, his hand rubbing the rough bark. No nightmares would dare come near him, no snakes under the bed, or wild beasts down from the mountain and up the stairs. He kept watch in the darkness, blinking his lashes against the soft pillowcase, but was soon peacefully asleep.

WORKING

The darkness was complete, no moon out to mar the perfect night of deep stars. Distant suns and supernovas winked across the universe at a small planet, waves of light so ancient, guttering in a cosmic wind, gone already at the outer edges. And here, deep in the holler, another wind rustled the shaggy coats of the hemlocks and rippled through the rhododendron thickets.

Inside the barn, the cow snoozed in the straw, stomachs working through a day's grass from the high pasture on the ridge. A tuft of blond hair from the cow's side still clung to a barb on the wire running the perimeter of the farm, bait for the flying night wind.

Higher up in the last woods, in a tree that was never felled by even the first settlers, a creature called out, a horrible cry of the night, then fell silent. Shadow piled upon shadow, inky, murky, deep in the woods. On the worm-eaten carpet of leaves, there came an eerie glow, the luminescence of fleshy Indian Pipe, upright ghosts on the forest floor.

The creek ran all through the night, fed by a dozen ice-cold springs from high in the mountains. Occasional creatures crept out onto a sandbar and dipped greedy paws into the water, then scurried away across the sand, leaving their prints at the scene of some nightly slaughter. Mist rose from the stream and fog drifted beneath the hemlocks and across the yard and around the house.

Before daybreak, a yellow light flooded the bottom between the two mountains, spread like butter from the kitchen of the old farmhouse. Wylie walked out into the chill, boots leaving prints across the dewed grass. The first birds were singing. The shadows thinned, the darkness diluted by the dawning light; there would be no visible sun for several sweeps of the clock's hands.

The cow was already on her feet when the lantern was lit in the stall, the smoked globe illuminating the blue flame drinking from the well of kerosene. Wylie patted her warm flank, "Come along, girl."

She didn't protest his rough hands tugging at her teats, but swished her tail as he relieved the udders, milk squirting out, ringing against the tin pail, frothing against the rim. He patted her flank again, and let her loose, to make her way out of the stall door and through the back gate. She lumbered out of the barnyard, out of the glow of the lantern light, a shadow drifting up the mountainside, toward her long day's graze of the high pasture.

He carried the pail to the spring house and poured the raw milk into the metal can set in the trough of icy water. In the kitchen, coffee was already on the stove, bubbling black in the glass button of the percolator. With a potholder, he picked up the pot and filled his favorite stained mug, and dumped in sugar and a dash of raw warm milk.

The world was taking shape outside, shadows became forest, became trees, became branches. The barn and the shed and the house stood apart in the first light. And the mountains on either side were rimmed now with red of the approaching day.

Wylie came out now in new overalls and started his car, let the engine warm up while he went to fetch the twenty-five-gallon milk can from the springhouse. He wrestled the can into the bed of the truck, and clipped a chain through the handles so it wouldn't tip over during the curves over the gap.

The headlights washed over the house then swept beyond the bridge and across the trees. The truck turned toward town, twenty twisting miles over the gap, led by the faint beams of light cutting through the fog. The radio signal went in and out, tuned to a station that gave the weather and the obituaries and yesterday's prices for hogs and grain and produce. The world was barely light when he dropped off his milk at the town's dairy plant, hoisting the sloshing can from the bed of the truck up onto the loading dock. He could feel the first twinges in his back, the muscles' premonition of a long week of lifting and hoisting. He was getting on and too old for this kind of work. He dug his fist into the small of his back, kneading his knuckles up and down his spine, then he climbed behind the wheel of the truck and drove the empty main street.

He turned onto the campus and parked by the green Dumpsters behind the college cafeteria. He cut the lights, switched off the engine, and pocketed the keys in his blue coveralls, with his name stitched in red over his heart.

Monday morning. Time to earn his keep in the world.

WALKING

Awake in the mountain morning, freed from the crushing quilts of the strange bed and the night's terrors, Dwight Martin took a running start into a day of nothing but play. He slid down the banister, varnished wood burning his thighs, before the newel post caught his butt at the bottom. He dismounted and slipped out the front door, careful not to let the screen slam behind him.

"Geronimo!" He parachuted off the end of the porch and landed with a grunt behind enemy lines. From behind the boxwood, he sprayed a hail of gunfire across the unsuspecting tobacco field. He ducked his head around the cinder block foundation of the porch and fired off a few rounds at the impregnable fortress of the rock by the barn. He zigzagged across the no-man's land as enemy airplanes strafed his steps. He made the cover of the woodshed, and threw a few grenades of green apples, annihilating the enemy bunker. Mission accomplished.

He stood at attention as the President bestowed the gratitude of a grateful nation on Dwight Martin for his bravery in the field against terrible odds.

Sometimes, Dwight couldn't be certain what was real and what he might have imagined. His grip on reality was up for debate in those conversations his parents carried on when he was out of the room, but never quite out of earshot. *"At least, he has an active imagination." "Well, so long as he's not making imaginary friends . . . is he?"*

Dwight dreamed of ending all argument by walking in and plugging both his parents with his new pop-gun. They would plop to the floor, kicking heels up high, clutching hands to their wounded hearts. Before they closed their eyes, they would beg Dwight's forgiveness. "Oh son, how we misunderstood you." He would blow imaginary smoke from the barrel of his pop-gun, then his mother would hop up to make them dinner.

He was just playing, pretending. Deadeye Dwight, cold-blooded killer, a bad man with a gun. No one was there to laugh at him, or to tell him to grow up or act his age.

Pop had gone off to work. Mom and Gram were in the kitchen, marshaling the mason jars for the canning campaign ahead. Steam already floated in the room, flushing their faces, the tension building like the pressure cookers on the stove. Dwight could sense he was in the way as the women disagreed over this and that. Finally, Gram had given him a whole dollar to be a good boy and play outside, and for once Mom didn't protest that he was being spoiled.

The gun wasn't working as well as yesterday. The ramrod that Pop had carved seemed to have warped during the night and it stuck when he pushed it through the bark barrel. Besides, he had targeted all the inanimate objects around the yard. Only one creature dared stand its ground against the mighty Dwight.

His mortal enemy eyed him through the slats of the barnyard gate, slowly swishing her terrible tail. She lowered her huge head and with soft lips tore up a tuft of green grass thick with dew. Dwight crept closer, reached through the gate and touched her brown flank with the tip of his gun. The beast grunted and stepped back a bit, startling the boy. He fought off his urge to run across the grass, back to the house, though his heart was already racing. He was deathly afraid of the cow. The devilish horns, the hard cloven hooves, the mask of black flies, the obscene udder hanging underneath.

He'd nearly sworn off milk when he was eight, watching Pop wrap his calloused hands around the thick teats. "Want to try her?"

Just then the cow had stepped backward, nearly crushing his foot.

Dwight hadn't forgotten. Two years later, he was several inches taller and twenty pounds heavier, but still nothing compared to the brown beast. He forced himself to stay by the fence, eye to eye with his worst fear.

"I could shoot you," he whispered.

He looked at the ground and picked up a sharp piece of rock. His hands were shaking as he loaded the end of the barrel with the projectile, inserted the ramrod into the back of the barrel, and he aimed point blank into the unblinking eye.

"I could kill you," he said more loudly.

The cow gazed at her would-be assailant, green grass drool hanging from her fat pink lips. She tossed her polled horns, then turned her back on the boy and hoisted her tail. A great, green Niagara of shit cascaded between her hind legs, splattering across the boy's shins.

Gagging and retching, Dwight retreated downwind. His left sneaker was soaked with the putrid stuff, and his skin stung with the hot excrement. Dwight ran to the creek and tried to clean himself as best he could in the muddy water.

Beside his right sneaker in the shelf of sand on the bank, he saw the print of a fellow creature, some furtive night visitor searching for a midnight snack. The tiny paw print was evidence that the water wasn't entirely poisonous. Something lived in the water besides the giant snakes in the shadow of the bridge.

He had read in fairy tales about the troll that ate the billy goats beneath the fabled bridge, but there were no goats on his grandfather's farm, and he knew trolls weren't real. But snakes were. After his mother's warning about the snake-bit little girl, Dwight was on the lookout for the slightest slithering motion underfoot, although he had yet to see a real serpent on the farm.

He suspected they would live under the bridge over the creek. The dark shadows, the curling briars and loose rock looked like perfect nests for diamondbacks, timber rattlers, water moccasins, copperheads, and coral snakes, all the poisonous serpents of the Continental U.S., according to the library book he once read. Black widow spiders and tarantulas, too.

Snakes and spiders aside, the bridge itself was scary; the huge planks had big cracks into which he could wedge his whole shoe. Sometimes looking down at the glimpses of fast water flowing beneath the bridge, he grew dizzy and afraid that his bones would lose all substance and his flesh would fold up paper-thin and he would slip through the crack. In his nightmare, he imagined a whirlpool beneath the bridge where he would spin and drown, snakes slithering out into the stream to feast on his small corpse.

He forced himself to walk to the edge and look over the brink. A face in the water stared up at him. He whipped his head back so fast, he could hear his neck pop, and then he braved another peek. It was only the silhouette of his own skull, like the Kilroy cartoon he sometimes saw drawn on graffiti walls, the bulbous nose and hands hanging over a fence. He spat into the water, aimed his pop-gun at the shape. *Kapow, kablooie*, he made gun-like reports deep in his throat.

Inspired, Dwight jumped up and ran to the tree to gather fallen apples for ammunition in his war against the water snakes. He piled the rotting fruit in his outstretched shirt, and with his pop-gun holstered in his armpit, ran back to the bridge. Too late, he could hear his mother's warning: *Don't run, don't drag your feet, watch where you're going.* The rubber toecap of his sneaker caught against the warped uneven planks. Down he went and hard, teeth jarring, skin scraping on splintered wood, apples everywhere, and the pop-gun rolling out from under his arm, and dropping into the inevitable crack between the planks. He heard the faint, fated splash beneath.

Dwight scrambled to the side and looked everywhere, but saw nothing but rocks and water. He raced to the other side. Still nothing. He waited, wondering if the snakes had gotten the gun. Then it came shooting out, caught in the flow of the creek, faster than he had expected, headed downstream.

He crossed the bridge and ran down the road alongside the creek where the pop-gun bobbed and floated along the rapids, farther and faster downstream. If he stayed on the gravel shoulder, he could stay abreast of the lost gun. The banks were steep and covered with thorns and vines, offering no easy access to the creek. He kept running along the shoulder, jumping every few feet for a better view of the pop-gun's voyage.

Up ahead, he could see a cow path down to the water. He slid down the muddy bank, his feet slopping into hoof prints left by thirsty, dirty cattle. But the pop-gun beat him and sailed only a foot away from his fingertips and on downstream.

He slogged back up the bank, lost his footing in the mud and then lost one whole sneaker as it was swallowed by a wet, green cow pie. He pried his foot free and then picked up the shoe itself from the shit and clambered up the mucky incline, jamming a briar into his wet sock. Howling, he gained the shoulder and hopping, pulled the offending thorn from his sole, and then reshod his foot and tied the slimy laces.

The gun was long gone, carried off by the current or perhaps the water snakes that lived along the rocky banks. He meandered up the road, the squish of one wet shoe, trying to be brave and see if the gun had caught against any rocks along the way.

When he looked back down the road, he saw he had lost sight of his grandfather's farm as well. He had gone all the way around the curve. And now he was in unfamiliar territory. Dwight decided to keep walking. Here was the road ahead, and the creek on his right hand, and who knew, maybe somewhere up ahead, the waterlogged pop-gun washed ashore. He walked until he reached an unfamiliar fork in the road. He wished now he'd paid more attention riding in the car with his mother. Was it the right or the left they took whenever they were headed for home? He usually had his eyes closed, faintly nauseous with the twisting hairpin curves and the dips in the road, trying to ward off carsickness until they were onto the main highway over the gap.

Dwight squinted at the sun, hoping for a sense of direction that Pop had attributed to his namesake. The sun was straight up, all right, and it was round like a clock face, or a compass, but that was all it told him, since he'd not been watching which way it moved through the blue sky.

He kept to the banks, following the right fork. Around the bend, he came across a farmhouse that looked somewhat like his grandparents', except older and abandoned. The white paint had flecked off the sides of the house and lay like dirty snow around the foundations, the porch had sagged and collapsed on one end, and weeds grew through the broken steps, the windows were all broken in the sashes. As if he had dreamed it, Dwight was afraid that he had been gone so long that his grandparents had died and their house fallen into ruin.

Dwight also began to believe he might die as well, walking the endless road. His legs ached and his stomach grumbled. He felt a hot spot on his heel that was fast becoming a blister worn by his damp sneakers, and the sun was burning the back of his neck. Still he kept going, one black canvas sneaker in front of the other, a fading *squish* on the left, a drier *flop* on his right. *Squish, flop, squish, flop.* Mesmerized by the music of his own marching, he stared at his feet as he went. He could imagine walking so far west that his shoes would begin to disintegrate, the black canvas turning gray and thinner and coming apart at the seams, his uncut toenails growing through the rubber caps, until shoes and laces came apart and he was walking barefoot; then watching the flesh peel away from the bone; and then someday, he would collapse in the midst of a western desert, a jumble of bones topped by a small boy's grinning skull.

He heard an awful commotion ahead and saw an old farmer hunched over the wheel of a red tractor, climbing up the grade. Dwight stepped to the shoulder to let the machine pass. He debated asking the man on the tractor for help. But the tractor passed by and in the noise, there were no questions or directions to be asked, the elderly gentleman nodded curtly, and Dwight returned the salute, his chin trembling. Dwight watched the tractor, and the decrepit driver bouncing on the seat, go down the road and around the bend and disappear, but it took even longer for the noise to pass.

Dwight mumbled to himself. "Can you help me? I'm sorry. Please don't think I'm a stupid little boy, but . . ."

But it was too late, and there was nothing left to be done but to keep walking. It seemed important that he keep moving as long as there was road ahead and daylight left. He would try not to think about what would happen when the night came.

He was so busy trying to walk and not think that Dwight didn't know what was behind him until the sound of a horn made him jump.

He turned and saw Pop's pick-up, its bumper not more than three feet from his backside, and the old man's head hanging out the open window of the cab, his face all angry-looking.

"Boy, where you been! Come on, get in."

Pop reached over and opened the passenger door, and Dwight slid across the seat.

"You about scared the daylights out of those women. When you didn't come home for lunch, they figured you'd wandered off. Called me over at the college to come join the search. They've been calling up and down the cove. Finally, Clay Wilson said he drove his tractor past a boy walking all by his lonesome, and I said, 'Bingo, that's my grandbaby.'"

Dwight was safe at least, but he knew his punishment was coming. They would whip him or ground him or starve him. There was nothing he didn't deserve. "I'm sorry," Dwight whispered.

"Sorry ain't an excuse."

"No, I mean I lost it. I didn't mean to, but it fell in the water and I knew I better find it."

"Lost? Find? What you talking about?"

"The pop-gun you made me, it fell through a crack in the bridge and then it was in the water, but I couldn't get it out. It just kept going down the creek and I ran after it, but I lost it."

Pop just stared at him. It was a look of pity, Dwight thought, like the old man wondered how could he be related to someone so stupid.

"Why did you keep walking is what I want to know?"

"I dunno. I guess I wanted to see how far I could walk. Maybe out west like you and Dwight Sparks."

"Whoa, now." The old man braked, and pulled off the road. "We better think this through and here's a good place to think."

Pop switched off the rumbling engine and they hung their arms out the open windows of the cab, patting the warm metal sides of the truck like a faithful horse. They stared out the dusty windshield at the creek. The brown water ran clearer here, rushing over large flat rocks. The sound of the water grew louder the longer they sat in silence.

Dwight stole a sidelong glance at Pop, trying to gauge what kind of trouble he was in.

"I'm thinking you're going to tell your mama you got a notion to go wandering down the road like I did. I'm thinking I should have told you a little more about me and Dwight Sparks."

Dwight dutifully reached in his pocket for a coin. But Pop waved him away. "Naw, this one's free."

The old man scratched at his whiskery cheeks.

"You ever hear of a moral to the story? I don't particularly care for morals that tell what a story's all about. Kind of a letdown at the end. Or it's like this lesson that the story's supposed to teach you, but that's what school's for, I figure. A story is just something you like to listen to, and the stories I've been telling you don't necessarily fall into the moral type."

Tired of explaining himself, Pop blew out all the exasperated air in his old lungs, blubbering his lips. "Look, here. The point I'm trying to make, well, you get it, don't you?"

Dwight shrugged.

"The moral here is: Don't leave home without telling nobody."

Dwight felt his forehead crinkle as he tried to think harder. "But you said you and Dwight Sparks went west without telling anybody."

"We did. I won't lie to you, that's the truth of the story." The old man nodded. "But I felt bad about that. There's a big difference between walking off one day and running away. All Dwight Sparks had for kin were his two old aunts, and I'm not sure what he told them. But I had a whole houseful of brothers and sisters. I was the runt of the litter, the littlest one at the table, having to duck all them elbows and pigtails flung in my direction. I didn't figure anyone would miss me if I left. I also didn't figure I would miss them as much as I did later on."

The sound of the water grew fainter and the ticking of the engine cooling under the hood, as Dwight leaned in, listening to his grandfather start again his story.

—

We commenced to walk west the day after school let out. Most of the stuff we left stashed under the Rendezvous Rock. It would have taken a couple of wagons to haul all that stuff, and we just had our two strong backs, and what Ivy would let us tie on her neck. We went barefoot at first, feeling our toes in the good, soft, firm dirt. The winter passes were long melted, and the sun was warm now, and the roads mostly dried out. There were some soft muddy spots in places, but nothing two boys and a cow couldn't pass. The boots we had strapped on our backs. We were saving them for colder weather and harder terrain ahead, the desert and such. Dwight said he heard tell of plants called cactus with needles for leaves, longer than locust thorns. We'd wear boots for sure when we reached the west.

Over Georges Gap, we went down an old Indian Trail that buffalo had first blazed. The world was newly green, the baby-bud green of early spring, when you've gone all winter long and realized you haven't seen the color green in what seems forever, and here is the first green, warm day. And everything is new and possible and spread out before you.

We waved to farmers in the fields, hitching up the first plow. We waved at the women beating the daylights out of rugs that had lain all dusty and sooty in parlors all winter long. Even Ivy let out a long farewell mooo to the cattle we passed in the pastures.

"Here is it is." Dwight had led the way and now he halted us with one hand raised.

"Welcome to Tennessee."

"How can you tell?"

Dwight gave me his hurt look. Again I had doubted his direction and time-telling talents. But Tennessee sure looked like what we'd left in Carolina. Same sorts of trees and rocks.

As we walked, a strange sadness started to pull down my high spirits. I wasn't picking up my feet. I began to think about my mama and my daddy, and my brothers and sisters. How they would all be sitting down to dinner along the long table, and they would be praying over the bounty of the Lord and passing the platters of chicken and chops, and beans and bread. And then it would all stop at my empty place, and all eyes would settle on the empty seat. "Where's Wylie?"

And I wouldn't be there to answer "Gone west."

Maybe I should have left a message, carved it out like old Pelham did in the door of his cabin. GTT. Gone to Texas. I could have scrawled a mystery in the soot of the hearth, a code my mama or one of my sisters might see sweeping out the hearth. WWW. Wylie's Wandered West.

Oo-gah, Oo-gah.

I nearly leapt out of my skin. The rope around Ivy's neck jerked my arm hard as she about bolted. We turned as this Tin Lizzie came tearing up the road, an open-seater horseless carriage bearing two begoggled beings. The driver kept squeezing this great brass horn, which let out an awesome noise. *Oogah, Oogah.*

We stood in the ditch with our cow to let the automobile pass. I tried to get a closer look at the folks riding in such style, but they were disguised in great dusters. I could see the driver of the machine bent hard over the wheel, chewing on one end of a great mustache as he navigated the potholes and ruts of what was nothing more than a cow path, really. But the one who took my breath away was the lady riding in the passenger seat, veiled like some sultan's daughter. She had one gloved hand holding the brim of her great hat, the other clutched to the outside door for balance or perhaps to make a quick exit in the likely event of a crash; the only flesh visible was her wrist and the long white of the back of her neck, but you could tell from those hints, here rode a real beauty. The vision took my breath away, and when my lungs remembered their purpose I was choking on the dust from her mechanized chariot.

When the dust died down, Dwight and I stared goggle-eyed at each other, mouths hung open.

"Did you see that?"

"What was it?"

"One of Mr. Ford's latest from Detroit, I suspect," Dwight said.

"Imagine if we had one of them to ride out west."

"What would we do with the cow?"

"Tie her to the back and let her run. 'Course, riding ain't the same as walking west."

"I bet one day you could ride one of them things all the way west on a real road."

"Did Boone or Crockett have a car when they went exploring, huh? Not my great Uncle Pelham neither. There's rules to do it right, you know."

An hour later and two miles later into Tennessee, Dwight and I were still debating the merits of riding in a car as opposed to walking when we descended the hillside and found the car leaning precariously in a ditch.

The two inhabitants of the machine had alighted on common ground. The man presented us with his ample backside. He was halfway under the back wheel, trying to pry it loose. The woman was likewise obscured, with her head draped beneath the black cape of a camera set on a tripod. She was evidently making some fancy photographic plate of the road they had just traveled and the mountains they had just crossed, when we came wandering into the picture.

No horn blast greeted us this time, but the woman cried out "help" or maybe "halt." It was hard to hear her clearly, muffled beneath the black cloth. She surfaced for air and glared over the big camera. "You there. Stay right where you are. Don't move."

Dwight pointed his own finger at his chest. "You mean us, ma'am?"

"Yes, you." You could see her green eyes flashing even at this distance, the great red halo of her hair, not an angel, but an archangel easily bored with mortals who were sore afraid. "I said, don't move. You're perfect right where you are. Move a muscle and you'll ruin everything."

And so we froze in our tracks, Dwight and me and even Ivy transfixed, while the woman aimed her camera. I could see her white hands moving all sorts of knobs and controls on the camera box. "That's it, perfect, perfect, perfect," her voice muffled under the black cloth. But her white hand was raised in the air, commanding respect and stillness.

The only sound came from under the car, where the feet of the man were moving, as he wormed his way though the dust, cursing a blue language the likes I'd never heard among the polite churchgoers of Beaverdam.

"All right, that's one. I need another pose. You boy, you have a name?

"Dwight Sparks, ma'am."

"And your friend?"

"This here is Wylie Rominger."

"Master Sparks, if you could please trade places with young Rominger, and stand on the other side of the cow." Her head popped out from under the cloth. "Is that a gun?"

"Yes, ma'am, but we mean you no harm. We're not desperadoes, or highwaymen, just yet."

"No, I expect not yet. Master Sparks. Would you mind though if you perhaps held up the firearm? That's it, young Dwight. How ferocious. And you, Wylie, if you would raise your arm and put your hand on the cow's horn."

And I spoke up for the first time. "Her name's Ivy."

"Pardon?"

"Ivy's the name of my heifer."

"Of course." She smiled and then ducked under the hood.

Now, I knew what she was up to, wanting to take our photograph. I had ancestors, there were plates of my grandparents hung in the parlor, daguerreotypes they had taken in Boone. One a picture of a man in a uniform with braid and a sword, Capt. Josiah Sherrill, who had fought the Yankees and came home minus an arm and died twenty years before I was born. He scowled from the parlor wall. But I was no soldier or deacon or personage important enough to have my profile recorded for posterity. It was hard staring at that one eye of the camera machine, and it staring back even harder, like it could see not just the shape of your head, but maybe some of what you were thinking inside your skull. I didn't want to appear addle-pated or plain stupid.

"Yes, yes." The woman's hand held us still, like the angel saying halt, no further. And then as the exposure went on an eternity or two, I wondered if my face was turning blue as it turned white in the camera plate, since I wasn't breathing, and I sure wasn't thinking.

Her fingers slowly clenched into a fist, pumping the sweet air of Tennessee. She threw back the cape in triumph, her hair even further askew and red, and her face flushed with triumph. "Yes. Perfect. Bravo."

Her male companion had crawled out from under the car and sat spread-legged in the middle of the dirt path, a grimy wrench clutched in one hand, looking like a large baby with a rattle. He was worth a picture himself.

"When you're through, Evelyn, maybe you could ask the yokels to help push the damned car out of the ditch."

"Language, Mr. Wilkerson. These are but lads. Don't mind Mr. Wilkerson, boys. He's not as gruff as he makes himself out to be," Miss Evelyn said. "But perhaps you would be good enough to lend him a hand."

The lady spread a blanket in the grass and ate her picnic. She read a small book, waiting for Mr. Wilkerson and ourselves to repair their transportation. Dwight suggested a lever and we took a sturdy locust rail off the fence. And a couple of rocks in the road for a fulcrum, with Dwight and the driver on the back of the rail, we got the car lifted enough for me to wedge another rock under the axle. From there it took Mr. Wilkerson no time to get the wheel off and the tire patched. On the count of three, we finally got the machine rolled back on the road.

Mr. Wilkerson cranked the car in front and the engine sprang to life.

"I believe we have cause for celebration," Miss Evelyn said, and she produced a large bottle of French champagne from her wicker basket. She poured a glass. "Would you carry this on over to Mr. Wilkerson?"

I took a whiff of the stuff as I walked over to the driver, and frowned. He took off his gloves and took the glass, smelling it, too. He wrinkled his nose, too. "A beer would be better on a hot day like this." He drained off his glass and wiped his mustache.

"What about refreshment for yourselves?" Miss Evelyn called out.

"Oh, we took the pledge. Wrote our oath in the family Bible. No alcohol," I said, suddenly panicked I'd have to drink that stuff.

"Yes, too young for the grape, I suppose," she said. "How old are you, anyway?"

"Thirteen and fifteen," Dwight said, pointing to me then tapping his chest.

"You are both strapping young men, such gentlemen." She was fishing in her purse for some money, some reward. "Let me leave you with something."

"Oh, that won't be necessary." Dwight waved her away.

"For the picture. I like some recompense for my subjects."

"Ma'am, if you could, please write my folks in Beaverdam, and tell them you saw us safe in Tennessee," I said. "Care of William Rominger, last road up the cove in Beaverdam, North Carolina. If you could send a picture perhaps of the two of us, I'd appreciate that as well."

She smiled at me. "Consider it done, Master Wylie. I'll also be sure to include how helpful you two boys were in our circumstance."

Mr. Wilkerson kept twisting his fists tightly around the steering wheel, muttering dark oaths under his breath.

"Just a second, Harry, be a dear now. Please hold this for me." Miss Evelyn gave the glass to Dwight, while she gathered her skirts to mount the jalopy.

From the corner of my eye, I could see Dwight sniffing at the glass, then sipping it a little. "Dwight," I cried. But he tossed it back like Mr. Wilkerson had. "Sorry, I was thirsty," he said, wiping the grin on his face with the back of his hand.

"That's quite all right." The lady smiled demurely herself.

She took her glass but Dwight grabbed her hand and kissed her fingers. At the same time, Mr. Wilkerson honked the great horn and released the safety brake. The car lurched forward and lips and fingers separated as I watched in wonderment.

Miss Evelyn waved over her shoulder, her white scarf floating around her in the Tennessee breeze. "Good luck, my young adventurers. God speed you west. I won't forget your request."

And we stood transfixed in the road in Tennessee, watching the departing car. Dwight licked his lips and whistled. "I'm in love."

"Nice lady," I agreed.

He grinned and punched my arm. "'Course, the world is full of women is what my daddy once told me. I'll bet there's all sorts of ladies, nice or not, out west."

"I could have stayed home if I wanted to play with girls," I scoffed, but I secretly thought of Ruth Wilson, the girl who sat two seats over from me in the schoolhouse we'd left behind.

Dwight studied my pained look. "You still homesick?"

"I ain't homesick."

"We could be back in Beaverdam before dark," he said quietly. "If you want, Wylie."

"Or we could be closer west."

I swallowed hard, dust from Miss Evelyn's horseless carriage nagging the back of my throat. I commenced to walking, tugging Ivy's rope, and Dwight's whistle bringing up the rear. . . .

———

They had been sitting in the truck, watching the water go by for a long time now. Dwight had drifted off with the old man's story, and then dazed by the long silence afterward, that he just now noticed when Pop spoke again.

"Didn't see that pop-gun go by, did you?"

Dwight shook his head.

"Things sometimes get lost. Sometimes they get found." The old man cleared his raspy throat. "I ain't real good with stories that got morals, but you're a bright boy, no need for me to belabor the point."

Dwight nodded, not a clue as to what his grandfather was saying.

"Next time, you go wandering west, tell your ma. That's the best advice." Pop started the truck. "So you want to go home?"

The way the old man asked, Dwight knew he meant his real home, where all his toys and his bike and his comic books were, where there were cartoons on television and pencil sharpeners, where his real life was as a boy, not a guest on good behavior here in the mountains.

The old man was asking him honestly. Dwight knew what he said might hurt the old man's feelings.

"Not yet. Not for a while. I could stay at your house some more."

The old man grinned. "So we're off."

Halfway to the house, his grandfather cupped his hand to his ear, and fiddled with the hearing aid. "What's that, where's that coming from?" Perplexed, he turned the radio on and off, then he stared at the boy. "Is that you, Dwight?"

Dwight heard the noise too, except it was coming out of his own pursed lips, a whistle.

"I'll be, I'll be." Pop said.

So two weeks shy of turning ten, Dwight Martin learned how to whistle. And when he grew up, he would never exercise his constitutional right to own and shoot guns like his grandfather, but he whistled often at close shaves, stray notes of relief when the world grew familiar after he thought he was terribly lost.

In that long ago summer in the mountains, he had learned the heart is a liquid compass, and its desire is the red needle that bends always to the future, bearing towards home.

GROWING PAINS

The summer he turned thirteen, Dwight Martin lived in daily dread of the bathroom mirror.

An unguarded glimpse in the glass brought new horrors: the Adam's apple knotting his throat, the thick brow beetling out, the eyes burrowing deeper, the very bones of his face shifting beneath his coarsening skin. He poked at his nose and cheeks, digging out blackheads, popping clogged pores between his gnawed nails. He watched and waited for the first whisker, when the fuzz on his sharpening chin would bristle, ready for the razor.

He leaned closer until his eyelashes brushed the cold glass. In the mirror image of his eyes, he could see another, smaller reflection of himself, that imp peering out of his pupils. He stood before the mirror, mouthing the words "Who are you?"

Dwight was becoming someone else, someone he didn't know, and the thought terrified him.

He wasn't very tall yet, a little less than average, shorter for the first time at school than many girls, those suddenly horsey amazons, angry at their adolescence and prone to kick the shins of any boy who dared approach them. Now that he was nearly a teenager, he was expected to deal with girls, to impress them, date them, somehow convince them to kiss his blotched face. Even Brenda up the street, the bespectacled Brenda he'd known forever, since first grade, had suddenly grown breasts and hips that made him blink and stare.

Alone before the merciless mirror, Dwight slipped off his T-shirt and flexed his thin arms, inspecting his biceps. He knew he wasn't very good in gym, where students had to shimmy up ropes, vault over pommel horses, and throttle their throats against the chin-up bar. Even worse than these exertions was the humiliation of the locker room, the odor of socks and athletic supporters. There was Dickie Pounds, suddenly hirsute over the summer, with coarse black tufts sprouting from his chest, belly and even his back, leering as he lathered himself between his legs in the shower for all to see, a spectacle that made the class snicker when Coach Carter called roll—Morgan, David; Pounds, Dick.

Dwight kept his own thing hidden as much as possible. In the showers, he turned discreetly toward the tiles, trying not to look at the marvels of nature in what was happening in Dickie Pounds' direction.

Of course, Dwight had gotten a *C* in sex ed class. He'd misspelled ovaries and testicles on the quiz, and he'd never quite grasped the mechanics of reproduction. In the side-by-side models of male and female equipment, he didn't see the connection, as it were, until weeks later he was fiddling with a complex set of directions for a model airplane. Tab *A* goes into Slot *B*, illustrated with forceful arrows. Then it clicked in his brain. *Oh*, he thought. He felt his face redden. *Uh oh*, he thought, sizing himself up in the shower.

—

"Dwight, are you coming out or not? Your grandparents are going to be here any moment." His mother's voice came through the door; the knob rattled but he was always careful to lock it.

"In a moment." His voice cracked and his pride crumbled. "Hang on," he tried again in a gruffer, more manly register. He slipped his shirt over his scrawny chest, frowned at himself in the mirror and washed his face again until the skin was an angry red.

He could hear the toot of a horn. Oh God, it was bad enough his grandparents were coming, did they have to announce themselves to the rest of the neighborhood? What if his friends saw them? What wisecrack would John Mark make at Dwight's expense?

Only son of the latest residents rotating through the Methodist parsonage up the street, John Mark Vogler was a good two years older and a bad influence on the rest of the neighborhood kids. Hell-bent on avoiding the boring heaven his father preached every Sunday, John Mark smoked cigarettes, drank beer, and cursed freely. John Mark boasted he once tore out the pages of his father's Bible, somewhere around Obadiah or Micah, somewhere no one ever looked, but nothing happened, no hellfire licking at his feet or lightning bolt at his head. Around adults, he would smirk and say, "Yes, ma'am," "No sir," in this smart-aleck voice, but once the back of authority was turned, he would give them the crooked middle finger he broke trying to catch a line drive in Little League. John Mark sang an obscene version of the church campfire classic, "Kumbaya," which Dwight couldn't get out of his dirtied mind.

But the Voglers were away this week in the mountains at some church retreat, thank God, where John Mark was trying to get lucky with Methodist virgins. If Dwight was lucky, he wouldn't have to introduce or explain his embarrassing grandparents to anybody he knew.

"They're here! They're here. Hurry up, Dwight," Mom called in the falsely enthusiastic voice that adults reserved for young children. *"Ice cream truck!" "Santa Claus!" "Hey, sport!"*

"Yeah right." He shuffled out on the porch, slouching, hands thrust deep into his pockets, with a practiced, pained expression that found this world sadly lacking.

The tooting horn kept closing in, along with the roar of a rusted muffler, until the familiar pick-up turned the corner. He could see the pair of them sitting upright in their best clothes in the cab. They started waving furiously out the window, and his mother returned the silly salute.

"Wave," she hissed.

Dwight reluctantly raised his arm. "Just like the Beverly Hillbillies," he said.

His family never missed the TV show about a clan of Ozark mountaineers who struck it rich and went to California, freaking out the rich people. At the end of every episode, the cast came out the doors of the set and waved like idiots to the audience. Kids at school watched the show, but it was too close to home for Dwight.

"Yes, just like the Beverly Hillbillies," Mom said. "Now wave."

The pick-up clattered into their driveway and came to a sudden, shuddering halt; the ancient engine just died. They emerged from the cab. His grandmother showing her stout leg, the waddles of flesh and purple veins visible on her thigh as she pulled down her paisley dress. His grandfather came limping around, tugging at the crotch of his pants after the long ride.

Since the Sex Ed class and the huge overhead projections of reproductive diagrams, Dwight couldn't help but notice the nuts and bolts and sockets and the sexual machinery everywhere. Even his family. Especially them. It was nightmarish to see the world sexually every waking moment and even in his sleep. The worst part was the stuff that came leaking out of him at night.

"Law me. Look at him," Gram waddled up the walkway. "How he's grown."

"Go give Gram some sugar," his mother prodded.

"Geez."

"Go." She gently shoved.

And into the bosom of his own grandmother, he could feel those big, old-lady breasts pressing against him, and he quickly fought his way out of her fleshy arms.

"You getting grown up, huh? Think you can dodge me?"

Dwight manfully stuck out his hand for a formal handshake, but Pop caught him in a bear hug redolent with the sharp tang of tobacco and an old man's sweat.

At least, his father wasn't here, frowning at this humiliation.

Frowning herself, Gram noticed the absence. "Where's Gary?"

"Oh, New Jersey needed him at the last minute and he had to fly up for a few days, troubleshoot a system for them."

"Working on them rocket ships, I reckon," Pop said.

"Well, it is a government contract, but Gary doesn't discuss his work with me."

"Too smart for the likes of me. Bet you take after your dad, huh." Pop pinched the nerve in Dwight's shoulder until he squirmed.

"Make yourselves at home." Dwight's mother was still trying to make the best of it. "Who knows, Gary might make it back before y'all leave."

"Leave? We just got here," Pop said. "We might stay a spell."

Finally Pop released the boy, and Dwight tried to recover his dignity, shuffling into the house after the grown-ups, but his mother stopped him at the door. "Dwight, please go get their things."

Dwight sighed in exasperation, but didn't let his mother see him roll his eyes. She complained bitterly about this new streak of independence Dwight exhibited, or what his parents called "attitude." He never directly disobeyed his parents, but he wanted to let them know that, at almost thirteen, he had his own timetable, and before he played bellhop, maybe he better go check the mailbox first. No longer a pre-teen but a full-fledged teenager, the troublesome topic, it seemed, of all his mother's magazines that he found in the mailbox: "Tips on the Terrible Teen Years," "When Your Baby Hates You: Loving Your Adolescent," "Recognizing the Juvenile Delinquent."

"How's it hanging, Martin?"

He didn't hear John Mark until it was too late. His neighborhood nemesis had skidded his bike to a stop only a few feet from Dwight, spraying loose gravel against his shins. John Mark sported a fedora with a bright red feather in the felt band, probably stolen from his old man, to lend some class to his torn T-shirt and cut-off blue jeans, his black canvas sneakers.

"I thought you were in the mountains, church camp." Dwight's eyes smarted—the gravel had been sharp, but he couldn't let the older boy see any sign of weakness.

"Let's just say me and this girl from Alabama got caught playing Adam and Eve out in the bushes one night. So what's been happening around here, Martin?"

"Nothing," Dwight admitted.

John Mark stared suspiciously at the pick-up in Dwight's driveway. "I see your family traded up to a new set of wheels."

"Oh, no, that belongs to, uh, guests. My mother has company."

John Mark scowled like he didn't quite buy Dwight's explanation, but to Dwight's relief, the older boy let it go. John Mark balanced on the pedals, and made the bike bounce up and down. Then he lounged on the banana seat against the sissy bar. "You coming out tonight for war?"

Behind their neighborhood, a decrepit dairy farm had been cleared to make way for a new subdivision. Lots marked off by wooden stakes, and the grading had begun. In the lingering dusk of daylight savings, after the workers had gone home, the neighborhood kids fought great battles, hurling clods of red clay from atop the piled mountains. Naturally, John Mark was king of the hill, pushing all challengers down the red slopes, staining their shorts and T-shirts with dirt. Last week, Dwight had come home, his forehead marked with dirt and blood where John Mark had popped him with a well-aimed missile.

"I can't tonight. Company. I have to be nice to them."

"Yeah, that's so hard for you, Martin. Being nice."

John Mark didn't believe in Christian names, only surnames, as it was more grown-up, but also less friendly, easier to bully and boss younger kids. So Dwight was no longer Dwight, but Martin, now, although this rule didn't seem to apply to John Mark.

"I probably didn't come back a moment too soon to save you from being a momma's boy."

As if on cue, his mother poked her head out the door. "Dwight, where are the suitcases?" She shaded her eyes, peering at her son's companion. "Oh hi, John Mark. Did you have fun at church camp?"

"Hi, Mrs. Martin." John Mark doffed his hat. "Great time, ma'am. Very spiritual."

"Dwight, Gram needs her suitcase," she called again.

John Mark cocked the fedora on his forehead and muttered. "Martin, your mom's a real looker. Kumbaya, you know."

"I better go," Dwight said, tight-lipped.

In the bed of the truck, he found a battered suitcase and a box of preserves, canned beans and potatoes, lashed to the sides with a sisal rope that smelled like it last came off a mule's back. The bed itself was scraped and covered with hay chaff, dried clods of dirt and cow pie. A hundred miles from home and they couldn't help but bring the barnyard smell with them.

The suitcase looked a little more respectable, its yellow paper sides tattered, leaking the smell of mothballs and camphor, old lady, old man odors. He dragged the prehistoric suitcase along the walkway, up the porch and through the front door, hauling it to his bedroom where his grandparents would be staying, kicking him out of his own bed, banishing him to the couch in the den for the duration.

Returning for the box of potatoes, he double-checked to make sure John Mark wasn't circling around the cul-de-sac on his bike. His grandparents had brought enough food here to last for months, it seemed. And Dwight had the terrible thought. What if they did stay that long?

After all his efforts, Dwight wanted to check the mirror, to see if his face was burning from shame or a new outbreak of acne, but the bathroom door was closed. Inside, he could hear the stream echoing in the toilet bowl, probably Pop who relieved himself as loudly as a plowhorse when he had to go.

Dwight moped out to the kitchen to pester his mother. Pots boiled over on the stove, steam was rising into her face, and the suspicious smells of vegetables boiling and burning flooded the house. His mother looked a little overdone as well. She kept pulling at her sticky blouse, blowing a loose strand from her damp forehead. He came around the counter to the range, where he tipped one pot lid and was hit in the face by a wicked smell. "Eew, what's that?"

"Turnip greens." She slapped his hand and replaced the hot lid.

"Why can't we just pick up pizza, like always?"

"Always? We don't always have pizza. I can cook, you know." She turned to the counter, chopping onions. Her eyes watered. "Besides, your grandparents don't like pizza."

"Everybody likes pizza."

"I'm not sure they've ever tried pizza."

"Well, how do they know if they don't like it if they've never tried it?" Dwight threw in her face a familiar argument he didn't know how many times he'd heard.

"Ouch." She turned with her finger in her mouth, then looked at the bloody cut on her finger. The tears were for real now, not just onions. She pointed her bloody finger at him. "Out. Out. Now."

—

The food was bland, but everyone made a fuss over it at the dinner table. It was as a bad as eating in the school cafeteria, great globs of congealed and stringy textures, lumps and knots that slapped on the tongue and against the teeth. Everyone chewed carefully with widening eyes.

Pop swallowed hard, dutifully clearing his plate. "Think I might have seconds, that's so good."

"Here let me get that." His mother leapt from her chair, grabbing for his plate.

"I can get it, girl. Quit fussing so. We're not guests, we're family."

He winked at Dwight. "How about you, boy. Looks like you need more meat on them bones of yours. Seconds?"

"No thanks." Dwight daubed the napkin to his mouth pointedly, politely. "May I be excused?"

He didn't wait for an answer but scraped his chair back and fled the room just as his mother and grandmother began fighting over who would do the dishes. "Mama, don't." "Oh, June, let me just help." "Please, Mama."

Dwight turned on the TV when he heard the crash of a dinner plate and a terrible silence emanate from the kitchen. He turned up the volume and settled into the couch, half-sitting, half-reclining, his legs jiggling in front of him, a posture that always infuriated his mother who nagged him, "Sit up straight, you're going to warp your spine."

But his mother didn't dispense with her usual advice when she checked on him. She had a harried look and a broken dish in her hand.

"Dwight, what are you doing?"

Anyone could see that he was watching TV. He always watched TV in the summer right after dinner, although everything was re-runs and boring. But he knew she hadn't really asked a question. She was about to tell him what he was doing.

"Pop's outside. It would be nice if you'd go out and keep him company."

"Outside?" Dwight protested. No pizza, no TV. His comfortable life was in chaos. "What's he doing outside?"

"Why don't you go see for yourself?" She whirled toward the kitchen when she heard the tap suddenly running. "Mama, don't. We have the dishwasher now."

Outside, Dwight found his grandfather inspecting the shrubs his father had landscaped around the house and already savagely pruned back for next spring. Dwight's dad was as meticulous about plants as he was about slide rules. He had actually drawn a grid of the yard on graph paper and mapped where each and every plant would grow in his perfect kingdom.

Pop snapped off an azalea shoot and started picking his teeth.

"I wouldn't do that." Dwight didn't want to explain the mutilated plant when his dad returned from New Jersey.

"Do what?" Pop chewed the woody stem.

Dwight let it drop, and he let his eyes drop to the ground. He continually found himself looking down this summer, browbeaten by adult inquisitions. He toed the grass underfoot.

"I mow this, you know," Dwight announced. "For my allowance."

Pop squinted, the tight look he had any time money was mentioned. The sprig jumped from the left side of his mouth to the right. "How much?"

"Five bucks a week." Enough to keep Dwight in comic books and colas from the convenience store a short bike ride away.

"Looks a little long now, don't it?" Pop toed the ankle-deep turf.

Actually, that was what his father had said right before he drove away to the airport. "Grass needs mowing, son."

"I was going to do it before Dad got back," Dwight defended himself.

Pop nodded knowingly, clasped his calloused hands behind him and strolled around the half-acreage. Dwight followed behind, obediently but bored. They looked over every bush and flower bed, the new white pines bordering the property line, scrawny sentinels spaced at six-foot intervals, each tethered with wire and hose to wooden stakes, as if his father were afraid the saplings might wander off at night, or someone might steal them, a tree thief. Actually it was only to train the trees to grow up in the perfect lines as their fate had been charted on graph paper.

"He just planted those," Dwight explained.

Pop pushed aside a pine bough and peered into the distance. "You're getting neighbors, I see."

A dozen construction sites beckoned beyond, and Dwight could hear the shouts of kids playing king of the mountain. He could be having some fun if his grandparents weren't holding him hostage at the house. The games were short-lived, with tight schedules for the houses. Soon the mountains of red dirt would be graded away, and then framing quickly raised, the skeleton outlines of yellow lumber outlining identical floor plans. And not long after, the house would be sold and a new family would move in with some strange kid who would show up at the bus stop come fall.

"Shame how the city overtakes the country these days. Didn't they used to graze cows here?"

"Used to."

Dwight remembered the farm's dwindling herd. Sometimes the cows got out of the rusty fencing on foggy mornings and slipped into suburbia, bovine intruders in the dawn grazing great, sweet clods of fescue and bluegrass out of homeowners' manicured lawns, leaving steaming droppings in their wake. Dwight remembered waking in the middle of the night, and hearing a soft step outside his window. Monsters, he thought and crept to the window. Outside in the moonlight, he saw hulking shapes in their yard, horned creatures milling about the driveway. He rubbed his eyes and the shapes seemed to melt away into the woods across the street. Dream cows.

"Cows really stink. I'm glad they're gone."

"Well, I don't know if I go so far as that. Cows are sensitive creatures, you know. Don't take much to hurt their feelings. I learned that the hard way when me and my buddy, Dwight Sparks, walked a cow across country when I was about your age. I ever tell you about that?"

"Yes," Dwight muttered. "About a million times."

Already he had his fist clenched around the two quarters in the

pocket of his cut-off blue jeans—all that was left of his allowance until
he mowed the lawn again. He really couldn't afford to humor Pop and
his tall tales.

But his grandfather was paying him no mind.

"The cow just lay down one day . . . "

The old hand held down a green bough of the young pine tree and he
looked over the former pasture now divvied up into house lots as if the old
man could still see cows, see grass, see the past when he was young.

Dwight waited, half-listening, half-nodding his head, wondering when
it would be over. He watched the network of wrinkles working in the old
man's face, like some road map, like every road and route and path he'd
taken in his long life could be read in his very features, and slowly those
wrinkles and lines vanished, and Dwight was looking into a face not
unlike his own, a mirror, and he could see how his father said he favored
his grandfather, the same shaped eyes, the same nose and mouth. And in
his mind he could see Wylie as a boy, and he could see what Wylie was
telling him, see it through his eyes. Dwight walking back through the
high grass, the cow that wouldn't get up. . . .

. . . The cow just lay down one day, 'round about Kansas, I reckon, at
least we thought it was Kansas, the land being so flat. We hadn't seen a
tree in quite some time, but the grass grew knee-high and when the wind
blew it lay down at your feet, rustling like green snakes slithering away.

We'd been walking two weeks since we made it over the river. A fort-
night later, I was still sloshing in my skin. I'd scratch my head and bits of
Mississippi mud came flaking down like brown snow, and I could still
hear the big river rolling inside my ear, and try as I might, jumping up
and down and banging the side of my head, I like to never get that sound,
that water out.

Dwight Sparks kept a good quarter-mile up ahead. A fast walker and a
head taller than me, his stride measured out to exactly two inches longer
than mine. And he had calculated that over the course of a morning's walk,
that two inches would translate into two feet, then two yards, and soon two
hundred yards, then two miles. If Dwight didn't stop to let me and Ivy
catch up every once in a while, he'd hit California two days before me.

I was counting all this in my head, when I was jerked up short. The halter I had in my hand raised a red welt in my palm, and my arm about popped out of my shoulder. Ivy had gone down on her front knees, and then flopped on her flank.

"Come on girl. Get up." I pulled on the halter, but she shook her horns and wouldn't budge.

"Upsy-Daisy now," I tried sweet-talking her.

She closed her eyes, and her long pink tongue hung out of her white mouth.

"Dwight, hold up," I cried out across Kansas.

He was getting smaller on the long horizon. I don't think he heard me at first. So I hollered again and waved my hands. There was nothing but big sky overhead and I don't know where they came from but suddenly there was a buzzard circling overhead. Uh oh. I hollered even louder until Dwight finally turned, and then grew bigger and bigger until he stood by my side, two inches taller.

Now there were two buzzards overhead.

"What's the trouble here?" he said.

"She ain't moving."

Dwight looked up and frowned. Now the two buzzards had grown into a dozen, come out of nowhere in the big sky, circling right overhead.

"Can't be hungry. All this grass around it must be pasturing paradise for a cow, and there's been plenty of water."

I slunk cross-legged beside her and patted her heaving haunch. "I think she's still mad at you for Memphis."

"Memphis? Lord, let it go, Wylie. You're talking water under the bridge."

"That's the problem. Weren't no bridge if I recollect."

And Ivy let out a low moan as well.

"Can't y'all forget about that?"

"No," I shook my head. "Cows don't forget, and me neither."

"Wait a minute! You said you were in Kansas. Memphis is not in Kansas!"

Almost thirteen now, Dwight was no dummy. He knew his geography and he wasn't going to let the old man insult his intelligence.

"The better question might be how we got across the river, you know. Besides being sensitive, cows aren't the best of swimmers." Pop stripped a handful of green needles from the branch of the pine tree. "Usually stories involve some kind of choice. You pick."

The old man extended his two closed fists. Dwight couldn't believe how lame this was. He reached over and tapped the right hand. His grandfather turned over his hand and slowly opened the palm to show nothing. He grinned.

"Try again. Bound to get it right this time." The old man motioned to the other.

Dwight impatiently pried open Pop's strong fingers. It smelled like Christmas, the crushed needles in his hand.

But Pop wiggled his fingers. That old game between them. Dwight had lost and it would cost him. He dug out one quarter and put it in the old man's calloused palm.

"Pay attention." Pop pocketed his spoils. "And don't be eager to interrupt your elders. Sometimes things turn out in the end if you give it enough time. So where was I?"

"Kansas?"

"No, let me back up a bit."

—⁓—

Tennessee took two weeks of walking before we came to the Big River. There were plenty of streams and creeks we crossed along the way, but nothing like the Mighty Missipp. Books always call it the Mighty Mississippi, but until you see all that water, it's just words to you. It looked more like an ocean than a river and there were wild waves out in the middle lapping at the shore where we stood, and far off glinting to the west the other side, like a whole another world across all that water.

"How we getting across?" I asked Dwight Sparks as we stood atop the Tennessee bluff. No bridge long enough to go over in those days, only barges charging two dollars a head for even a cow to cross.

We trooped down to the first wharf, only to be stopped by a Nubian giant, the first Negro I'd seen in his coal-black flesh.

"Hold it there. Bossman charge two bucks."

"How about we pay you on the other side?" Dwight smiled, but the ferryman wasn't buying.

"This is up-front money."

"We could swab your decks, maybe row a little if you needed us?"

"That, white boy, is my job." The man made a show of turning his broad back on us as he would on any poor trash blown across the sticks of Tennessee.

Up and down the river, along the wharves and docks, we went but it was the same story. River Rats have no heart. The blood that swam through their tattooed and torn bodies was exactly the same cold ooze of the river that stood behind them. The price went as high as five dollars, especially if you were wanted or were carrying stolen goods. The best fare was an honest dollar, still more than we had in our skinny pockets. For all the gear we accumulated on the Rendezvous Rock, what we really needed in our adventuring was cash on the barrelhead and lots of it.

"We could roll the dice," Dwight suggested as we wound our way through the back alleys of Memphis. "Rely on Lady Luck."

I shook my head. Gambling was a sin in Beaverdam, and I wasn't far enough from home to start risking hell-fire. We walked by stockyards where Ivy's kind milled behind wooden rails. At one end of the enclosure stood a wooden ramp leading up in a chute to a narrow gate where a heavy sledgehammer leaned against the railing. I knew what that was all about, and Ivy knew instinctively, too; I felt a shudder go through her. Some big black man would stand there like the angel of death. One swing of that iron hammer and life would be knocked clean out of a cow's skull.

Ivy hurried her step some as we went by, but Dwight Sparks dawdled by the fence, pulling on his chin whiskers, a sure sign of deep thought and more than likely trouble to come.

"What if we sold the cow?" he suggested.

"Over my dead body." I crossed my arms over my chest, like I was already laid out in my coffin.

"No, we could sell her in the morning, then come back and steal her at night."

"But don't they hang you for stealing livestock?"

"Horses. They hang horse thieves out west. You might draw a prison term for a cow."

"Let's keep moving."

Down the muddy street, we passed by the substantial doors of the local Mercantile Bank and Trust, so trusting the doors were wide open to patrons and even passersby. I nudged Dwight and nodded toward all the loot within. "If we're going to settle on a life of crime, maybe we ought to rob a bank."

"Wylie, you can't waltz into a bank without the proper weaponry. You have to have pistols like Jesse James or the Daltons. Tellers take one look at desperadoes without six-shooters, they wouldn't be able to hold their hands over their heads, they'd be holding their sides and slapping their knees, they'd be laughing so hard."

We kept on walking, and just to let us know what lay in store, if we went the wrong way, we happened to walk right by the Memphis jailhouse. You could see the fists of men clinging to the iron bars. Hoots and hollers, screams and the clanging of heavy doors echoed from the stone walls. And in plain view in the courtyard was a scaffold and gallows. A row of three thickly knotted ropes dangled from a heavy crossbeam, the nooses swaying slightly in the breeze that blew off the river. I could imagine me and Dwight and even Ivy strung up by our scrawny necks, to be taught our last lesson.

"Maybe we ought to keep walking until something better occurs to us."

So we walked on down the river, debating how to get across. The river didn't get any less wide nor the ferries any less expensive. Until we were clear out of Tennessee and before we knew it, down into Mississippi. Dwight said it must be Mississippi because of the cotton fields. It felt hot and humid, the air not at all cool like back in Beaverdam. It must have been a hundred degrees but all the ground as far as the eye could see was covered with white, like a snow had fallen in the middle of summer. This was the land of cotton. As we walked the river road, we could see dark heads moving through the white rows, and the sound of mournful songs being sung.

Down the road, a man sat on his horse at the edge of the fields. The haunches of the horse showed, and the man kicked black boots against its piebald ribs. He was the whitest man you could imagine. His hair was white under his straw hat, and his skin that showed under his hat and his shirt was like a sheet of paper no one had written on. His hat looked too small for his head, or maybe it was the brim was too stingy with its shade; he had to pull down hard over his pink blinking eyes. Those eyes were watching us now.

"Howdy," Dwight said all neighborly, like albinos lived up and down the cove where we came from in Beaverdam.

The albino man said nothing.

At the edge of the field, you could hear the voices of the workers carried over the cotton. At first, I couldn't understand the words; they were so slow, like molasses coming out of their black mouths, like the words were sweaty. Then my ear slowed down to their speed, and they were singing of deliverance and Promised Land and milk and honey.

"They sure sing nice," I said.

"Yeah," the albino man leaned over his horse and spit a thin stream of tobacco that raised a plop of dust in the dry road. His pink tongue flicked out and took off a little black spittle from his thin lips.

"If they shut up, they might pick a little faster. I got a hundred acres here, and I don't think these boys are going to get it done in time." He glanced nervously at the sky, which was boiled white as the cotton fields. Not a cloud or bird or anything to be seen.

Dwight nudged me. "Mister, maybe you need another pair of hired hands."

The horsemen rested his white hands on the horn of his saddle, and those pink eyes blinked beneath the straw hat.

"Y'all boys ain't from around here," he noted. "Tennessee?"

"Beaverdam, that's in the Carolina mountains," Dwight said proudly.

"Uh huh," the albino said slowly, chewing his words slowly along with his plug. "They pick cotton in them parts?"

"Mostly burley tobacco," Dwight had to admit.

"Nice looking heifer there," the man mentioned.

"Thank you, sir. She's mine. She ain't for sale," I added, not liking the look in that pasty face.

"So what say, sir? Need some good hands?

"I usually only do shares around my land. Tell you what, go help Pervis and his family. They're pretty far behind from the looks of it."

"And what's our pay?" Dwight asked.

"Penny a pound, when we weight it, minus what you eat and where you sleep."

"Fair enough, Mister —? " Dwight wiped his hand on his jeans and reached up to shake his new boss's hand in good faith.

"Snow," said the man, who evidently wasn't the handshaking kind of man. He spurred the mare to make her rear up in the road, like she was about to kick us. "Tell Pervis, Snow sent you. He'll show you what's what."

Then the horse came down and settled into a slow plodding walk, swishing flies away from its rump.

I tethered Ivy to a shade tree by the road, and we waded into the white rows to commence our careers as cotton pickers. "Hey, any of y'all name of Pervis?" I cried.

Slowly, the black heads lifted from the field of white, and blinking big eyes like cotton bolls considered us. The sun was hot but not as fierce as the glare of those eyes. Finally, one of the women said. "What you white boys want?"

"Mr. Snow sent us. We're here to help." Dwight said.

You would have thought it was the funniest joke these folks had ever heard. They opened their mouths and such rich laughter rolled out among the rows of cotton. Then just as suddenly, the laughter dried up, and their looks were like throwing knives in our direction.

"Tell us another, white boy."

"Honest Injun," Dwight said. I could see the smile twitching on his face, and his neck was starting to turn red in a way I reckoned wasn't just sunburn.

"Careful what you say. Pervis is half Choctaw," the woman said.

"We meant no offense," I explained. "We're just walking our way out of Carolina and need to earn us enough money to get over the river."

"I'm Pervis." A gaunt black man stepped across the rows. "Snow says you're the hired help, I reckon that's the way it goes. Just don't be getting in the way."

He threw us a pair of sacks. "Go help my young'un Pearl down at the end of the row."

Pearl would be the same sassy girl who had taunted us. She was no bigger than me, but her hair was done up in braids that stuck out from beneath a straw hat. She wore jeans like us and a long shirt tied up around her waist.

"You Pearl?" I asked. "We're here to help."

"Huh, y'all don't look like cotton pickers."

"Mostly tobacco, but I figure we'll catch on."

"Now this here's complicated," she said. "You pull all the white stuff and you put it in this here sack."

"I think we can manage." Dwight straightened and slipped his arm through the sling. "Once you suckered tobacco, can't nothing be any worse than that. Am I right, Wylie?"

"Well —"

"Where we come from, suckering tobacco is a terrible chore," Dwight kept bragging and making up stuff. "Grown men have been known to break down and cry. You go through and pull all the small leaves off and let the big leaves grow. And this sap glues your fingers together and the cutworms nibble at your fingers. That's why they don't let girls do it, men die suckering tobacco."

"Oh yeah?"

When Pearl squared her shoulders and set her fists on her hips, she looked as fierce as any boy you'd fight in a schoolyard, except she had the makings of a woman's breasts pointing through the white sweaty shirt.

"I was picking cotton when I started crawling out of the cradle. They tied a bag to me, and let me crawl down the rows on my hands and knees, and I picked the cotton and sucked on it a while, and then they learned me to put it in the bag. I picked a hundred pounds of cotton before I was out of diapers."

"Well, it goes to prove my point then—if babies and girls can pick cotton, it can't be all that hard, now can it?" Dwight kept goading her, which I wasn't at all sure was a good idea.

"Tell you what, white boy —"

"Don't be calling me that. I go by Dwight. And this here's Wylie. Now tell me what?"

She hushed for a second and studied us hard. "Well, Dwight and Wylie, I'll race you. First one to the end of that row gets all the cotton in the other's bag. Beat me, you might make it over the river a little quicker."

"You're on."

Dwight and me got down like we were going to run a dash. Pearl just stood there, hands on her hips when she said go. Dwight and me jumped like rabbits, grabbing cotton handful after handful and stuffing it into the bags that unfurled behind us. Looking back, I could see Pearl's white smile under the shade of her battered straw brim, her hands moving slowly but surely along her row of plants.

"Like the man said, Wylie, penny a pound. Two hundred pounds a piece, we'll be sailing over the River in no time at all."

—

"Lemme see them hands, boy." The old man's grip was astonishingly strong, a vise of rough calluses and knobby knuckles.

He turned Dwight's palms over for inspection. "You using ladies lotion on 'em? Not a working man's hands for sure. You ain't ever picked cotton, I can tell, or hoed a row of taters."

No," Dwight said defensively, pulling free and shoving his hands in his pockets. He was a student, not a farmer, not some redneck. He had hands like his father's, soft and manicured.

—

Fifty years now, it's been and I can still feel my fingers pinching and poking at all that cotton. Like when the arthritis flares up, I fetch the aspirin,
and what do they pack in the top but this ball of cotton, so you've got
your fingers all pinched up, trying to fish this white wad out, and it hurts
something fierce to get to the pain pills. That's what picking cotton's like,
plant after plant, row after row, hour and hour, like trying to pull the cotton balls out of a million aspirin bottles until your fingers are on fire.

Now, imagine the bottle has broken and you're picking cotton out
of broken glass. Soon I noticed all the cotton bolls I was picking were
turning red from the blood on my fingertips. Them brown spikes of the
splayed bolls are sharp as pins to prick your fingers. Soon it's not like
having hands but claws, and you're crawling like a crab all hunched over
since the plants don't come up much higher than your knee. And you
wouldn't think something as fluffy as cotton would weigh so much, but
the bag starts filling up and stretching out ten feet behind. By the time
you reach the end of the row, it's like you're dragging this cloth ball and
chain. And after a while, it feels like you're carrying the sun on your
shoulders as well. The heat bores down on your back and you come to the
end of the row and you try to stand up straight, and you hear this snap in
your spine, like you done broke your own back, and the blood suddenly
leaves your head, and the world goes all white and things are swimming
in your eyes . . .

The sun was fierce. And after awhile I had to squint my eyes to see
anything. The world was burning white. It looked like a snowfield in
December, and the funny thing was I started shivering all over. I could
hear them singing but the words kept getting slower and slower, like
molasses in my ears. And then it was all like humming. They sounded
like angels now. I looked back over my shoulder, at Pearl coming up the
next row. I pitched headlong into the cotton and that's all I remember.

"Wake up, Wylie! Wylie, you with us?"

I came to under the shade of a pin oak by the edge of the field. I lay
on my own sack of cotton, on a pillow that Pearl was holding under my
head.

Then I realized that pillow was, well, her bosom. She was softer than she looked, and lying there, under the shade of the pin oak, I didn't want to ever get up.

"Here," she lifted my head and gave me a dipper of water. "Nice and slow. That's it."

"Who won?" I said weakly.

Pearl laughed and showed her strong white teeth. "It wasn't you white boys. Y'all owe me two sacks of cotton. I already got his. Yours, you can lay on until you feeling better."

I tried to lift my head but the world started swimming before my eyes again.

"No, now. You lay still. I reckon you mountain boys ain't used to Mississippi sun."

"Problem, girl?" a voice called out.

Pearl stiffened with fear, and behind her I saw the albino on the horse.

"This boy laying down on the job already?"

Dwight straightened himself. "He got a little light-headed in the sun. He just needs a breather and we'll be back at it."

Snow spurred his horse forward. "Good Lord put only so many hours into one day. 'Course God's got all eternity, but I ain't. Y'all get a move on."

"Yessir, Mr. Snow." Pearl ducked her head and gathered her bag, but not before her hand squeezed mine.

The albino rode on, and I could hear Dwight saying to Pearl as they headed back into the field, "Double or nothing?"

—

The sun was down and fireflies were starting to swirl about the yard like the ember of the old man's cigarettes. Pop snuffed out the butt beneath his brogan. He yawned and rose with great cracks sounding in his joints.

"I believe it's about bedtime for this old farmer. Just talking about that cotton picking tuckered me out. Hard habit to break after you been getting up to feed chickens and milk the cow long as I have."

The old man sauntered off to Dwight's bedroom to join his ancient bride already turned in for the night. It was all of nine o'clock.

Dwight was displaced to sleeping on the sofa in the den, which wasn't so bad, since he could stay up late watching television and his mother couldn't yell at him, at least not in the deaf earshot of the old folks. "How long do you think they're going to be here?" he asked his mother.

"Dwight, I do wish you wouldn't mumble. What did you say?"

Dwight wasn't brave enough to repeat himself in a louder voice. "Who's feeding his chickens and cows if he's down here? Did he leave enough food for the chickens and cows?"

"Oh, he sold off all those pullets, and that old cow last winter."

"What?" Dwight was shocked. "Sold them?"

"The cow was getting old. Your Pop's getting along in years. Things are getting to be a bit much for him. He's not a spring chicken himself."

"He wouldn't sell his cow."

"If you say so. Don't stay up too late now."

Johnny Carson was swinging a make-believe golf club at the end of the monologue. Dwight kept the volume down but not low enough to drown out the whistles and rasping snores of the two old people lying in his bed, making the model airplanes spin over their dreams with their ancient lungs. They competed in a sleep symphony; the old lady took the high nasal notes and sniffles, while the old man boomed out a raspy lower register.

Dwight turned on his side under the sheet his mother had given him. He sighed and he punched the pillow behind his head, then wondered what a girl's breast would feel like: would they be as soft as Pop made them sound?

CHORES

Dwight awoke on the sofa to the rustle of a newspaper, and in the still half-dark world before the summer sunrise, his grandfather sat in Dwight's father's chair, reading. The black eye of the television stared from across the room, though Dwight had no recollection of turning it off, or of anything other than the black-and-white image of the red-white-and-blue American flag waving across the airwaves as the station ended its regular programming for the day and signed off to the tune of the national anthem.

The old man peered over the daily paper. "I was wondering how long you were going lie there like some lump on a log."

"What time is it?"

"Time to be getting up. Daylight's a wasting. You get to be my age, you want to savor every single moment the sun's out. Night's all dark, same thing you get when you close your eyes. But the day brings something new to look at."

Pop wet his broad thumb and turned the pages of the classifieds, tilting his head up and down, squinting at the tiny type. "Look here, says a man can earn six dollars an hour with vacation and health benefits for laying pipe."

"It'd be healthy at your age, not to worry so about work," Dwight's mother suggested from the kitchen where she was cleaning up from the unusual breakfast.

"Somebody's got to." Pop rustled the paper and peered down the next fine-print column of possibility. "I might need that money to buy this used pick-up the man is selling. Best offer, he says."

But then he forgot all about such work, abruptly folding his paper. "Chores to be done. Ready to mow the yard?"

"No."

"Grass is growing, sun is shining. We ain't got all day."

Dwight got dressed, and scrubbed his sleepy face, checking for any new adolescent pox. He was still yawning when he went down the basement stairs, and to his horror, found Pop dismantling his Dad's push mower.

"What are you doing?"

"I just thought I'd oil this engine a bit, then I saw the blade needed sharpening. Come on outside, we'll get this filed up nice and sharp."

Not mechanically inclined, Dwight had no idea how the infernal machine actually worked, only that he should never mow the yard barefoot and never put his hand under the body. They carried the blade around to the front and sat on the porch stoop. "Here, run this file like so, up and down. At an angle. There you go. Nice and slow."

Dwight held the blade awkwardly between his knees and ran the long file down the blade with a satisfying metallic rasp. "Okay, now what?"

"Well feel the blade again with your thumb. Feel any sharper to you?"

"Nope."

"Then keep doing it." Pop lit a cigarette, sipped his cold coffee, and then casually asked, "I was telling you about my cotton-picking days yesterday?"

Dwight said nothing. If he didn't encourage the old man, maybe he wouldn't rattle on with one of his stories.

"Now there's work you have to keep at. Dwight Sparks and me learned that the hard way down in Mississippi, trying to pay the fare for a ferry ride over the river . . .

Dwight kept rasping the file up and down the mower blades, listening reluctantly as Pop started again with his tall tales.

———

Over the course of three days, Dwight Sparks had lost every race down the row to Pearl's more experienced cotton-picking, and I'd learned not to even try to keep up with that girl. She was more than a good sport about it, and gave the cotton back to Dwight, but sweat certainly came cheap in those days.

Sunset came and went, that great red ball tottering on the levee for a few minutes, then rolling into the river itself. You could almost hear the hiss as the fireball burned out, and the air seemed hotter for a second just before the cool of the evening came on. We picked the last of the rows, the white flames of cotton lighting the way, our eyeballs burned out from the long white afternoon. And we came out of the fields like giant glow-worms, the sacks of cotton trailing behind us. Grasping and ungrasping the air to straighten out aching fingers, slowly achieving a full stance from the crouch we'd worked from all the day long.

For all our work, Dwight and me weighed out at just under a hundred pounds apiece, not hardly a bale worth toting, according to Mr. Snow. The albino wet his pale thumb and turned the page of his ledger. With a pencil stub so small, he marked what we'd made that day, twenty-three and twenty-four cents respectively, minus the nickel for renting a place to lay our heads overnight in the black man's barn.

What if we sleep out by the fields then, Dwight suggested. "That way we could be right in the fields a little quicker come daylight."

"Suit yourselves," said Snow. "You boys need to pick up the pace any-how. I can't wait until the next big storm blows all that cotton off the bolls and into some bales for me."

So priced out of the barn and into the outdoors, we tied the cow to the tree. Pearl came out with two plates of rice and beans and greens, good eating like we hadn't had since Beaverdam. And we sounded like pigs, clattering over our plates, while Pearl waited to take the plates when we were finished.

Off in the distance, there was a mournful sound. A train passing in the night, headed upriver.

Pearl sat with her arms wrapped around her knees, swaying slowly back and forth. She sighed. "I'd like to ride me a train, see the world outside of Mr. Snow's cotton field."

"You could come with us," I said.

"We don't want no girls with us," Dwight protested.

"Technically, Ivy's a girl."

Dwight spat loudly in the dark. "Huh, girls can't keep up."

"Look who's talking, white boy who can't pick cotton."

"You talk to me when you sucker tobacco."

"Can't you two knock it off," I said.

Dwight flipped the empty plate in her direction. "Thank your mama for the food. Very good. Can't say the same for the company."

"Hmph!" Pearl had her arms crossed.

"Hmph to you too!" Dwight flopped himself down hard on the ground, but before long he was snoring us a serenade.

I thought Pearl might leave as well, but she lingered.

"I thought you got tired of these fields," I said.

"Well, don't think I'm gonna stay here forever. I'm leaving these parts some day. Daddy's talking about up north anyhow. Where you can live in a city and not a tarpaper shack. Where they have schools you can go to, and real jobs and there ain't no cotton, and snow up North is what falls from God's sky, and it ain't some funny old white man who rides up on a nag to pick at you and how you pick cotton. And I don't need no white boy with a cow to come rescue me. Just you watch, just you see."

"Hey, I believe you. Don't be yelling at me."

"Sorry," she said. But she still didn't leave.

There was a bluff off in the distance and as the moon rose, I counted thirteen columns standing in the light. "What's that?"

"There's the old Snow place," Pearl said. "My people have been here as long as his. They say back before the war, that place was lit up like Christmas all year round, and the big boats coming downriver used it like a lighthouse to steer by the shoals. Snow calls 'em damn Yankees that burned the place out, but I say good riddance, even though the war never ended for folks like us. Just last year, they hung my cousin there from the columns, there, the thirteenth one on the end."

"He didn't steal a horse, did he?"

"No," Pearl shook her head. "Men in white robes came riding up and hogtied him and took him up there. They say he was fool enough to steal something else. They say he stole a kiss from a white woman."

"And they hung him for that?"

"A black-and-white kissing gets you killed hereabouts."

"That don't seem right."

My lips began to itch, my throat tightened, and I felt this hollowness filling my ribs. Who knows what possessed me, but I leaned in close against the blackness. I couldn't see where I was going so I closed my eyes and followed my nose to the sweetness of her skin, and my mouth brushed against hers, soft and full and moist.

She was the first girl I'd bussed.

When I opened my eyes, she had jumped clear across a row of cotton and stood in the next furrow in the full moonlight. "I've got to go. My daddy don't like me out after dark."

I saw the stars in the sky and I still felt her on my lips. I don't know how long I sat like that in wonder.

"You through with your courting, Mr. Rominger?" Dwight was no longer snoring.

"How long you been awake?"

"Long enough to hear you all getting all mushy. Keep your mind on the job, Wylie, or we're going be picking this cotton until kingdom come."

———

"You kissed a black girl?"

Dwight had never thought of Pop putting his lips on anybody other than Gram and that was about a hundred years ago, let alone getting all romantic with a black girl down in Mississippi. The story was getting interesting.

"What happened?"

But Pop took the lawnmower blade from Dwight's hands and inspected his whetting work. "Yep, now you're in business. Let's go put your mower back together."

Back in the basement, with the mower on its side, Pop showed Dwight how to bolt the blades on the crankshaft with the wrench. "Better give it another twist. That's it. Wouldn't be good if that thing came flying off while you're cutting grass this afternoon."

Dwight could barely contain himself. "Mississippi. Pearl. What happened?"

Pop scratched his head and left a streak of grease over one temple. "Oh right, Pearl." He chewed his lower lip, trying not to grin too broadly. "She's not one you can easily forget now, can you?"

———

Three days passed like that, hot white heat and then darkness that never did cool anyone off. We were in an oven. And though we went through the rows, picking cotton all day long and into the dusk, we didn't seem to be getting much closer to the three dollars we needed to make it over the Mississippi. But then nights came with Pearl, and I didn't much care.

Pearl might have slowed her pace, or picked it up, but it seemed we were all the time passing each other, and she would reach across the row of plants and touch my hand and smile. She had a smile whiter than the cotton.

"Hey, sugar."

"Hey, you."

But I couldn't help glancing over my shoulder as I crouched along the cotton, looking back at the burned-out plantation on the hill. Those thirteen stone posts up there on the hill, about as unlucky a sight as could be. I could almost see Pearl's cousin hung against the white stone.

The sky was white with heat overhead, and then suddenly a great black cloud loomed over the pillars on the bluff. A wind started to blow hard, and cotton sailed into the air. I felt something hard and cold hit my back, and I wondered if Pearl was lobbing rocks at me, but how I wondered did she get them so icy. At my feet, there was white gravel amid the black dirt, slowly melting away.

"This hail will kill us!" I slipped my arm free of the cotton sack, and I grabbed Pearl's hand. "We got to get out of here."

The ground started to shake underfoot, the straight rows of cotton turned crooked, and we were running from side to side, and then uphill.

"Oh lord, the levee!" Pearl screamed.

I looked over my shoulder to see the ridge of mounded dirt wiggling like a worm, then a wave of brown water came breaking over the top. Mr. Snow was riding the levee on his piebald mare, putting the tiny spurs to that poor horse's ribs. The horse reared and the albino lost his hat. And then the levee disappeared beneath them and the water closed on top, and horse and rider were gone.

Pearl and I scrambled up the bluff, just a few steps ahead of the surging water. The ground was still shaking, and the pillars were falling, like Sherman's Yankee ghosts had come to topple the last survivors of the wake of that old war.

Pervis, Mrs. Pervis and Pearl's baby sisters were waving us up the hill. "Run boy, run girl, run for your lives,"

And when we turned, we could see the field of white cotton all swept away by the wall of brown water. Amid the rumbling and lightning and thunder, I could hear a cow bellowing.

"Wylie!" Pearl gripped my wrist, but I peeled her frightened fingers off and wrapped her arms tight against the pillar of stone that once was Snow's house.

"Sorry, I've got to save her, save him."

And I ran downhill and stepped into the raging waters. I could see the top of a tree where Ivy had been grazing, the same willow tree in whose shade I regained myself and lay in the lap of my first girl. I went under and knew I was going to drown, but I got my feet down in the muck and the water pushed me upright again. I dove under and felt the cotton plants underneath. My hands were moving like claws, and I held my breath as long as I could, picking my way underwater toward the tree where Ivy was tied.

The poor cow was already floating up amid the willow branches at the end of the long halter. I grabbed hold of her udders and righted her. We were floating, now past the hill.

"Hold on, hold on," Dwight was hollering.

Me and Ivy rolled under once more, and there was nothing to see but mud and when we came up again into blessed air, I could see Dwight's head next to mine, sputtering and blinking. "Son, you can swim?"

"I'm learning pretty fast." So we were holding onto the cow's horns, one on either side, Dwight had the cotton sacks with him, and they were ballooned up in the water, able to keep our heads up.

Below all that water, I couldn't tell if the earth was still quaking or not, but the river was running backwards and taking us with it. We floated fast past the hill, and I could see the Pervis family clinging to the stone pillars and they were singing in the downpour, to keep from screaming. I reckon. The longest suffering people I ever met.

"Pearl, Pearl," I cried.

The wall of water crested, and in the oncoming swell, I could see a man and a horse rise up. It was Snow and the piebald mare, and it was like he was charging us, his mouth open and his pink eyes fixed in anger. And then the wall came crashing down and the horse turned its four stiff legs up, carrying its rider under, black boots caught in the stirrups.

"Hang on, Wylie, hang on," Dwight kept hollering as we were swept past the hill with the thirteen pillars and Pearl hanging there.

Cows can't swim, but they float O.K., and I held my breath and reached under the water under Ivy's belly, and quickly milked her dry. The milk streamed white in the red water, but the air in her udders would now keep her afloat. So we held on tight and rode right across the river.

We were in the water so long, we about grew fins and gills, and by the time we washed up in Missouri, we couldn't walk. We had to crawl a ways, then up on our hands and knees, and it took us about a day or two to get fully upright, but we were still making progress all the way into Kansas. By the time all that Delta mud had dried on our backs and then slowly fallen off, we were in the prairie, and that's when Ivy took her notion to lie down . . .

—

"Now hold on," Dwight protested. "Just wait a minute."

Pop coughed as if he might spit up still some of that old river water after all these years. He had the wrench in his hands and was tightening the bolts back on the underside of the lawnmower. "Yeah?"

"You were in Memphis, right, then walked on down into Mississippi, and then during the flood you got over the river, but then you wound up in Missouri? How can that be?"

Dwight knew his geography, and the states of the union were facts you couldn't argue with, facts that the teachers drilled into your brain by sheer repetition until you got it or you flunked. It was a fact Missouri was north of Mississippi and the river went in the other direction, not north. There was no way that two boys fifty years before could have lashed themselves to the horns of a cow and floated over the river from the Delta and landed up north. Just no way.

"Well, you caught me there." The old man stretched out his legs. "Look there. Let me see your legs. Go ahead, stretch 'em on out. Know how you can tell a city boy from a mountain man?"

Dwight shook his head.

"One leg's always longer than the other on a hillbilly so he can walk sideways on a mountain. Then the hillbilly sits down, they tell him a story and pull his other leg even."

Dwight let out a long whistle of exasperation, blowing back his bangs from his creased forehead.

"So I might be just pulling your leg." Pop said. "Then again, you're a bright young'un. I bet if you looked it up in that big ol' encyclopedia you got, you might read about the earthquake that make the river flow in the wrong direction. Earthquake or hurricane. It was old Dwight who told me and I ain't ever forgot, Old Mother Nature can be a real b----."

But the last word was lost in the roar of the engine as Pop jerked the starter cord.

—

That afternoon, as Dwight pushed the mower up and down the lawn in the precise lines that his father insisted upon, he worked up a sweat and the sun beat on his browned back.

He saw John Mark out in the street, tossing a football. He motioned for Dwight to come play. Dwight shrugged helplessly and pointed at the lawnmower.

As the oldest kid in the neighborhood, John Mark dictated the games they would play. When school let out for summer, and you could start safely going barefoot, the preacher's only son stepped out into the June air and decreed that it was football season. None of that flag fag stuff like you had to play at school. Or two-hand tag, where you're trying to touch the guy's ass, all the time. Coaches were fairies for making you do that kind of crap, according to John Mark. No, the real game was like on TV, where you played tackle.

Being more athletic, John Mark bossed around the other boys, chose up the teams, and always played quarterback. In the huddle, he drew the secret play on the palm of his hand: buttonhole, left, down and out, go long, hook, do a flag. He had all the jargon down, maybe from his father who'd played football before he discovered the faith. The church marquee advertised upcoming sermons like "Jesus as Coach," "Winning at the Game of Life," "The Eternal Touchdown," which Dwight's dad always read with a completely straight face every time they drove past.

Dwight still smarted at the memory of the first time they'd played football. After the umpteenth touchdown John Mark had made by straight-arming Dwight to the ground, the older boy lined his team up for the kick-off. John Mark gouged the grass with the heel of his shoe, then teeing the ball, then backing up ten steps. He raised then dropped his arm, the signal for mayhem to begin, and started running forward with a blood-curdling scream, kicking the helpless ball with a solid thump.

Dwight watched the ball sail end over end, floating against the fleecy clouds, then descending like a deadly missile. He positioned himself roughly underneath, held out his arms, and closed his eyes. The ball took a wicked bounce at his feet, grazed his right ear, and flew over the barbed wire fence that marked the end zone.

"Touchback. What a fabulous kick. The crowd goes wild." John Mark clapped his hands, providing his own play-by-play, then stopped. "Well, don't just stand there, Martin, go get the ball."

Dwight went down the honeysuckle-covered fence line to a clearing, where he could see the field and some unexpected spectators. While the boys had been playing ball, a herd of cows had gathered on the other side to graze, their ropy tails swishing the flies from their flanks, their pink noses and eyes. The ball was in the midst of the grazing herd.

"Get the ball, Martin, hurry up. You want to get penalized for delay of game?"

Dwight looked at John Mark, then at the cows, caught between peer pressure and his bovine phobia. He crawled carefully under the bottom strand of barbed wire into the field. The cows backed away uneasily, except for the largest, blackest of the beasts with polled horns. Looking underneath, there were no udders, but the low-slung sacs even a city boy like Dwight knew as the business end of a bull.

"Nice boy, nice boy," Dwight whispered, creeping toward the football that lay between him and the balky herd. Slowly he reached for the ball.

"Yaah!" John Mark hollered at the fence, and the cows turned in a stampede. Dwight grabbed the ball, but then he slipped and fell into something green and wet. He scrambled on all fours for the fence, and underneath, but then something—the horned bull?—grabbed the seat of his shit-flecked jeans. He kept crawling in place, all elbows and knees, but going nowhere, until he heard a distinct ripping sound.

He finally stood and got a look at what had happened: the seat of his favorite jeans hanging like a flag on the rusted barbed wire, and a draft at his backside where the underwear his mother lovingly washed white now showed green with an alien excrement.

Dwight flipped the ball with as much nonchalance as he could muster. "I've got to go."

"Looks like you already went." John Mark smirked.

His eyes burned with shame as he walked home, with John Mark leading the laughter at his back.

When Dwight finished mowing, he went in for a Coke from the fridge. He took the bottle out on the porch, letting the sweat drip from his skinny chest on the brick steps. The roar of the engine still throbbed in his ears and in his hands. He looked at his handiwork, the straight lines. He breathed deep the smell of the trimmed grass. He was tired, but pleased with himself.

"Looks like you earned your keep for the day," Pop said. "Gram said to give you this. A dollar."

"Thanks." Dwight slid the twice-folded dollar into his pocket.

Pop lit a cigarette and blew smoke into the summer air. He didn't say a word, but Dwight knew he was waiting.

Dwight tried to resist, but the longer he sat there, the more curiosity got the better of him. It was like he was addicted. He just had to know what happened next. It was all made up, a lame tall tale that fell woefully short of any credibility. But he had to know.

"So, the river ran backwards during this big old earthquake, some kind of rip tide or current that ran back-river for a hundred, two hundred miles and you're floating on either side of the cow, lashed to her horns, and you wash up in Missouri and walk out all the way into Kansas, and the cow decides to lay down. Then what?"

And as if the old man could read his mind, Pop held out his horny palm, and Dwight fished the wadded George Washington from his shorts. Pop slid the tribute in his shirt pocket behind his ever present smokes.

"Lemme see. Where was I?"

"Kansas." Dwight sighed. "The cow was laying down in Kansas."

———

. . . Dwight Sparks was getting put out with Ivy. He nudged her flank with his boot. "Get up, ya dumb beast,"

She swished her tail twice in the tall grass, but she wouldn't budge.

"I don't think she's feeling good. Are you not feeling good, girl?" I asked my cow.

"I said get up," Dwight said louder this time, and his nudge of his boot turned into a swift kick.

Both Ivy and I protested. She said *Moo*. I said *Hey!*

Dwight kept kicking her, which was a real mistake in hindsight, since his boot came undone, half-rotted as it was, from our trek over Tennessee and then mildewed from the Mississippi. The toe flew off, and then the knots in his broken laces snapped, and the sole went sailing in the Kansas wind, and soon he was just kicking her ribs with one bare foot.

"Up, I say. I have half a mind to butcher you here and now, you good-for-nothing cow."

"Stop it!" I shoved Dwight Sparks aside. "Can't you see she ain't well?"

"She's lazy is all. She can get up."

"She's sick, Dwight."

Ivy was rolling on her back, her four legs now straight up in the air, bellowing bad.

"Then let's end it now. I need me a beefsteak and some leather for some boots. And I tell you another thing, all that milk is starting to give me the runs."

"Back off!" I screamed at him.

"Get up!" He screamed at her.

And we were screaming at the top of our lungs just to be heard over the wind that had all of sudden picked up. The wind was blowing so hard, it pushed the brim of my straw hat down into my eyes. "Uh oh," I heard him say. I got the hat brim out of my eyes and looked in the direction Dwight was looking. The vortex of vultures was swept from the sky, and the empty sky was now filled with black clouds and off in the distance, on the horizon, there was a shape headed our way. It wobbled like a drunk back and forth, but stayed always upright, growing larger and darker the closer it came. And the closer it came, the worse it looked. A bank of black clouds, with flashes of lightning and that dark tail dancing along the ground, was coming with a sound so loud you could hardly hear yourself think the only thing in your suddenly empty brain: tornado.

And then the next thought that comes to mind: run.

But Dwight had other ideas. "Get down." And he pushed me backwards over Ivy's leg, and hunkered down himself. It was upon us in the next second.

"Hold tight!" Dwight screamed.

Hanging on to whatever I could, I had my fingers dug in the dirt, and my teeth chewing on the grass, and I think even my eyelids clamped down on a dirt clod, hoping that twister would just roll right over my back. The racket kept getting louder, pounding on my eardrums until they were like to burst. "Hang on. Just hang on," Dwight kept screaming, or maybe it was me, or maybe both of us, not just something you said, but that you felt in every muscle and bone. Then I made the mistake of opening my eyes and saw what little we were hanging on to. The whirlwind was right over us now, and I could feel the earth trembling beneath, as if dirt and grass could get as scared as two boys. From the corner of my squinched eye, I saw the sod slowly shaved away, like a knife cutting a curl of cold butter. Suddenly, all the earth exploded; dirt, grass, pebbles, clay and us flung upwards and airborne.

I couldn't see anything, it was like we were swimming through the murky Mississippi once again, the rain was turning everything to mud, and then a bolt of lightning flashed by and I could see Dwight hanging on Ivy's horns. I reached out and had a hold of her tail, and I was getting sick to my stomach swirling around in midair in this clockwise direction. I looked down but I couldn't tell how far up we were, a few inches or a few miles. I closed my eyes and gritted my teeth, and waited for the end.

Much to my surprise, I wasn't dead when the wind stopped blowing and I opened my eyes. We were lying in the grass again, much in the same position where we'd started. I raised my head and spit out the dirt between my teeth. Ivy roused herself and finally got to her feet, wobbled there like a drunk. Dwight lay very still between her legs, and she about planted a hoof on the side of his head.

"Dwight? Buddy?"

Oh Lord, I hoped it wasn't what I thought. I shook his shoulder and his head rolled from side to side but he wasn't really moving, and his eyes stayed closed. I didn't know what was going to be worse, having to haul his body all the way back to Beaverdam or bury him here on the lonesome prairie. Either way, without Dwight's built-in compass, heck, without Dwight, I'd be lost and lonesome and, I'd about die as well.

I pumped on his chest, hoping to get the breath back in the bellows of his lungs. Heck, I would have even put my lips on his and breathed in, if they'd invented that mouth-to-mouth resuscitation in those days.

But Ivy had the right idea. The cow seemed concerned, standing over my shoulder as I furiously pressed on Dwight's chest, or maybe she was just hungry, considering the bit of turf on his cold cheek. That caring cow bent down to his face, kissed him with her big wet cow mouth and brought him miraculously back to life.

"Get that beast away from me." He sat bolt upright, coughing and sputtering and wiping the slobber off the side of his smudged face. "Where are we?"

"You tell me."

We seem to have been set down on a promontory higher than the plains we had been on. Where this sudden hillock came from, I had no idea, since there'd been nothing visible on the flat horizon before the tornado came our way. I looked all around; the sky was clear blue and empty, no vultures circling overhead. And off in the distance, I could see white glittering peaks.

"Well, we sure as fire ain't in Kansas."

Dwight closed one eye, then opened it, wet his thumb and held it to the wind that wasn't. "Colorado, I make it."

———

"No! No way." Dwight jumped up shaking from the porch stoop.

He'd come this far, drawn on by the old man's saga, but now he had to halt this nonsense. He'd forked over all his allowance to the greedy grandfather, enough to catch the next matinee of the Godzilla picture at the double cinemas, and the old man couldn't even keep the geography of his lies clear. *We ain't in Kansas no more.* Jeez, please give a guy a break. What was next? Flying monkeys, or tin men that talked or dancing scarecrows? Even a listener soon to turn thirteen knows larceny in a story. No one forgives the storyteller caught stealing.

"You don't believe me? What part don't you believe? Floods and tornadoes are terrible acts of God. I ain't making them up."

"Mississippi to Missouri, then Kansas and now you're in Colorado? I mean, come on."

"Well, stories aren't like real life, and maybe some of what might have happened gets stretched here and there over time with all the telling, but that's not to say the heart of it ain't true."

"So it's a lie?"

"Careful now." Pop narrowed his eyes. "Careful."

"No, it is," Dwight insisted. "It's all just one big lie."

"So what are you calling me, then?"

Pop's voice was different now, husky and low. And it hung in the heavy summer air between them. The old man fumbled with the fat wallet in his pocket. He laid a twenty-dollar bill on the bricks and slapped shut the cowhide folds.

Dwight wanted to take back what he said, but he couldn't. He hadn't meant to hurt the old man's feelings; still he wasn't a stupid kid who'd believe anything an adult told him.

"Wait, I didn't —"

But Pop had slammed the storm door behind him.

ARROWHEAD

"What did you do to your Pop?" Dwight's mother demanded, yanking him into the kitchen, out of earshot of the old man.

"Nothing." Dwight jerked away, rubbing the funny bone in his elbow that she had set tingling.

"What did you say to him?"

His grandfather was sulking around the house, sighing on the sofa and gazing out the bay window. Dwight's mother automatically suspected he was the culprit in Pop's suddenly low spirits.

"He was telling me a story about how they got from Mississippi to Kansas. I might have said it was stupid or something."

"Dwight, it's just a story. If you go picking everything apart, you won't ever be happy. Just enjoy it."

"But he had this cow, and they were going the wrong way on the river, and then he says this tornado came along and —"

"You have an imagination. You don't have to be like your father where everything has to be so logical. Help me out here, hon. God knows, I have to listen to your grandmother and you don't see me second-guessing everything she says, though that's what she does to me. But never mind, that's not really your business. Forget I said that. Just go out there and ask your grandfather to tell you a story."

"He charges me money."

"He what?"

"He makes me pay a dollar every time he tells me a story. He says nothing's free in life and I need to learn that lesson."

"Well, that's true. That's not a bad lesson."

"But it's my money. I don't want to spend it on some old guy's lies."

"Dwight Martin, do you want to be grounded for the rest of the summer?"

He knew he could push it only so far with his father away and his grandparents here. Sooner or later they would have to leave, then he could get his real life back. He closed his eyes and rolled his eyeballs secretly.

"Here." She dug through a drawer where she kept the household bills. "Here's a dollar. Go ahead, you don't have to use your own money. Give this to your grandfather and ask him to tell you a good long story, as y'all go up to the store. Maybe he'll buy you a comic book there if you ask nice."

And she brushed the bangs from his oily forehead and planted a quick kiss there like always; that told him no matter what his mother still loved him. He pocketed the dollar and then thought better and went to his room and exchanged the bill for two quarters, and slipped the folding money far into the back of his desk drawer into a cigar box with a few bubblegum cards.

Outside, he found Pop at the edge of the yard peering at the oak tree. "What is it?" Dwight had to ask.

"Squirrel having a set-to with that jay there." Pop pointed to a branch, at the squirrel barking, the bird squawking.

"What are they fighting about?"

"What's it matter to you, Mr. Know-It-All?"

"I don't know everything." With a dry gulp, Dwight tasted the bitterness of pride going down his throat. "The bird and the squirrel in the tree, why are they fighting?"

"Who knows? Old squirrel did something to ruffle old bird's feathers, or maybe the bird got cocky and rubbed old squirrel's fur the wrong way. All animals have feelings, you know, not just cows."

And old people, Dwight thought. I get it, already.

Pop palmed his cigarette and took a short toke, the same way Dwight had seen older kids puffing in the bathroom at the junior high, acting cool. The gesture was shocking, years suddenly stripped away from the old man, and Dwight glimpsed someone closer to his own age, someone not so wise, but more of what John Mark would have mocked as a "wise-ass."

"Look, I'm sorry I doubted your story. I shouldn't have interrupted." Dwight said though he wasn't sure what he was supposed to be saying he was sorry for, he hadn't exactly said anything or done anything mean to the old man. They loved each other, though it was understood that was never to be spoken between them. These conversations, these stories had been edging up to that embarrassing articulation. *You're all I got, so appreciate what I'm telling you.* Or: *I hear you, you're older, wiser and think you've got something I need to know.*

Dwight held out the change from his pocket as a peace offering.

"Huh," Pop snorted with smoky contemptuousness. "Money don't mean sorry, though sorry people sometimes think it."

He put the money back in his pocket. "O.K., fine, then."

Put out with Pop, he walked over and kicked at his bicycle lying in the grass. Then he jerked the bike up and got on, riding up and down the driveway. He pulled up on the spider handlebars, leaning back on the banana seat and the chrome sissy bar to pop a wheelie.

"You're pretty good on that bike, aren't you?" Pop had to concede.

"Well, yeah." Dwight shook his head, trying to look humble.

"You ride that thing a lot?"

"About every day. After school and all," He suddenly remembered the manners his mother was always trying to drill into him. "You want to try, the bike I mean?"

"Lord, no. Never been on a two-wheeler in my life, probably not the best idea at my advanced age to start such foolishness. Bicycles were rare back in the hills, back in my day. Besides it's the problem I got with one leg longer than the other walking sideways on the mountain." And the old man turned and started walking in a hilarious circle, dropping one shoulder with each step.

Dwight knew that they were friends again.

"Mom thought you might like to walk me up to the store and buy me a comic book," Dwight said, pushing his advantage.

"Comic books. How much money you spend on them things?"

"A quarter usually for a Captain Marvel. Fifty cents for the last Justice League double issue, but you get about a dozen superheroes in the deal."

"Never did understand comic books. Garish pictures if you ask me. I try to read the funnies in your mama's newspaper when I come down. You ever notice everybody talks with these white clouds over their heads? I don't see white clouds coming out my mouth lest it's a cold day, and I ain't never seen my words spelled out what I was saying."

Dwight opened his mouth, gawking at the old man's stupidity, before he realized Pop was right. It was kind of stupid how they always had *POW* and *BLAM* in these dynamite explosions. And once you read a comic book about a dozen times and traded it to some kid at school, you might as well be talking in big balloon letters yourself.

But Dwight and Pop had so little in common, the years between them. Dwight was running out of ideas to entertain an old man. "You want to see something else?"

"What you have in mind?"

"They're building new houses over there."

"Show the way." Pop pulled out of his halting mountain walk and started a normal stride while Dwight slowly pedaled, slaloming to and fro in front of the old man.

"That's pretty good. You ever fall off?"

"Nope."

Dwight was tickled Pop had noticed his daredevil talents as an Evil Knievel rider. Just get him closer to the construction site and Dwight would show him a trick to knock his white crew socks right off.

He sped down the hill, dodging the potholes left by the dump trucks, and hit the dirt ramp piled to one side of the future basement. Up in the air he went, about to yell, "Look at me," one hand waving over his head, like a rodeo rider on the back of a bucking bronco, acknowledging the wild cheers of the invisible audience Dwight wanted desperately to believe watched his every move.

Of course, he'd practiced this particular maneuver at least a dozen times the week before under the squinted eye of John Mark. But he had not counted on the construction crew tampering with the dirt ramp the boys had worn with the repeated assaults of their Schwinns. The ramp was angled a little higher, he was sailing a little farther, the front wheel was turning slightly as he turned one-handed to watch the anticipated look of wonder on his grandfather's face.

Next thing he knew, he was face first in dirt. His bike lay upside down a few feet away, the chrome of the sissy bar buried in the red clay, the front wheel still spinning uselessly. Dwight spit grit between his front teeth along with a trickle of bitter blood. He could smell the blood in his nose. Tears were red in his eyes from all the clay crammed in his eyelids.

Pop took his time to see if Dwight was still alive. "Nice trick. Looks like some fun. You didn't break anything we need to tell your mother about?"

Dwight shook it off. "Naw, I'm O.K."

He pulled the bike upright and sat on the saddle, ready to go again, never mind the scraped knees and the mud that was clinging to the front rims of his tires. Just say the word, he'd do the jump again. John Mark made them all jump over the ramp, double-dared them if they weren't pussies or pansies. But his grandfather didn't seem that interested with doubling the derring-do.

"This what you wanted to show me?" Pop kicked at the clay.

"Yeah, they dig out the basement with a bulldozer. Then they start on the foundation, they lay all this cinder block, and it's like you're in a dungeon or a castle or something. So it's pretty cool."

"What's this?" The old man bent down with a loud crick in his knees. "Could be. Well, I'll be. It is."

His hand opened and Dwight's eyes widened at the object in the old man's palm, a perfectly formed flint arrowhead. "Is it for real?"

"I reckon so. Ain't seen one of these in a while. Fairly big one. I'd say it was either meant for a deer, maybe a man. Could have been an old hunting ground here for the Cherokee or the Catawba. Might be where a war party happened on some scalps."

"You really think so?" Dwight's voice broke in his excitement. A low exclamation that suddenly, inexplicably cracked high.

Pop laughed, then quickly added. "Sorry, just a funny sound you made there. I ain't laughing at you."

Dwight was sorry too, for thinking so low of his Pop. Here Dwight and the other kids in the neighborhood had been clambering all over this clay for the last two weeks, and the only buried treasure they'd found was a few empty beer bottles left by the workmen. Pop walks over and right away happens upon Indian artifacts.

"Can I touch it?"

"Here, you can keep it. Careful, you could cut yourself. Flint, if you strike it just right, will hold an edge a hundred, two hundred years, which I reckon is about how long ago that Injun flaked that point out. And usually, you find one in a field, you're likely to find more. No telling what that bulldozer might dig out. Kind of a shame, we might be on some burial grounds. Kind of like what happened to me and Dwight when that tornado took us over into Colorado and parked us on that promontory."

Dwight relented. He pulled the two quarters from his pocket along with a handful of red grit and a pebble or two that seemed to have worked its way into his clothes during his spectacular crash.

"All right. So the tornado took you and Dwight and Ivy from Kansas to Colorado. Next thing you knew you were on this high ground. You thought Dwight Sparks was dead at first, but he was just sort of knocked unconscious or playing 'possum or something. So what happened next?"

"You got a good memory," Pop said. "Probably better than me. Maybe you ought to be telling the story."

Dwight still held out the two coins. "Here. Go ahead and tell me the rest."

"You sure? It ain't no comic book or TV show what I'm telling you."

"I want to know," Dwight insisted.

"Why don't I hold that arrowhead and you hold that money, and if at the end of the story, you think it's better than a comic book, that's fine. At the end, we'll just swap even, arrowhead for those fifty cents. Deal?"

"Deal. So what happened next?"

"Now where was I? Oh, Colorado as I recollect."

We seem to have been set down on a promontory higher than the plains we had been on. I had no notion where this sudden hill came from, since there'd been nothing but flat level land before the tornado came our way. The eastern horizon was stacked with retreating thunderheads, flashing jagged bolts. And in the other direction, the skyline was bright with high clouds.

Dwight closed one eye, then opened it, wet his thumb and held it to the wind, then announced. "Colorado, I make it. And them's the Rockies."

We were halfway from home, halfway toward our hope, and I wouldn't have believed we would have made it, and it was a sight, standing up on that little hill over the Plains, looking west. We must have stood there minutes or maybe hours just taking in the view, when the sun dropped amid those white peaks and what was white was now on fire, like seeing the Pearly Gates flung open, streets of gold and mansions in the air.

"Look there."

We were smack in the middle of the wide open Wild West and we were whispering like in some fancy church, which to my eyes it was, it truly was. "Wylie, you ever thought you'd live to see such a thing?"

Never. I had seen the promised land, the finest firework show. Sunsets are never better than after a bit of rough weather. And we'd surely seen that. If Dwight Sparks had said, well, that's the best part, we've seen the west, best turn back and head for Beaverdam, I would have gone willingly and never regretted it to the end of my days.

Then, it was like the Lord Almighty put out the lights. The sun dropped over the Rockies a hundred miles away, and the sky turned two shades of gray, dusk hurrying on, and the shadows of the storm gone to the east came racing back over our heads and we were in the great night on the Great Plains.

"Leastways, we picked a good place to land," Dwight said. "Let's pitch camp here for the evening."

I agreed, although this was a mighty peculiar promontory where the tornado saw fit to land us. The hill stood maybe fifty feet high above the surrounding plain with a base of about hundred feet all around, the only real elevation for probably a hundred miles, and there weren't even any little mounds or rocks or little rises to get you ready for this high one. Like I said, mighty peculiar.

Fortunately, we hadn't lost any of our gear in that sudden gale. Supper would be some beans and maybe some johnnycake we would lay on the ash of our cook-fire. Problem was finding fuel to build us a fire most nights. We hadn't seen a honest-to-God tree in weeks, and the bushes and shrubs were getting shorter the further west we went.

"Reckon I better scout around for something to make us a—"

Dwight turned, took one step and was suddenly gone—a blur in the corner of my eye. I had barely blinked, but my partner had disappeared into the thin, darkening air. I looked all around, but there wasn't anywhere for him to hide for miles about. He was as gone as gone could be, like he had stepped off the side of the promontory and off the planet as well.

"Dwight?" I whispered. Then "DWIGHT!" A yell that the Pervis family could probably have heard all the way in Mississippi. But still no answer.

Now I was getting real worried. Night was falling fast in the west and it was just me and a cow in the wilderness, and my guide and best buddy suddenly whisked away. Maybe a tornado had come by and lifted him up when I wasn't paying attention, but I'd felt no shift in the wind. This was getting spooky.

I began to fret over the stuff I'd heard preached in the church about the Rapture, how all the real Christians would go flying into the air when the angel blew the trumpet and Jesus came hovering down to collect all the living and dead corpses popping out of the ground and the oceans. But I hadn't heard any trumpet, but then I wouldn't if I wasn't saved, and if I wasn't saved and Dwight was, what was the use of getting my head dunked in Beaverdam Creek where I was baptized all of nine years old to join the saints? After the Rapture came Tribulation for all that was left behind, famine and pestilence and general hard times. Even if Dwight hadn't disappeared in the Rapture, I could prophesy Tribulation up ahead for me if I didn't find him fast.

While all these thoughts were slamming inside my skull, I was busy yelling my fool head off. "Dwight, Dwight Sparks. Where'd you go? This ain't funny, Dwight Sparks! Show yourself! Now, I mean it! *Dwiiiiiight!*"

My throat was raw before it occurred to me that I was screaming so hard, I couldn't hear if Dwight tried to make himself heard. I shut up and listened.

And in the lonesome night, I heard nothing but the wind rustling the grass like a giant snake that slithered across the land, or like the brush of a big dark wing against the sky, or maybe it was the sound of the shiver up my spine or the faint knock of my knees together. Then the wind turned into a groan that seemed to come from the ground itself.

"Dwight, buddy? Where are you?" I was whispering, half-hoping that sound was Dwight's, fully dreading what it wasn't.

The groan got louder underfoot. Something inside me said, "Watch your step," and I held my foot in midair and brought it down on—nothing! There was a hole in the hill, and I jumped and turned in midair to keep from going right down it. I squatted and found the edges of the hole with my hands. Even in broad daylight, you wouldn't have necessarily spied that hole, since the grass grew about a foot tall and lay over the sides, and it was no more than two feet wide, bigger than a gopher and just the right size to swallow, say, a boy as lean from weeks of walking as me and Dwight.

I parted the blades of grass and put my head down into the hole. A faint foul stench came drifting up, not just the rot of the earth or sometimes the sulfur boiling out of hell-fire, but more like a grave that had been opened up, the sort of smell that flips your stomach at the same time it lifts the hairs back of your neck. I held my breath and called, "Dwight, you down there?"

What went down little more than a whisper got thrown back into my face like a choir of a thousand demons, all amplified and echoed and all sounding like me.

I sat up and heaved in some fresh air and tried to think. The hole that Dwight might have stepped through went down a ways. I braved myself again, and knew what to expect of the echoing demons when I called again. "Dwight, Dwight Sparks, you alive or dead down there in hell?"

That long a sentence took a while to bounce around the inside of the hollow hill and the echoes to die down, and when it did, I could hear on the tail end a new voice that wasn't my own. "Wylie, that you?"

And I called "Dwight, that you?" And our "you's" went bouncing back and forth, echoing all over the place.

"You better quit fooling around, Dwight. Come on up out of there."

"I cain't see doodly down here. Toss me a torch."

"I ain't got no fire built. Remember? You went looking for us something to burn is the way you wound up down there."

"I don't mean to alarm you none, but I don't believe I can feel my leg. There's either a trickle of water keeps dripping down in my eyes, or, oops, I was afraid of that. Looks like I'm bleeding."

"Good Lord. Dwight what we going to do?"

"You got a good moon coming up in a few minutes, if last night was any indication. Look in my satchel and you'll see a few pineknots I packed for such an occasion. There's a stoppered bottle too. Get that. You know where the sulphur tip matches are."

Sure enough, I pulled my head out of the hole and into the night air, and in the time I'd been talking to Wylie amid all the echoes, a full moon had climbed the eastern sky and there was enough light to see where Dwight had stashed his gear.

It was more by feel than by sight that I found the splintery pineknot firestarters, the tin with the sulphur matches and the small stoppered glass. I unplugged it and took a whiff, and went *whew*. Evidently, he'd brought some flammable fluid for dire emergencies. I hurried back to the hole, making sure not to fall in and join Dwight in his dilemma.

"Hang on. I'm back, hold on," I hollered into the hole.

Now I don't know if you've ever tried to strike a match and light a sticky pineknot out on the high plains, but it's no easy feat. Even without a wind, the air's always in motion. I'd get the first match struck on a bit of sandpaper Dwight had fixed underneath the tin cap and it's like the wind from a hundred miles away would come rushing to snuff out the flame. My hands were sticky with resin, and I about burnt my fingers a few times.

"What's the hold-up up there, Wylie? It's getting even darker down here."

"Hang on. Hang on." Three matches spent and still no luck. I could have spent the rest of the night trying to get a flame going, when Dwight called up again.

"Throw me down that bottle."

"Ain't you afraid it might hit you and break?"

"Don't you worry none. I'll take my chances. The bottle, just let it drop."

I reached down as far as my arm would go into the hole and let the neck of the bottle slip from my fingers. Quick, I turned my ear down but heard no shattering glass, just a soft *oomph* I reckoned was Dwight.

"O.K.?"

"Tarnation, Wylie, you should have stuck the stopper in better before you dropped it. You done spilled half of it over me."

"Well, dry yourself off, I'm still working on this fire."

I heard a funny glugging sound for an answer. "Dwight?"

Up came an *ahh*, a sigh, then a cough. "Dwight, you all right?"

"I'm better since I drunk up the last of Auntie's' 'shine. Might take the edge off this leg aching so." He was trying to be brave, but I could tell every word was short and raw, worked out between gritted teeth.

I kept trying to light the pineknot. And I would have run through the last match we had for the whole way west, if I hadn't figured out to empty the can of matches, and light one inside the can to shield the flame against the wind. I held the match between my burning fingers until I got the pineknot crackling with fire, then I held the torch down the hole. For a second, I could see Dwight's white uplifted face illuminated below, his eyes wide and white and fearful. Illumination is not always a wonderful thing. Sometimes you only shed light on what is a worse situation. I must have flinched a bit at what else I saw, since I dropped the torch.

Dwight screamed at what he suddenly saw. He was sitting in a circle of skeletons, all upright bony arms hugging tight their fleshless femurs. It was like Dwight duplicated a dozen times, like once a decade some skinny boy came along this godforsaken plain and dropped down this hole in the

hilltop, to starve to death with his luckless predecessors. Dwight kicked
away from his bony companions and must have put out the flame trying
to get away from his fate. The light went out.

"Oh Lord. Lord. Something's moving down here. Wylie, God, they're
biting me. Oh God Almighty. Get me out of here! They're murdering
me!"

What scared me worse than the screams was when they stopped. I
worked as quick as I could, lighting another pineknot. I uncoiled some
rope and looked desperately around for something to tie off the bight, but
in the high plains on this lonesome hill, there was nothing more solid
than grass, and the nearest tree was a week's walk back toward the river.
Ivy looked at me looking all about frantic, and I had a sudden idea, the
best one you seize when you don't have much time. That old girl didn't
protest as I wrapped the end of the rope twice about her horns and tied it
off. The other end I quickly looped about me in a bowline.

I jumped down the hole, hanging onto the pineknot, and dropped
about ten feet before the rope caught me. I was dangling inside a hollowed
out cellar at the center of the hill, and I saw crossbeams that weren't the
work of hell's demons, but Indians. This may have been simply an old
earthen lodge, maybe a chiefs' council hut among a lost tribe long ago.
The air was dark and smoky and I could barely breathe. Swinging above
the white skulls, I saw what Wylie had been screaming about.

A tribe of rats had laid claim to this underground kingdom, probably
not long after the people had gone onto other happier hunting grounds.
The rats were singing too, gnashing their teeth like a million little knives.
They ran in circles everywhere, milling on the earthen floor. Perhaps to
their rodent minds, I was some god coming down with light and judg-
ment, or maybe they figured they had just been served from on high a
banquet of boy.

The bight was digging under my ribs and binding my lungs as I dangled in midair, but I managed to get some momentum, kicking my legs
back and forth until I was able to stab the pine torch in the side of the
wall, then kick toward the opposite wall, trying to reach Dwight Sparks.
He was passed out from fear or maybe the half bottle of his Auntie's best

'shine, his head lolling on his shoulder, his feet jammed in the ribs of a skeleton, like a ladder he'd been climbing above the swarm of vermin.

Swinging back and forth, I finally caught a handful of his hair, but with a rip, I came away with half of Dwight's scalp in my hand. I flung the hank of blood and blond hair down, and the rats went wild with this appetizer for the feast to come. I kicked harder off the far wall, putting my boot right in the yawing jaw of an old skull, and flew back toward my buddy. This time I grabbed a hold of his arm and hoisted him up. It was probably a good thing he was out of it. I could see his knee was bending the wrong way as I lifted him. Awake, he would have been screaming about murder again.

The rats had devoured what was left of his scalp and they were singing for more. As my feet dragged through the swarm of vermin, I felt their sharp teeth nipping at the thin leather of my boots. Dwight's bloody head hung against my cheek and I held his limp body close as we swung back. I grabbed the pineknot stabbed in the wall. I had only one flimsy hope to save us both, and it depended on my aim and the cow who anchored our slender lifeline.

"Now!" I cried and flung the flame straight up through the hole and into the night. Out on the dark plain, a man standing miles off might have seen the flare, and guessed it must have been a falling star, or maybe the first spark of a dead volcano coming to life. But I wasn't hoping for help from any man. I was counting on a cow who stood idly by in the darkness, minding her own bovine business, which was filling her stomach or closing her eyes for sleep, suddenly seeing the terrifying spectacle of a flame in midair. To her mind, it would mean nothing but the message: *Fire. Run.*

I heard her bellow and the rope yanked us up toward the air. And I knew that Ivy had gotten the right idea. Now the second part of my plan might still get us killed. The hole was too narrow for two at a time, so I could only hope the cow could run fast enough downhill to pop us right through that opening, or succeed in breaking both our necks against what would be the ceiling of our tomb.

I closed my eyes and ducked my head waiting to hit the pay dirt. We came shooting out of the top of the hill, and then started rolling down the slope. While a cow is a sensitive enough creature to scare into a one-heifer stampede, she wasn't smart enough to mind me hollering *Whoa*. Rather than have Ivy drag us all the way across Colorado to the foot of the Rockies, I pulled out my knife and cut the rope.

I tried standing up but my right foot buckled beneath me, so I crawled back up the Indian mound. The hole that had been a trap for wayward boys was now a crater that opened half the side of the hill. I crept to the edge of the opened grave for a look. The rats were drowned in dirt and the ancient dust was beginning to settle. In the moonlight, I could see the skulls of a few chiefs in the circle. The mouths of all the skulls were open and between their teeth they bit into flint spearheads.

Only later on, talking to Indian tribes along our journey, would I guess what had happened here. The chiefs had been defeated in a terrible battle by a rival tribe and buried alive in the captured council hut, chewing on their own severed tongues, so no one would hear the screams. Even after they slowly died under the earth, their ghosts would never speak their own words again, but echo only what unfortunate travelers might say.

We were the cursed travelers all right. I counted only four and half toes on my left foot when I finally unlaced my bloody boot. Dwight lay at the bottom on the hill, alive, but with all the skin and hair gone from the crown of his head. You could see the white bone of his skull in the moonlight, and what was stranger, the hair around his ears and neck had turned snow white as well with the terror he'd witnessed.

And far off in the moonlight, I could hear a frightened cow bellowing across the empty plain, with a cut rope bound about her horns, running a thousand miles from home.

—

Dwight gaped at the arrowhead in his grandfather's hand, like an object the old man had snatched from the dirt of the distant past. He could imagine the blood dripping from the flaked edges.

Pop's story was a thousand times better than any comic book. He had seen it all in his impressionable mind as the old man told his tale, the

Indian mound, the moonlight, the matches flaring futilely in the wind, and then the descent into the grave, the rats swarming and the grinning skeletons all around them in the burning light. He marveled at the man who had survived that ordeal, just a boy, not much older than Dwight was now.

He reached in his pocket for the two quarters. Dwight was ready to ride back to the house and empty out his bank to hear that yarn once more.

Usually after a story that good, Pop had a grin that showed all his long yellow teeth and every wrinkle in his ruddy face, but instead of looking triumphant, the old man stared at the stone in his hand with mournful eyes, like he wasn't looking at what he held, but at something he had lost long ago.

"Pop?"

"Here." He thrust the arrowhead at the boy. "It's yours."

"Really?" said Dwight. He couldn't believe Pop would willingly part with such a treasure.

"Keep it." His grandfather snorted back some fugitive moisture deep in his throat and turned away.

Up the road, Dwight saw the first person he could impress with his new possession. Brenda Cook was out on her pink bicycle with its plastic streamers and the white wicker basket on the front where she could carry her girl stuff. But even a feminine creature like Brenda would be impressed with a real Indian arrowhead. He rode up to her.

"Hey, Brenda, want to see something cool? Look, it's a real live arrowhead."

This was as close as Dwight had come to a thirteen-year-old girl. She was actually holding his sweaty hand, as she bent over the amazing artifact. Brenda Cook was nearsighted and wore glasses at school where she always got straight As, but away from class and her mother's scrutiny, riding her bike out in the summer dusk, she had left her spectacles on her nightstand.

"Is it for real?"

He could feel her warm breath on his skin. And she looked at him, long lashes and blue myopic eyes. "Where did you find this? Is this really yours?"

Dwight knew he could lie and impress her, claim all credit for himself and the girl would believe him and think better of him, but then he knew that wouldn't be right. He looked over his shoulder, looking to credit to his grandfather, introduce him to the neighborhood's best looking girl, maybe let the old man wow her with the story that was better than any comic book. But without his noticing, the old man had disappeared into the summer dusk.

"Ooh, it's sharp," Brenda was still holding his hand and smiling at him. And now she was brave enough to run her white thumb against the sharp edge of the point and the soft skin of Dwight's palm.

"Look who's holding hands."

John Mark suddenly appeared out of nowhere, skidding to a noisy halt at their side on his rusty dirt bike.

"Hey John Mark," Brenda said softly.

Dwight couldn't help but notice that girls liked John Mark, his pouting lips, his brooding looks.

"Hey kiddos. What you doing?" He rode in a tight circle around them. He'd outgrown the bike the year before. His bare knees pumping nearly to his chest, he didn't sit on the bike so much as slouch, like he was lying on a sofa, somewhere in his preacher dad's rectory. With a battered fisherman's hat pulled hard around his ears, he wore a pair of yellow-lensed sunglasses that gave his eyes a jaundiced look, daring you to say something, anything to him.

"Dwight was showing me this arrowhead."

"Oh yeah? Let me see."

Dwight felt a sinking in his chest and a tightness in his throat, as Brenda handed the arrowhead to John Mark.

He stared at it for a while. "You found this?"

"My grandfather did, over in the dirt."

John Mark kind of smiled, but it wasn't a particularly nice or friendly smile. His teeth were too wet. "So he told you this was an arrowhead? Looks like a rock to me."

"No. See those edges? They're really sharp." Dwight found he couldn't breathe very well in this conversation. He felt dizzy.

John Mark flipped the pointed stone and let it fall in his hand. "Hey Martin, go long." He flung the arrowhead into the air.

Dwight turned pale and speechless, watching the pointed stone fly into the dusk and disappear into the mountain of clay and clods.

"Oh, look what happened. You going to cry in front of your girlfriend? Grow up, Martin. It was just a stupid rock."

John Mark was sitting on his bike, balancing himself as his feet spun the chain backwards. He was leering at them, waiting as usual for Dwight to turn tail.

Dwight couldn't believe what he did next. His hand took on a purpose of its own. He leaned forward and simply touched John Mark's bicep with his first two fingers, a sharp jab just enough to disturb the older boy's precarious balance.

First his feet kicked out on either side, and flailing in mid-air, John Mark and his bike toppled over. His yellow sunglasses flew off his surprised face, his hat flew off his head and his ear smashed the pavement.

Brenda laughed, then clapped her hand to her mouth.

"Man, I'll get you." John Mark tried to get up, but his feet were tangled in the frame of his bike and he kept floundering on the pavement, like a turtle turned on his back, snapping at the air. "I'll get you good, Martin."

But his threats were lost in the laughter that burst out of Brenda and Dwight. They were about to fall down themselves.

"What's so funny? What's so funny?" John Mark demanded as he slammed the hat sideways on his head and tried to put his bent sunglasses back on his red face. He got on his bike, and rode away, the frame swaying from side to side as he furiously pumped the pedals.

"Whew." Dwight gasped for breath and his ribs ached from laughing so hard.

"That was so mean of John Mark." Brenda said sweetly, then she added. "I'd hate to be you. John Mark's really going to get you."

But he wasn't worried about John Mark so much as what he would tell Pop. The arrowhead was gone. It was too dark and the mountain of dirt too big to ever hope of finding the point again. The next morning, the workmen would be back with their bulldozers, the arrowhead would be lost again for centuries, buried under a seeded lot.

"Well, I better go." Brenda blushed. "Thanks for showing me that arrowhead. Sorry you lost it."

Brenda pedaled off, swinging her legs slowly on her pink bicycle as Dwight watched in wonder and regret and terrible longing, lost in the middle of the street as the first street lamp clicked on overhead.

RATS, SNAKES, GRASS

Out of the dusk, Dwight came riding down the hill and glided up the drive, a practiced motion, to see how far the bike could travel on pure momentum. The wheel wobbled back and forth as he fought to keep his balance, standing on the pedals, until he reached the walkway, swinging his leg over the frame and stepping off to let the Schwinn topple into the freshly cut grass.

Pop was guarding the stoop, the ember of his cigarette glowing against the ravines of his leathery face. He drank the cold coffee from a mug set between his unlaced brogans, and swatted away mosquitoes that flew around his jug ears. "We ain't got these little boogers up in the mountains. Lord, how you stand these things?"

Dwight sat to Pop's right side, positioning himself in shouting range of the old man's best ear. He was quiet, bruised and bleeding, not knowing how to begin. He'd pushed the bully over on his bike, but he'd lost the arrowhead that Pop had given him. It was shameful to admit, but Dwight also knew he had to be man enough with the old man.

"I looked around for you, but you were gone," Dwight said.

"I thought you might like a little time with that pretty little girl. I could see you were sweet on her."

Dwight felt his face burning in the cool of the evening. "No way," he lied.

"Well that's good. Good looking as you are, no need to get so settled so soon."

"Look—listen," and Dwight launched into a breathless account of his confrontation with John Mark, the bully who threw the priceless arrow-head back into the dirt where it came, where it was like looking for a nee-dle in a haystack, a sharp rock in a couple tons of dirt and debris scooped out from the past for a modern day basement, how Dwight pushed John Mark over, and how he was probably going to get his butt kicked once John Mark quit blushing so bad, but mainly how sorry he was about the arrowhead.

Pop just nodded his grizzled head as he took a sip of his cold coffee, another drag off his cigarette. "Sounds like he might have been sweet on her too. Reckon he didn't care for you pushing him over like that."

"It wasn't a fight, not really, more like an accident," Dwight tried to explain, since teachers at school frowned on kids having fist-fights. "John Mark got all tangled up in his bike and fell down and looked so funny, we had to laugh. He was the one who ran off, not me."

"Sounds like you did fine."

"I'm sorry."

"About that old arrowhead? Don't feel bad about that. Main thing was we found it, you and me, right?"

But Dwight was trying to apologize for everything, for doubting Pop and his stories, for being so snotty the past week.

Pop bent to pluck a stem of grass and starting picking at his teeth, as if to change the awkward subject. He spit out a stem, and picked a fleck of green from the tip of his yellowed tongue. "A body gets old and forgets things. Like the taste of grass."

"Cows eat it," Dwight blurted out.

Pop shot him a sideways look. "So they do."

"So what happened to that cow who ran away? Did you ever find her?"

It was getting darker, and Dwight caught either a gleam or a glistening in the old man's eyes. He swallowed a few times, coughed and snuffled, sounds of ancient fluids and phlegm, the faulty plumbing of an old man, like he'd swallowed that cold coffee down the wrong pipe. Pop cleared his throat and spit, the last moisture he was going to betray before the boy this evening.

———

It was weeks later when we did find Ivy or she found us again on the Great Plains. Dwight Sparks and me were busted up pretty bad, him with his scalp half gone and his knee all twisted, me with four toes intact and one gnawed away. It took me about three days before I could set any weight on it at all. We stayed put on that collapsed Indian mound. I got me a fire going from some brush and dried cow chips and nursed Dwight back as best I could, hopping about the campfire on my one good foot.

It was strange but on the second day, I saw black birds circling overhead. I first thought the buzzards were waiting us out. They came from all directions, and caught a spiraling breeze that blew straight up over the ancient grave. They were hawks, a whole kettle of them circling overhead, like a feathered tornado. One by one they dove down into the hole with terrible bird screams, and came flying out with a hissing rat writhing in their claws.

What was good for hawks may be good for busted-up boys. I found one of the hawks' half-eaten rats dropped from above and cut a bit of the rat tail and hooked it on a rope with a pin.

I can tell you, rat is a rare treat, especially to its rodent relatives. I threw the bait in and heard the commotion. Soon as I felt the strike, I'd haul up a hooked rat. I'd cut off the tail for fresh bait, and skin the rest and throw it into the pot.

Dwight Sparks was still in and out of it, though the blood had turned black and scabbed on his scalp. He didn't twist and turn so in his fitful sleep, nor did his eyes roll back in his head. I lifted his head on my lap and tried to spoon him some of the broth, like I remember my mama did for me when I was feverish.

He took a swallow of the soup and licked his lips. His eyes bulged and his mouth puckered. "What's that funny taste?"

"Just a little something I cooked up."

He dumped the broth from his bowl in disgust. "Lord, ain't bad enough them ghost Indians nearly took my scalp. Now you're making me eat what about ate me."

I took the pot myself and turned my back on my finicky friend, and had my own feast of rat. Drank up every bit of the broth, and chewed on the little morsels, closing my eyes and trying not to think about what was between my teeth and slipping into my stomach.

The rats have their revenge even if you eat them. It was an hour after dark, that I felt a fierce gnawing in my gut, like I'd swallowed their teeth, like they were trying to get out. I held down my meal, but commenced to shiver in the dark. The stars came out, cold and gleaming, eyes looking down at me, like heavenly vermin they were marching over the sky, over my skin, and every hair on my head seemed to be standing up straight.

I was sick for days, lying beside that Indian grave in the middle of nowhere out west. So now it was Dwight's turn to care of me. He was letting the wound air now under his bandanna. The scab had turned dark, and there was no pus now. His head was perfectly bald on top, like Popish monks you see in old pictures, with a fringe of hair all around, but nothing left on top, snatched clean off like he'd been scalped.

He wandered further off from camp each day, he later told me, circling, scavenging for food. He fashioned a bolo from rocks, and found a jackelope, a rabbit with long pronghorns, which he fed me in my worst delirium. You could see the rack of horns in the stew, if I remember correctly.

There were even hoop snakes that rolled in across the prairie, great wheels of them, with their tails in their mouths. They rolled across the plain and into the hole to eat their fill. Dwight reached out and snagged one of the reptile doughnuts and he cracked it like a whip to break its skinny back. Into the pot it went. He found wild grasses to season it with, and fricasseed the serpents. A lot of rib meat, but tasty, like chicken, only longer cuts.

But then for days, he couldn't find anything. We were doomed. The hawks had flown off, replaced by buzzards, silently circling over us. I'd close my eyes and the black spots still swam around under my eyelids.

"Promise me one thing, Dwight, don't bury me with the Injuns, please. You'll carry me home?"

"Son, if I have to drag you all the way back to Beaverdam, Lord help me, I will."

"Promise. Don't let my bones rest in the west. I want to go home when I die."

"Wylie, hush all this talk of dying."

I kept closing and unclosing my fists, digging my nails into the hard sod. Lord, I'm done for, I thought, and I licked my lips that felt like sandpaper.

I thought of Pearl back in Mississippi, how her mouth had felt against mine. I thought of all we had seen and come through and how I'd never see the salt water of the Pacific. I was about to cry, I felt so bad, but there weren't any waters left in my eyes, barely spit enough in my throat to work up a swallow. When all the juice dried within you all that's left is the dust. Dust to dust, I understood the preachers now, what seemed only the oily words they poured from their mouths over the coffins of all the kin folks I'd seen buried.

Then it was like Pearl kissed me back, some big angel planted a sloppy wet smooch on my mouth and nose, too. I sat bolt upright and banged my head against Ivy's bony knee.

She licked my face with her fat tongue and mooed in my ears. I stood up for the first time in days and hugged her neck.

"I do believe your cow is with calf," Dwight Sparks observed.

Ivy flicked her tail girlishly. She was all aglow, something I'd never seen before in my heifer before. She'd been a dry cow for days crossing the plain, now two weeks later, she was brimming with milk, her teats swollen.

"What happened?"

"Birds and bees," Dwight said. "And maybe buffalo."

We looked far to the north and there was a black cloud moving there. Stray shaggy things that rumbled across the plain. We watched them pass and Ivy let out a little heartfelt *Moo*.

"Simmer down, Juliet. Romeo done went roaming." Dwight Sparks laughed at us, me red-faced and the mother to be.

The old man's words trailed off. It took a second for Dwight to hear the silence and that the story had stopped. Pop stared off into the distance. The light of the sunset was in their eyes, the west all aglow with shafts of red and gold, like angels in all their glory, bright beings flying to the horizon. Then the sun went down, a big red ball the size of a silver dollar his grandfather had given him once and never once asked for in return for a story.

"That was some sunset." Pop whistled softly, and Dwight understood him to mean not just this one, but the one way back in his story, before they fell into the Indian grave, and Dwight Sparks got banged up and Wylie had to save him from the rats, and then Wylie got sick, and it looked like the end for sure, but then the cow came back and saved them.

"So you lived happy ever after." Dwight leaned back and felt the cold brick of the porch stoop, his bare knee bouncing against the old man's threadbare pants leg.

"Naw, you're thinking fairy tales."

"But the cow saved your lives. You made it out west and back. Everything turns out in the end, right?"

"I reckon." But to Dwight's ears, he didn't seem so certain. "It's just a story. Seems to me you might be getting a tad too old to listen me jaw about some old cow."

"But I want to know how it all turns out."

Pop smiled. "You learn a lot of things from your ma and your dad. In fact, they're probably going to teach you nine-tenths of what you really need. The rest is book learning, reading and writing, and if I recollect, you like the reading and writing, and I think you'll pick up the numbers just fine if you mind your schoolteachers. But there are things you might not know, and you don't even know yet that you don't know them.

"And tell you the truth, I lie awake nights sometimes and I think back just how easy things were walking west. Just me and Dwight putting one foot in front of the other and not having to think real hard or real quick it seemed, and that was easy compared with the kind of adventures you're probably going to have in your life."

Pop pinched the glowing ember of the cigarette between his broken thumbnail and the horned callous of his index finger. Sighing out the last smoke, he pocketed the butt rather than throw it onto the pristine yard of his son-in-law. Then he leaned his whole weight on Dwight's knee, as he struggled to get to his feet. Dwight reached out his hand, suddenly afraid his grandfather was going to fall on top of him. Then Pop regained his balance, and with the terrible crack of his joints, he was standing upright.

"We been in your mama's hair long enough, reckon it's time to head on back to the hills."

"But you've just got here!"

Too suddenly, it was time for his grandparents to go, just as Dwight had gotten used to sleeping on the sofa. Suddenly, the summer looked to be at an end. School was coming up, all the fears he'd forgotten, anxieties that normally consumed him, he would have to shoulder once again.

"First thing, tomorrow morning. We like to get an early start. 'Night now."

"Good night," said the boy.

An early start was no exaggeration. It must have been about five o'clock when they left, still dark out as Pop tied the suitcase in the back of the truck. Dwight felt like he was still dreaming the departure, a repeat of the scene from a week before, but running backwards now. The hugs from his grandfather and kisses from his grandmother, before they hobbled out to the truck and slowly got in, the engine coughing on the first try, then roaring to life as Pop gunned the gas, and if people were still sleeping at five in the morning they were wide awake now across the neighborhood.

Dwight was standing next to his mother, waving his hand, she waving hers, the truck creeping back down the drive and around the corner, and finally out of sight, the chugging engine still audible for blocks away, and then nothing but bird song and silence again over the house where they lived.

"Now that wasn't so bad. Was it?" Mom hugged him, looking in his face for an answer he wasn't sure how to give.

They went back inside and went back to bed, she in the bedroom where she slept alone. He didn't go back to the sofa but to his own room, now strangely not his again, he crawled back into the bed where the old people had slept, still warm under the sheets where they had lain, snoring up their storms.

And it was all like a dream, when he got up later that morning and stretching, stepped back out on the porch. The slam of the car door surprised him. He swallowed his yawn and opened his eyes.

The familiar sedan was in the driveway, dusty from a week's parking at the airport where his father had taken the plane to and from New Jersey.

"Hey, want to give your old man a hand?" Dad was pulling the suitcase from the trunk.

Dwight leapt up, then caught himself, for his adolescent slouch. Time to act his age. He had his own life back. Enough of Indian graves, and tornadoes and rat food and cows.

Time to get real.

CALIFORNIA, 1969

The summer Dwight Martin turned sixteen marked the first year in his young life he did not visit his grandfather's farm in the North Carolina mountains. Instead, he flew cross-country on his first plane ride and stayed a month in California with his old man, that stranger who was his father.

He had not seen his dad since December when the family gathered for what would be their last Christmas together, and many more holidays apart to come. His mother and his father sat on either side of the Christmas tree, gaudy with the lights he'd put on and the glass balls she had hung. All their presents underneath the evergreen were lavished on him, none exchanged between them except for hard looks. They competed in their attentions toward their only child, watching him dutifully rip the wrapping paper from boxes of shirts, socks from his mother, a pocket knife from his father, a pen and pencil set from her, a wristwatch from him, the most loot he'd ever gotten over the holiday, although he'd asked for nothing.

They had already opened and fawned over the gifts he had gotten them. A set of Louis L'Amour paperbacks for him, "Whoa; westerns. Thanks, Son." A bottle of perfume for her—not knowing what scent she would like, Dwight had picked out the one with the strongest bang for the buck. She had the same reaction he had at the store, taking a whiff and her eyes bulging a bit. "Thank you, that's very nice." Then she stoppered the bottle.

His mom gave him books as well—Wolfe's *Look Homeward, Angel* and

Thoreau's *Walden*. She had entertained not-so-secret ambitions for Dwight ever since his precocious novels when he was ten. He frowned at the massive Wolfe book, thumbed slowly through the Thoreau. Actually, he was more into Tolkien and Tarzan, but it was hard to explain Hobbits or the Ant-Men to his mother.

She cradled a ceramic Santa Claus mug, her slippered feet curled beneath her, and the faint stubble showing on her shins beneath the terrycloth robe. Dwight's dad sat with his elbows on his knees, slowly wringing his hands, as Dwight unwrapped his last present. An intricate model of a souped-up roadster with Rat Fink details and California surfboards stuck in the rumble seat. Quickly, his father snatched the box from his hands to point out the specifications of the engine. It was what Dwight would have liked about three years ago, but not now, not really. The only interest Dwight had in cars was getting his license and driving off in one, a recurring daydream where he pulled out of the driveway and headed west, south, north, somewhere that took him anywhere from this house.

"Well, it's Christmas, that counts for something." His dad handed back the box. "Sorry I can't be around to help you put it together, but I know you'll do just fine without my help."

His mother coldly eyed his failed father, sipping black coffee from Santa's merry skull.

That was as close as they came to formally announcing their separation and impending divorce.

His father flew away the day after Christmas on another business trip, and simply didn't come back. A week went by, then another. He didn't call, but his mother didn't act surprised.

One night after supper, clearing away the dishes from their table, his mother paused, put her hand on his face, and brushed back his hair from his forehead, tenderly, something she hadn't done for a while. She had seemed preoccupied, and seemed to notice him for the first time in weeks, his quietness, his sullen mood.

"You know, don't you?" she asked. He kept his eyes down, but nodded, swallowed hard the last bit of meat. She kept fussing with his hair. He wished she would stop that, would leave him alone.

"Anything you want to ask me?"

The question caught him off guard, something he swore wouldn't happen. His eyes welled with hot angry tears. He shook his head.

So close to sixteen, sullen and silent, Dwight knew everyone assumed he was different now, grown up or at least an inch taller than last year. But it was the world that had changed all around him, not him, not inside.

—

In those spring afternoons after school, he shot basketball at the goal his father had bolted over their garage. He wasn't very good at dribbling. Every time he tried something fancy like between his legs or behind his back, the ball got away from him. But he got so he could sink more free throws than he missed. His father had always encouraged him to work hard at whatever he was playing at. "Pay attention, bear down, discipline yourself, you'll be amazed at what you can accomplish with the right attitude," Dad insisted, and now that he wasn't here, Dwight almost believed the man.

By the time school let out for summer, he had worked up to shooting a hundred consecutive shots, making strings of ten and twelve buckets, one after the other, a grove of nothing but net, air and space, perfection, every awkward muscle finely tuned, completely focused, and free of any thought. One night he made a miraculous twenty-seven buckets in a row, before the twentieth-eight shot whirled around the rim and heartbreakingly out.

O.K., concentrate. Soon he was back down to only four or five in a row, then he would miss and miss badly, an air ball, or one that sailed past the backboard and hit the roof and bent the gutter. His father wasn't going to be happy about that, but then he realized his dad wasn't going to be back anytime soon to yell at him about anything.

After that week, Dwight slacked off. What was the use? Instead of success, he quit after failure, when he had two air balls in a row. Then one night, he wouldn't even try making the basket, but hurled the ball against the backboard, *wham, wham*, a horrible racket, the ball ricocheting back and he would catch it and heave it with all his meager strength against the goal, the garage door, then pounding the ball harder and harder into the asphalt, letting it bounce ten and fifteen feet into the air. But even that game lost its appeal.

When he walked in the house, the ball tucked under his arm, his mother was on the phone.

"Hang on," she said, scowling to the caller. "Where you've been?"

Why the inquisition, he wondered. "Out," he said, showing her the ball. Obviously.

"Here." She shoved the phone receiver at him.

"Who is it?"

"Your father. He wants to talk to you."

"Me? What's wrong? I didn't do anything."

He bounced the ball even though he'd been told a thousand times not to bounce the ball in the house. His mother was afraid the vibration would upset some porcelain gee-gaw from the mantel or cause a china dish to crack in the dining room breakfront. He didn't even get a rise out of her. She shook the phone like a club. He took it.

"Yeah? What do you want?" The words came out harder and quicker than he'd intended.

His father was two thousand miles away. In the distance, he could hear static, a blur of distant voices, millions of people, thrumming in the background. He thought he heard music, someone speaking what sounded like Russian, a woman laughing.

"Dwight? You there?" His father sounded different, less sure of himself.

"Yeah." Dwight drawled.

"Everything going O.K., huh?"

"Sure."

"You're minding your mother, aren't you?"

Dwight bounced the ball and caught it. His mother didn't even blink. "Uh huh."

"Listen, son. I was wondering if you'd like to come see California. Your mother and I've been talking about this. You know, come on out, visit for a while. See Hollywood, Disneyland, you name it. We'll do it."

The words seemed ordinary enough, but out of the question. *Come to California.* All the way across the country, two thousand miles and a three-hour time difference? A different world.

"Sure," said Dwight, deciding his fate.

"Great. Great. You won't regret it. We'll have a good time. We'll hang out."

Hang out. His father was using slang. Was this something he'd picked up in California?

"I'll send the ticket in a couple of days. It will be so good to see you." A pause, then all of a sudden—"I miss you, Son."

"Yeah," Dwight didn't know what to say. "Me too." The words seemed to rush out, running ahead of his heart.

"Well, I better go. Long distance. O.K. I'll take care of everything. Bye." Dad hung up.

His mother hadn't moved since she handed him the phone.

"What did you say to him?" she asked, even though she had stood there during the whole conversation, had heard Dwight's reply.

"He wants us to come visit him in California."

"No, he doesn't. Just you." She would not relax her grip on her thin arms, crossed under her thin breasts. The gray in her hair made her look more tired than usual. "And you said yes."

He didn't know what to say. He hugged the basketball before him, pressed it tight into his solar plexus, into the hollowness inside him.

"You're not going?"

"No, Dwight. I'm not going."

Her mouth made a tight smile, but her eyes cut right through him. It was a terrible look to show anyone, let alone your own son. He wished he could say something to make it all right. He pressed the ball harder into his gut, until it hurt.

"I guess you won't be going to see your grandparents this summer. I know how much you'll miss seeing the farm."

Dwight gnawed his lip. Why would he want to go see the same old rundown farm, when he could go out to California? Beach girls, surfers, hot rods. Versus what? Rocks, a dying apple tree, a broken-down barn.

And he did miss his father in a strange way. What would be so wrong about seeing him?

"Pop won't be pleased. It'll about kill your grandmother." She sighed dramatically, a new habit of hers, Dwight had noticed. "But don't worry. I'll try to explain it to them."

"Maybe I'll go see them when I get back."

"Sure." His mother mimicked him, cruelly if unconsciously. Everything she said had an edge to it; conversations with her lately were like trying to pick up razor blades without slicing your fingertips.

It was getting dark outside, nearly summer in the Carolinas. In California, clocks were moving three hours behind. And his father was watching the unending sunlight, waiting for his son to come visit.

———

Flying was like going to a funeral. His mother insisted he wear his polyester blazer and tie, a white shirt. "You're taking an airplane. This isn't a Greyhound bus. There'll be professionals," she said.

The kid next to him was decked out as well in a bowtie, blue blazer and shorts. He looked terribly uncomfortable and kept squirming around under the seatbelt. His little oxfords banged the seat in front of him. The airline evidently put the orphans together, those kids put on planes by their parents with a kiss and a wave, who then watched them take off with terrible tears.

"Hi, you must be Petey." The stewardess beamed.

She leaned across Dwight to strap Petey into his seat, and Dwight experienced the full frontal assault of perfume and makeup and feminine proximity. She paused in her wrestling with Petey and tucked back a wing of her black hair behind a perfectly formed ear. On the lobe glistened a single, brilliant gemstone. Rouge on her cheeks. Hairsprayed bouffant and thick mascara. Her lips were full and painted red, her teeth were dazzling. Her eyes dark, skin tanned. Her name was Marcie, according to the silver pin that bounced on her tightly buttoned blazer. But Dwight couldn't help but study the swelling of her white blouse, like the undercarriage of a bomber, the payload inches away from his face.

She got the little guy all buckled in, while leaning over Dwight, the lapels of her blazer about to poke out his bulging eyes.

Finally, she stood up. "And who are you?"

"Dwight Martin, ma'am."

"Aren't you the well-mannered young man. Well, Dwight Martin, can you do ol' Marcie a favor?" She smiled.

Anything. Say the word. He would swear eternal allegiance. He could worship at the altar of those breasts behind the white blouse, behind the tightly buttoned blazer, behind the silver pin of her name.

"Keep an eye on Petey, will you? He's going to get off at Cleveland. I want you to be like a big brother to him. Petey, meet your big brother for this flight. This is Dwight. Say hey."

"Hey Dwight."

"Hey," Dwight repeated dutifully.

"I've got some little presents for you when I get back, but why don't you two get acquainted with each other? It's an hour or so into Cleveland."

Dwight watched Marcie's backside as she walked back down the aisle, bending over to check on passengers. When she glanced back and saw him looking, he gave her his best-mannered smile.

The plane began hurtling down the runway, the engines growing louder, the frame beginning to shake. Dwight had never flown before, and he understood that this was an unnatural act he was committing, leaving the solid earth for the thin air. The kid next to him suddenly laced his sweating fingers into Dwight's own. He looked over at Petey, who had his eyes closed. That looked like a good idea.

Dwight felt his stomach turning with the revolutions of the propellers outside their window. G-forces pressed him back in the seat like an invisible hand. He felt the nose of the plane tilt up and then the wheels break free of the ground. They were up. He opened his eyes and saw the edge of the runway, then the green tops of the trees and then fields and houses, smaller below. They were flying. He was alive. They were flying.

The pilot came over the intercom and announced they were flying over Mount Mitchell, the highest peak on the Eastern seaboard. Dwight strained his head toward the window when the plane banked a bit, wondering if he could see his grandfather's farm from up here, but he really couldn't see past the little sniffly kid who sat with his nose smudging the round porthole window.

"Hey, kid, can you move over?"

And the little kid turned to him, sticking his tongue out. A panicked look in his eyes. He gagged. His cheeks ballooned. God, the kid was going to throw up on him.

Marcie deftly reached in with the airsick bag and covered his chin and mouth and nose. "Dwight, could you be a dear and hold this for me while I check on the gentleman in C-3? Scotch and water coming, sir."

She waltzed down the aisle, leaving Dwight holding the bag while Petey gagged some more. After the kid quit heaving, Marcie came back and took the bag with a smile and wiped the boy's chin with a napkin.

"Feeling better? That's a brave boy. You're such a brave boy for handling that takeoff. Captain Blanchard and the crew wanted to give you a medal, you're such a brave boy."

She held out a cheap metal pin, tin wings "like the ones pilots wear." She leaned over and pinned the wings just above the crest of Petey's blazer.

Again all that female apparatus just inches away from Dwight's red face. He could feel his elbow in his thick polyester sleeve, pressed against her hip behind the skirt and stockings and girdle or whatever else a woman wore. He was touching her. He closed his eyes and breathed in the smell of her skin, her perfume. He fell in love with the whorls of her white ear. It was worth vomit to be in love, he decided.

"Dwight?" She held out another one of the tin flight pins. "Go ahead. We won't tell anyone. Usually it's kids twelve and under, but I can make an exception."

Would it be well-mannered to decline? Actually, it was kind of a cool pin. And she was holding it; he could take her hand for a second, hold it.

He snatched the pin from her hand and pocketed it. "Thanks," he mumbled.

They would hopscotch from airport to airport, a route that would take them from North Carolina to Cleveland and then on out across the plains and deserts to Los Angeles, following the sun racing ahead of them. The strange thing was the time he would lose in the air. He would be three hours younger when he landed in L.A. He wondered when he should reset the wristwatch that his father had sent him, whether he was still on Carolina time or in the unknown dimensions of California, here at the midpoint across the country.

Petey kicked him. "I need to go potty."

Dwight looked up and down the aisle. He couldn't find the stewardess. It wasn't that big of a plane but she was nowhere in sight in the haze of cigarette smoke. With a uniform snap of their Zippos, all of the businessmen had immediately lit their smokes once the plane had lifted off the runway. There was the crunch of ice in the molars of the men, as they savored the last of their highballs before asking for the next round. And the drone of the propellers washed away all conversations, leaving a constant roar in the ears. Maybe Marcie had disappeared behind the blue curtain that concealed the mysteries of First Class.

Petey pulled at his arm again. "Potty. Petey potty."

Dwight caught a whiff that wrinkled his nose. It seemed this couldn't wait.

He got the kid out of his seat and pulled him past the sleeping passengers toward the back of the cabin. No one looked up. Men in coats and ties stared at the melting ice of their glasses, or snored with their heads thrown back against the cushioned seats. There was a nun in the back, no Bible or rosary, but with a *Life* magazine in her hands, slowly turning the pages.

They got to the bathroom, which was thankfully unoccupied. Dwight opened the tiny door and pushed the boy inside. But Petey looked up at him, quizzically. "Help?"

Who me? Help? Oh, God. Another whiff and Dwight could tell the kid really had to go. He knelt in the small compartment, the hinged door banging at his backside, enclosing them both inside. *I'm not going to hold*

Petey's peanut for him. But he did yank down the boy's pants for him, then the underwear, and lifted him up on the john. "Don't fall in. O.K.?"

And closed the door on Petey's problem.

The plane suddenly shook and threw him against the bulkhead. The red warning lights came on to fasten seatbelts as the plane bucked in the turbulence. The captain came over the intercom. "Sorry about that, folks."

Dwight opened the door and knocked Petey off the john as he fell inside. "Come on kid. Time to go."

"But I'm not finished."

"Sure you are. You know this part of potty." He grabbed the roll of toilet paper, crammed it in the boy's fist.

There was a knock on the door. "Boys, are you in there?" Marcie sounded worried.

"We're coming, we're coming." Dwight reached down and tried to yank up the boy's BVDs with the next bounce of the plane. Petey's peanut stiffened and shot out a yellow hot stream across Dwight's knees and hands. "Oh, great. Just great."

Marcie was knocking at the door. "Boys, this isn't fun and games. The captain wants you back in your seats right now."

Dwight wiped his hands on Petey's coat as he got the kid looking decent again, then he got the door open. Petey fell out of the john howling and wrapped his arms around Marcie's wonderful legs. Marcie gave Dwight a horrible look, and led the whimpering traitor back up the aisle. Everyone was looking oddly at him. Even the nun looked cross and frowned.

———

They survived the flight into Cleveland. And he could see Marcie leading Petey down the steps and across the tarmac into the waiting arms of a woman, who knelt on the tarmac and let the little monster wrap his shitty hands around her neck. They turned and hand in hand walked away, Petey evidently chattering away about his big adventure on the big airplane. The woman stopped and patted his backside, then glared back at the plane, shading her eyes. Dwight ducked away from the window.

They changed everything. Marcie was gone; a new crew of pilots and stewardesses came on. The new stewardesses were just as pretty, but none of them leaned over him the way Marcie had done. He'd had a special rapport with Marcie, who secretly understood him and his good manners.

"Hi," he tried to impress the new stewardess, a blonde named Nancy.

"Can I get you something?"

"No." He turned to the window, still smudged with Petey's nose prints.

The plane rolled down the runway, building terrible speed, but Dwight was a veteran now. He threw his own head back against the cushions, clutched the armrests tighter to intensify the experience, but it wasn't the same. They lifted off, leveled off, and the world of Cleveland and small houses and small cars disappeared below the cloud cover.

The flight took six hours across the heartland and into the desert, a journey that had taken his grandfather and his buddy Dwight and the cow Ivy ever so long to make. The landscape faded from green to yellow to brown, with faint lines of roads traversing the emptiness miles below.

He closed his eyes and crossed his legs under the seat. His feet were tingling, almost asleep. He stretched, rocked his soles across the floor, heel to arch to toe, toe to arch to heel. He tried to imagine walking like Wylie had done. He wondered what Wylie and Dwight and the cow would have looked like from the air. They were beyond even the buzzards. The clouds gave way to long, flat land. He tried looking down and seeing people or cars or houses or anything. He couldn't tell that the plane was moving except for the wisps of cloud that occasionally passed over the wing through the ever-whirling propellers. He thought of movies he had seen with toy airplanes circling a globe, indicating great travel on a hero's part. Dwight didn't feel like he was going anywhere.

This was the first summer he wouldn't go check on the trees he knew at his grandfather's farm, the gnarled apple tree by the woodshed, still standing, but half rotten at the trunk, the huge hemlocks high up on the slopes. He patted their bark, ran his hands through the short, dark-green needles as he passed under the lowest-hanging branches, breathed in their air of a constant Christmas.

At least he wouldn't have to pay for all those impossible stories that Pop used to tell, but sadly now he would miss those tales like he'd miss the trees.

His mother once let on mysteriously that Pop only told such funny stories because he was secretly sad. The remark had haunted Dwight through the years, because he often felt sad himself, and wondered if his mother felt the same when he caught her standing at the kitchen sink, staring off into a middle distance, or at the kitchen table with her cheek in her hand and the mug of coffee grown cold under her constant gaze.

⁓

Dwight's dad was not there to meet him at the gate, after his eight hours in the American air. People milled past him in the long concourse, a Babel of different languages and looks, Oriental, blacks, Hispanics, fancy white women in chic dresses, the pilots and stewardesses in their uniforms. He rubbed his hands in his pocket; his fingers against the tin wings Marcie had given him, a medal for a little kid who did not cry.

Dwight looked for his father's face amid the many men running and walking, talking into telephones or hunched in seats behind newspapers. But he was nowhere to be seen. A woman's curt voice echoed over the intercom, announcing gates for delayed flights, boarding calls, the names of lost children or passengers sought by longing families or higher authorities. But he did not hear his own name.

He trailed after a woman in a blond beehive and large sunglasses whom he recognized from his flight, until she ran into a dark man in a white suit. They kissed each other hard, black and white, on the lips, until Dwight looked away, embarrassed to intrude on their happiness. He followed the couple, their arms interlocked around each other, hip to hip, in a closeness he could never remember his mother and father sharing. They ambled against the stream of harried businessmen rushing for their flight, Dwight just behind the couple, wondering if they would notice him, ask if he was lost, just so he could say courageously, no.

At last they led him to the carousel where the suitcases and trunks and duffel bags were arranged on a conveyer belt. He watched the bags go around the circular conveyer belt and then disappear under a black flap into the wall, and reappear again. Slowly all the other passengers retrieved their possessions, and were reunited with their families and friends and ushered off, all smiles, into the City of Angels.

At last Dwight picked his bags off the conveyor belt, and headed toward the doors with his heavy Samsonite cases, over-packed by his mother with more underwear, socks, belts and sweaters than anyone would ever wear in Southern California. He stepped through the sliding doors and into the setting sun that blazed beneath a pair of palm trees over the parking lot. He blinked over the glinting chrome and paint of countless cars parked in the lots stretching forever. The air was different, full of a golden light, but the breeze was hot and dry on his face. He chewed at his chapped lips and felt instantly thirsty, like he'd stepped into a metal wilderness, a man-made desert. He went back into the air-conditioning, dragging his heavy bags that threatened to pull his right arm from its socket and leave him permanently listing to the left.

"Dwight. Where have you been? I thought you're were going to be at Gate 33."

"Hey," Dwight said. "Just looking around."

"You got your things? Let me take one of those bags."

Dwight had worried about this reunion with this disapproving man Dwight had almost called *Daddy* when his father suddenly appeared in the midst of the busy airport. Should they hug, or simply shake hands? Or better yet, not acknowledge the many months they hadn't seen each other? Awkwardly, their hands brushed, human contact made between their shared flesh and blood, as they distributed the luggage.

His father carried the heavy bag for him while he took the lighter one, and they went wandering into the wilderness of cars. "Sorry, traffic was a bear. I should have left an hour ago, but hey, that's California. Now, Row 3A, 3A," his father muttered, looking for where he'd parked the car. Which way was that? They squinted into the sun, looked one way, then

Dwight with the brighter, younger eyes, saw the number on the distant light pole off to the left and pointed the way.

Without Dwight's mother there, his dad seemed apologetic and lost, unsure of his bearings or directions. "I think you're going to like it out here, son. There are all sorts of things to do and see. I've got a light week of work, I hope, coming up, so you and me will have plenty of time for catching up. You like baseball? We can go see the Dodgers any day you want. Box seats. You'll see. You're going to like it out here."

His father stuffed the Samsonites under the front hood. He smiled at Dwight's look of disbelief. "That's right, the engine's in the back," and drummed his hands against the sleek roof of the Corvair. "Pretty snazzy, huh? Maybe you can drive it around a bit. You'd look good behind the wheel of this baby."

And Dwight said nothing, but blushed and grinned and cut his eyes and shuffled his feet, unused to such attention from this man, no longer his disapproving dad, but a hail-fellow-well-met. Dwight was no longer a child, but like a colleague, a traveler who could loosen his polyester necktie at the end of the deal and the day. So, this was California, the other side of the country. Dwight felt strangely displaced.

"What time is it?" Dwight looked at his new wristwatch, the one his father had given him for Christmas.

His father glared at his own timepiece, then tapped it and bent his wrist to his ear. "I just bought this the other day. Now look. American obsolescence. Can you believe it?"

Dwight set his watch back three hours anyway. This was a new time.

His father was right about one thing: the traffic. He'd never seen so many cars, whipping by in so many directions, overpasses and underpasses, and multiple lanes of big-finned, chromed cars, grim-faced drivers in wrap-around sunglasses barreling into the California glare and smog. It was like bumper cars, at 70 miles per hour, except no one hit each other intentionally. Dwight looked with new admiration at his dad, this middle-aged man hunched over the wheel, sweating profusely, muttering blue language under his breath. His eyes darting back and forth between rear and side mirrors, holding his breath as he made his "big move," a quick lane change, slipping right into the path of an oncoming semi that wailed its air horn at this maneuver.

"Yeah, you too, buddy. No one uses a turn signal out here. It's like giving vital information to the enemy."

Dwight sank lower in his strange bucket seat. He wasn't ready to drive, yet another adult skill he wouldn't be very good at, and not being good at this could be fatal. He wouldn't live to drive past sixteen. He wished he were back in the slow South.

"Did you see that? Did you see that?" Dad pointed out the imbecility of fellow drivers actually turning loose of the wheel that held their cars and lives in a straight line; he threw up his hands at the inexplicable actions of the car attempting to cut him off. "That's it, buddy. Go ahead and just try." He accelerated, closing off the gap. It was a deadly cat-and-mouse game with a big truck that whipped in and out of lanes as his dad barreled behind drivers until they surrendered their lanes and pulled over to what he called "Grandma's lane."

"Oh, that reminds me." His father's eyes darted between dash, windshield, mirrors and back again, a constant round robin, like his eyes were spinning in his head. "You got a letter from Pop and Gram."

Dwight wondered how they knew his father's address all these weeks, when as far as Dwight knew he had dropped off the continental shelf into the ocean.

When his father finally exited the freeway, there was no more yelling at the other drivers and nothing much more to say to each other. They drove up into hills, a dry, dusty, arid place. There were taller peaks in the distance, brown, raw mock-ups of the domestic blue mountains around his grandparents' house that seemed to graze like giant, gentle beasts. He knew enough of his geology to remember that actually the mountains were younger on this side of the country, still waiting for the eons to wear them down like the ancient tribe of hills he had climbed every summer.

They drove into a subdivision, down wide streets with evenly spaced houses with lawn sprinklers and no trees, and sidewalks that gave off wavy heat lines under the sun. Out past all the irrigation and green lawns, the land looked like desert.

"Well, here we are, home sweet home." His father pulled into a concrete driveway up to a bungalow that matched every other house on the long straight street. Dwight checked his watch. They had been on the road for an hour and fifteen minutes from the airport. He had left home at eight a.m. It was four p.m. Pacific Standard Time. His mind froze up at the math involved in calculating where he really was in space and time now; he had come so far, crossed an entire continent.

His father got the suitcases out from under the hood.

He fiddled with the key ring at the front door, betraying his own unfamiliarity with the lock, and at last got it open, backed up and bumped Dwight with the suitcase, then pushed his son forward. "Go on in, don't be bashful. Make yourself at home."

Shag carpet, white walls, modern furniture, a bigger and fancier TV than the one they had at home. It looked like a hotel room, like no one lived here. There was a kitchen, and a sliding glass door opening onto a back deck that looked out upon a small yard of brown grass and then a fence and an empty clothesline. He almost expected to see his mother out there, a clothespin between her teeth, the wet laundry in a basket at her bare feet, as she pinned white sheets to dry in the breeze.

But the only thing that hung there was a dried mop. He couldn't imagine his father doing laundry.

"You're back here." His dad led the way, scuffing the white hallway with the suitcases, muttering more language under his breath. It gratified and unnerved Dwight to hear his father swear. He had never spoken such things in front of his mother.

"Here's your digs." A bed and a pine dresser, a small nightstand. Blank walls. A small window that gave out on the same brown grass of the back yard, but with a closer view of the redwood fence. It had all the charm of a cell.

The telephone rang. "Oops. Bet I know who that is."

While his father took hurried steps down the hall to the kitchen to silence the insistent rings, Dwight looked at his new surroundings. He opened the louvered closet doors, set the few empty clothes hangers on the rack jangling together like a sad mobile with a brush of his hand.

He sat on the edge of his bed and saw the letter addressed to him set against the blue bedspread, against the pillow.

In the kitchen, his father was telling his mother. "We just got in. He's fine. A little tired. No, his flight was on time. It was the traffic."

Of course, he didn't tell her about the mix-up in the terminal, how the two Martin men wandered aimlessly through the crowds looking for each other, afraid to ask directions.

"Do you want to talk to your mother?" Dad called from the kitchen.

"Uh, can I call her later? I'm a little tired," Dwight fibbed, figuring his father was rich now, living in California. If he could spring for a plane ticket, he could afford the long distance. Besides, Dwight felt the distance between himself and his mom. He didn't want to talk to her just now.

"Sure, son." Then back on the phone. "He said he's a little tired. He'll call you later. Sure, it's my dime. I know, long distance. Yeah. I'll take care of him. He's my son, too . . . "

He opened the letter in his hand and read his grandmother's girlish handwriting in a blue ballpoint pen on ruled notebook paper.

Dear Dwight,

We're sad you couldn't come to see us this summer, but nobody should pass up a chance to see the world, your Pop says. The weather has been hot, but we are well as we hope you are too. Be sure to eat well when in the west. Your Pop says keep your bearings. It's only for the summer, but we hope you have a fun time, and see all those sights California is known for. Perhaps you can bring us back some California produce, grapes and lettuce would be interesting to taste, though ours are doing well this year. But you're a big boy now and know how to take care of yourself. The airplane ride must have been something. I'd be too scared to try something like that, though your grandfather says me and him ought to fly out west and see the Grand Canyon and the desert, although he just says those things, I think to tease me. I can't help it if I'm a homebody. From what all I've heard tell from folks I've talked to, most places, even California, don't hold a light to this holler we live in. I'd rather stay at home, thank you. The time to see things like

California is at your age. Your Pop keeps hollering from the porch for me to write you. "Keep your bearings and the cow pointed west." He says you'll know what that means, even if I don't.

Love, Gram and Pop (Rominger)

P.S. You need a little more than directions for California. I've enclosed a little something to line your pockets.

And in the envelope was money, ten worn dollar bills, that still warmed to the touch when she slid them into the envelope and entrusted her message and money to the U.S. Postal Service.

That first night together in the Golden State, they grilled steaks out in the backyard. His father, being his father, had to explain the correct way to build the perfect fire. "You have to stack the charcoal in a pyramid, concentrate the heat, so that the coals will start out burning evenly. Then of course, just a smidge of the magic potion." He squirted the lighter fluid from the can in a long thin stream, scribbling the dark briquettes with squiggles.

"You do the honors." Dad handed him the book of matches. "Careful now."

Dwight folded back the cover and struck the head against the strip. The paper match burned. And he dropped it toward the coals. He jerked his hand back, but not before the pleasing whoosh of combustion and instant yellow flame leapt for his face and singed the hairs on his knuckles.

"Whoa."

"Now we're cooking." Dad grinned.

The excitement of the fire didn't last long. The flames burned away the fuel and started to work on the charcoal. They stood over the metal grill and watched for a while, silently sipping their iced bottles, Dwight drinking orange pop, his dad, a beer.

"Takes about twenty minutes if you stack the charcoal just right. But that's the secret to the perfect steak, patience with the fire. Best way to ruin meat is to put it on a fire that's just not ready."

They followed the red edges nibbling at each briquette, the carefully stacked pyramid crumbling into white ash. "Yep, twenty minutes." His father held his hand over the fire. "See, it's barely hot enough to warm."

He held his hand close to his father's. He wondered what it would feel like to palm one of those red coals, if he had the courage. Heat is an illusion, pain nothing but a state of mind, he read of these Kung Fu masters who could ignore heat or cold and Indians who could hang pierced from sinews and thorns through the skin of their chests. He'd seen on TV where men walked barefoot through beds of coals. He didn't flinch, but kept his hand beside his dad's. Dwight noticed the white band of skin on his third finger. His father wasn't wearing the wedding ring anymore.

"Ouch," Dwight snatched his hand away from the heat suddenly real and searing the center of his palm.

His father flapped his hand as well in the evening air. "I was wondering how long that was going to take."

He switched the bottle of beer from his left to his right hand. Dwight did likewise and the burning stopped. He drank his soft drink and considered this stranger who was his dad.

Before he left home, Dwight had asked his mother just to be certain; this fall, his father was turning forty. But his dad looked different in the seven months or so since he'd last seen him, not older, really, but changed. The man had let sideburns creep down past his ears. It was 1969 after all, his concession to the times. Otherwise his dad dressed pretty much like he was still home in Carolina, back in their backyard. He wore a rayon camp shirt and loud Bermuda shorts, but the black socks and the dress shoes seemed incongruous. The old man would never be in or with it, or whatever.

Dwight, of course, dressed in carefully patched blue jeans and a tie-dyed T-shirt that his mother had made for him after psychedelia became all the rage in high school, but she put her foot down when it came to long hair. He promised to make his father take him to get a haircut this summer. "I don't want you coming back looking like a hippie," she said. Hippies were in the newspaper a lot, along with riots in Watts.

The full pale moon crept over the redwood fence. They watched it a long time before remarking on the latest headlines.

"Did you see Neil Armstrong on the moon the other day? Amazing. Never thought I'd see something like that in my lifetime."

Dwight had read all the stories about the race to the moon. Watched the broadcasts every time the rockets went up or the astronauts went for the funny walks in space, or the strange black-and-white landing. The pictures were right, it was bone white on that round moon staring at them over the fence.

"What did he say?" His father mused. "One step for man, one great something for somebody. I thought about your grandfather when I saw that."

"Pop?"

"Yeah, here's a man who's seen us go from the covered wagon to the Model T, to the Cadillac. He was around before the Wright brothers went flying down at Kitty Hawk and he's still around when men can fly to the moon. Think of all the things he's seen in his lifetime."

Dwight stared at the moon. The nursery rhyme was going through his head about the cow jumping over the moon. Dwight had no idea that his dad took Pop at all seriously.

"Mars won't be too far off. You could go there in your lifetime. You ever think about that?"

Dwight didn't. California was about as far as he was prepared to go. Realistically, he knew all the astronauts started out as scientists and fighter pilots. The one involved numbers, the other involved, well, probably flying over in Vietnam, and he figured he'd be better off avoiding both science and the service.

"You ever thought what you might do someday? I mean, after college. Work-wise. You were thinking about college, right?"

"I dunno." Dwight threw up his right shoulder in a half-hearted shrug, trying to brush away his father's question.

His father frowned, took another swig, then looked down at the empty bottle in his fist.

Dwight wondered if his dad was drunk. He'd never really seen his father drink beer at home. In one of his mother's strange asides, she had let on that his father's grandfather, Dwight's paternal great-grandfather, had lost an arm in a hunting accident, although it was never explained, somehow it was understood that the old man was loaded even before he picked up the loaded gun.

Bourbon and bullets don't mix, being the moral of that story, Dwight remembered his dad saying just once, but he never spoke of it again.

But now his father was drinking beer out of the bottle, something his mother wouldn't cotton to. And he was actually talking, something Dwight didn't recall them doing that much back home.

California seemed to have changed him. His father acted like he might not have talked to a soul in the last seven months, all the time he'd been out west.

"We're getting along here, aren't we?" Dad asked for some reassurance.

"Sure," Dwight said.

"Your mother worried we wouldn't, you know. But your mother worries a lot. She's a good woman." He kept trying to drink from the empty bottle, before he finally set it on the ground at his feet. He clapped his hands, then rubbed them briskly together.

"So, look here, twenty minutes and these coals are perfect. How do you like your steak?

"Medium rare," Dwight dared to be different.

"That's eight minutes and coming right up."

They took the plate with the eight-minute ribeyes back into the kitchen, since there was no picnic table out back. His father had fixed baked potatoes, and iceberg lettuce and sliced tomato for salad. "Great produce out here in California, they grow everything."

Dwight sniffed at the dressing, which wasn't the usual orange of mayonnaise and ketchup that his Mom mixed with relish for their iceberg. This was strong stuff that nearly made him gag.

"Blue cheese," Dad explained. "Steak house kind of stuff."

His dad never went to steak houses, at least not with Dwight and his mother. The only steak house Dwight knew was Staley's, out in the swank neighborhood where the doctors and lawyers lived. A giant steer stood by the awning that led inside into the nights of cocktails and

Sinatra serenades. That huge cow unnerved him whenever he rode by the restaurant.

When Dwight cut his steak, it was frighteningly red in the middle. Medium rare. Usually he had meat well done, especially up in the mountains.

Dad noticed his discomfort. "Your mother overcooks a lot of things. I never told her that, but I'll tell you." His father winked, then winced. "Sorry. I promised I wouldn't say anything negative about your mother. She's a fine woman. I want you to know that. I have the deepest respect for her."

Dwight felt the red juices squeezing between his molars and felt like a cannibal. He swallowed hard, then spit out what was on his mind.

"How did you know Mom was the one? I mean the right one to marry."

Dad chewed over the question and his steak a second. "I don't know. I woke up one morning and I just knew. Took me a while though to tell her. Saved up two months worth of salary and got her the best ring I could afford. High school math didn't pay all that well."

"How long did you teach high school?"

"About a year and half. Those kids were eating me alive. Fortunately I found the job as a technical writer at Western Electric. Good money, it's done O.K. by you and your mom, hasn't it?"

Somehow Dwight could both see and couldn't see his father at the head of an algebra class, clapping his hands dusted with chalk dust. His thin tie, waving his slide rule in the air, trying to keep order. *You, John Mark, go to the Principal's office. Donna Bright, quit kicking the back of that boy's chair . . .*

He'd seen a photo of his parents taken at their wedding, his future father with an unlined face, with a bowtie and a white jacket; Mom, little more than a girl, no wedding dress, only a dark dress and a white corsage, joined together in holy matrimony in some minister's pine-knotted study. In the background, there stood Pop with dark hair and Gram half-smiling at the ceremony.

Then later, a shot of them at some overlook on the Blue Ridge Parkway, probably not too far from Pop and Gram's farm. Him with his sunglasses and a wind-tousled hair, her with a scarf and a swelling belly. They had the formal, stiff look of a couple acting out their parts, but part of them uncertain; hesitant, they stand where they are supposed to, his arm at the small of her back, her belly protruding slightly over his lean form, like a half moon out of his side, what is to come. They don't blink behind their sunglasses, framed forever in the uneasy past, staring out into the unknown future.

But in all these figures, these calculations of the heart, the mathematics of emotion, Dwight asked only the quickest questions and his father gave the easiest answers. What couldn't be asked, what couldn't be answered was when he knew that his mother was no longer the one.

"Good steak," Dad said with his mouth full.

"Umm," Dwight agreed, and they stuffed more meat in between their grinding teeth.

THE SHORTCUT BELOW

Dwight dreamed of flying. His grandfather kept trying to push him off a crag into the wild blank yonder of the west. *Flap your arms, faster, that's it.* And the old man hooked his thumbs into the straps of his overalls and fluttered his own flabby biceps, his pointed elbows, until, miraculously, his shit-coated boots began to leave the earth. He was six inches in the air, trying to talk Dwight into stepping off the side of the Grand Canyon. *We could fly to the river, you know.* The old man looked so disappointed, sensing Dwight's disbelief. He quit flapping and his feet came back to the South Rim. *Yeah, you're probably right. I was lying all along.*

———

Dwight awoke in white light, in a strange room. For a disorienting instant, he didn't know where he was, or how he got there. Oh yeah, California. He sat up, rubbing his fist into his fold of his eyelid, to dislodge the grit of a hard night's sleep. He yawned as he rubbed his feet on the floor, feeling the shag rug squinch under his toes. He wandered, yawning, out into the hall of the strange rancher, not sure which way to turn, right or left.

He followed the sounds of silverware clinking in a cereal bowl and found his father sitting at the kitchen table already dressed for work. He was slurping coffee, sucking the last of his cornflakes from his back teeth.

"Hey sport, sleep good?"

A change had come over his old man since he'd hit the West Coast. Back east, he'd favored heavily starched, impeccably white, buttoned-down Oxfords, narrow black ties, and synthetic slacks. Out here, he favored bright, even psychedelic ties, comfortable slacks and pastel stripes in his short sleeves. His father looked, well, cool, the sunglasses clipped with the pens and pencils in the vinyl pocket protector that also displayed his company's security badge.

But why was he wearing any kind of tie on his vacation? And why did he keep shaking the stubborn watch on his wrist?

"You're going somewhere?"

"Sorry, sport but I've been called into the office. The code crashed on them over the weekend, and I'm the guy who has to pick the bugs out."

"Bugs?" Dwight imagined termites in his father's office.

"Computers. It's all in the code, one wrong line and the whole thing just goes down."

His dad unlatched his battered briefcase with the tarnished locks. Dwight remembered the leather-holstered slide rule, with its precise movements up and down a dizzying scale of minute numbers. It was like a magic wand his father could wave over his elaborate equations. Space men used slide rules, which definitely ruled Dwight out from outer space journeys.

But instead of the slide rule, his dad produced a thick stack of manila punch cards bound by a thick red rubber band. "I've got to run all these suckers here and find out what's the problem. One wrong hole in a few million, that's a bug and these big mainframes we got, they just go haywire. The whole thing blows up."

"Really," Dwight asked, still following along a little too literally. "Smoke and fire?"

"Well, no. All these little holes represent yes or no, yes or no. Say you're trying to ask the computer something like what do you want for dinner? The computer will say yes or no."

Listening to his dad explain computers, Dwight felt his stomach lurch at the same time his brain locked. He remembered fifth grade and his father trying to help with homework when math had moved beyond multiplication tables into fractions and integers, and word problems, stories that made no sense in the real world, no action, or heroes or villains, just these cars traveling at different speeds in different directions and where would they meet. It was always a head-on collision for Dwight.

"Look, I won't be long. I told the boss that my boy was here from the East Coast, and I can't stay cooped up all day when you're out here visiting California. So. . . . " His dad took a legal pad from the briefcase and slid it across the table. "Just jot down everything you ever wanted to do out in California, and when I get back we'll see if we can't start crossing things off your list. O.K., sport?"

He had a way of making fun like homework. Dwight tried to imagine what the next four weeks with his father would be like, what they would actually say to each other. He tried his own calculations. Twenty-four hours times thirty days would be, well, a lot.

"Well, got to go." His father finished his coffee, scooted his chair from the table. "Make yourself at home. You might need to rest after that long trip yesterday. Jet lag and all. Your mother worries you won't get enough rest with this three-hour time difference."

Dwight waved from the front door, watching his father get into the car and drive off. He sighed his mother's sigh and walked back into the empty house.

In the back bedroom, he went through his father's things. His rolled underwear. His socks neatly paired. The shirts were boxed by a dry cleaner, and suits shrouded with filmy plastic and placed in the closet. A Hawaiian shirt hung in the back, a vivid array of parrots and hibiscus like one of his mother's floral arrangement projects. He could not imagine his dad braving the daylight in such a gaudy outfit.

Dwight wasn't sure what he'd expected to find. Rubbers, girly magazines, liquor, women's lingerie, rumored evils he had only heard of from the school locker room? His mother hinted darkly at such transgressions: "I don't know what he does out there. I don't know what's gotten into him."

In the dresser drawer, there was the box with his father's wedding ring, a simple gold band. It lay useless near his ten-year service tiepin, a pair of engraved cufflinks, other bits of jewelry he never wore. Dwight slid the ring on his own finger, but it was too big and drooped about his knuckle. No wonder his father didn't wear it. Dwight suddenly panicked, that precious metal in his slippery fingers. What if his hand suddenly flew up, launching the ring into the air, to land on the floor and roll across the room to the vent near the floorboard, and dropped forever with a fatal metallic ping into the dusty airshaft? What would his father say? Would losing that ring forever separate his mother and father?

Dwight closed his fist over the ring and decided he wouldn't let that happen, wouldn't lose his father's wedding ring by his own clumsiness. He let the ring drop slowly into its velvet cushion, then he slid the drawer shut.

Dwight did find a pack of cigarettes in the handkerchief drawer. Figuring his father, the human calculator, wouldn't inventory all twenty cigarettes in a pack of Luckies, he shook out two.

In the kitchen, he searched for more clues. There were two cans of unopened beer in the back of the refrigerator and a jar of maraschino cherries, bright red orbs floating in syrup. Did his father alone at night, drinking beer and dip his fingers into the jar, pull the bright cherries out by their long stems and place them on his tongue?

In the living room, Dwight turned on the television, twisted the dial through a dozen channels until he found a wobbly picture instead of steady static. Not that there was anything on he wanted to watch, just a talk show evidently aimed at women, Merv Griffin talking to someone. He squatted on his haunches, turning the dial until he found a Tom and Jerry cartoon, the violence of cat and mouse and sledgehammers. He came two thousand miles for this, to feel childish, stupid. To feel more grown-up, he turned off the tube and sat on the sofa, flipping through the newspaper his father had been reading. He learned that Californians were worried about crime and car accidents, something called smog in the air, riots in the streets, student unrest, Governor Reagan making declarations from Sacramento, which Dwight remembered was the capital of the Golden State.

When he was through, he folded the newspaper the way his dad did, every section in place. His father was a fanatic about road maps too, and everything folded just so.

Dwight got dressed in a pair of cut-off blue jeans, fringed with white thread, a Carolina Tar Heels T-shirt, white tube socks, high-top black canvas sneakers. He had no shirt pockets, so he tucked the cigarettes behind either ear, brushed down his hair over them so no one would see. In the foyer, he caught a glimpse of himself in the mirror where his father checked the knot of his new ties and smiled, checking to see he had nothing stuck in the incisors after breakfast.

Now Dwight took his own measure, his goofy reflection. A cowlick on the left side of his head. A pimple pushing its way to the tip of his nose, whispery whiskers on his sharp Adam's apple where he missed shaving. Dwight frowned, then sneered. *You're a redneck, a grit, you're a hick, a cracker.* The words made him cringe. What worse things could anyone say to him other than what he saw? He stepped outside into California, closing the door on the constant air conditioning.

The air was dry out here; he could taste metal in his throat with every breath. He looked up and down the street; all of the houses seemed deserted. He tried to get his bearings, but all he could tell was the sun was nearly overhead. He wet his finger and held it to the breeze; there was nothing blowing his or any direction.

He meandered down to the sidewalk and closed his eyes, and then following his heart, decided to go left. He came to the end of the street and looked both ways for nonexistent traffic. There were For Sale signs in some of the yards. In the back, there were clotheslines hung with white bed sheets. Everything was quiet. The curtains were drawn in most of the houses, except for big bay windows looking in on dim living rooms where no one ever lived. Everyone had gone to work or to the store. He listened for children's voices, screams or shouts or laughs of little kids. Nothing but the hum of air conditioners, and the faraway drone of the freeways.

Over the rooftop of a split-level at the end of the next street, he could see a brown mountain. He headed in that direction. He cut across the backyards toward a fence line. He clambered over the chain-link, jammed his rubber-tipped toes into the diamonds and wobbling on the wave of wire, he rolled over the top and fell into sharp-leafed grass and rocks. He was out of the grassy lawns now and into the chaparral, the real

California, and not the soft green of Carolina. He clambered down the slope through the spiky brush, heard the high hum of insects, thorns and small creatures biting at his calves and shins. He crossed a culvert where an iron pipe ran out of the hillside into a dry gully. Picking his way across the loose scree, he scrambled uphill.

He checked his watch. It took thirty-five minutes of Pacific time to crest the hill. At the top, he came to a grove of tough-looking pine trees, Ponderosa he thought, little cousins of great redwoods somewhere in California. Beyond the trees, he came to a transmission tower. The power lines went up and over, carrying the sun like a track, hauling daylight up and over the hill, the mechanics of dawn and dusk. There were beer cans littered on the ground, amid strange scrub brush, little cacti. He came to a promontory, which gave a view of identical subdivisions and the freeway in the distance, and a brown haze.

Dwight had thought he might see the ocean from here, but then realized that was about an hour away. He sat down on a rock, after checking for rattlesnakes or Gila Monsters or whatever creatures might bite his butt in the Wild West, and lit up a cigarette.

He blew smoke up, watching a jet drag a white contrail across the blank sky. He wasn't much of a smoker, and the fumes were making him faintly nauseous. He thought of his grandfather, with his tar-stained fingers and his yellowed teeth and the smell of tobacco on his worn white shirts. He wondered if he would smell that way.

He went through all the Dwight stories his grandfather had told him, of that long cross-country trek with the cow. But he realized all of the stories were en route; there was never one that mentioned actually arriving in California, or seeing the ocean. Now that he was here himself, Dwight didn't know what had happened. Had Wylie, Dwight Sparks and the cow Ivy simply crossed over the mountains, and come to the end of the continent, to dip their toes and hooves perhaps in the surf, to watch the sun they'd been following for more than a year drop off into the water? After all that, did they decide, *Well our adventure's over, time to turn around and head back home?*

He imagined them side by side, the image he had always during his grandfather's telling. Maybe they sat on a hill like this, except closer to the sea and not just a city to look at, puffed away at their hand-rolls, while the cow grazed the strange California bushes behind them.

Two thousand miles and that's a view all right.

Well, Wylie, you about ready?

Yep, I think it's about time.

And the two travelers would slowly rise and dust off the back of their blue jeans, snuff out their smokes beneath the worn soles of their boots, and slowly turn to the east.

The sun beat down on his head, until he felt a slight pounding at his temples. He checked his watch again, sighed, got up and descended the hill toward his father's subdivision.

⁓

It was only eleven when he got back to the house, but he could feel his stomach starting to growl. Fortunately he had noted the street number and the color of the siding and shutters on the otherwise anonymous rancher amid the identical streets and cul-de-sacs. He went up the walkway to the front door, turned the knob, gave a shove with his shoulder. When the door did not give way, Dwight realized he was locked out.

He circled to the back and tried the sliding glass door to the kitchen. Locked. All of the windows were down and locked, while the air-conditioning hummed away inside. He could put a brick through the glass but he figured his father would get mad at him for being foolish enough to leave the house in the first place. He'd already stolen his dad's smokes. One transgression in the course of a morning was about all his conscience could handle.

He sat on the stoop and waited. Dad said he'd be home for lunch, right? Then they were going to drive somewhere, see something?

There was a basketball goal over the garage door, evidently left by a previous owner. No basketball, of course. He peered in the small windows of the garage, empty except for a couple of trashcans and brooms. He took a few mighty leaps, trying to see if he could swat the bottom of the nylon net, but he wasn't much of a jumper, either vertically or horizontally. His feet were sore anyway. He had a blister on his heel from his hike up the mountain to see the other side.

He went back to the stoop and took off his shoe and tube sock to check his feet. A car, the first one he'd seen in the subdivision all morning, came down the street and pulled into the driveway directly opposite.

Two blondes, a matching set in blouses and pedal pushers, kicked their long legs out the doors of the Thunderbird. The taller one had a scarf around her head and sunglasses. She opened the great finned trunk and pulled out groceries. He watched the woman bend over, and the way she handed off the bags of groceries to the blonde girl, evidently her daughter.

They turned and stopped, spied him across the street where waves of heat were already shimmering over the asphalt. He waved bashfully. They did not wave back, but talked to each other. The woman walked out to the end of her white driveway, shading her eyes with her hand, even though she wore sunglasses.

"Can I help you?" she yelled from across the street.

"I don't know," Dwight replied.

The woman marched across the empty street, across the broad sidewalk and into the yard.

"Excuse me for asking, but I haven't seen you around here before. Are you quite sure you need to be sitting here?"

"I'm waiting on my Dad." Dwight said defensively.

Close up, he could see she was an older woman, probably his mother's age. The other girl was younger now; she had drifted across the street as well. "Mom?"

"Sherry. Go back to the house." She waved a manicured hand of red-polished nails at the girl behind her. But the girl sat down in the grass and broadly chewed her gum.

"If you don't mind me asking, but who's your Dad?" The woman didn't mind asking.

Californians sure were inquisitive, he thought. "His name is Gary Martin."

"Can you describe him?" Dwight couldn't tell if she blinked at all behind the wrap-around sunglasses, but he could feel her eyes bearing down on him.

"Well, he's balding, bald I guess. A little taller than me. I don't know."

"That sounds like the guy." The woman finally relinquished her hard frown, and pulled her sunglasses up on her scarved head. "So who are you?"

"Dwight Martin, ma'am." He scrambled to his feet, belatedly remembering his manners.

"Ma'am? You're not from around here?"

"Me?"

"It's the accent. Somewhere in the South, I'd say." She held out her hand and he shook it firmly. "I'm your next-door neighbor, Marla Hopper. This is my daughter Sherry."

The girl blew a pink bubble from her mouth. "Hey," she said.

"Hey," he said.

"Well, it's always good to have new people move into the neighborhood. I haven't met your mom yet."

"She's not here. She's back home." Dwight said, flustered. He pointed over his shoulder, the general direction of the continent at his back. As if he had walked the whole way. "She, my dad. . . ." He shrugged.

"Oh," Mrs. Hopper said. "Oh, I'm sorry." Suddenly flustered herself. "Well, me and Mr. Hopper. I know that can be hard on you. Sherry can tell you all about that."

Sherry looked at her mother and crossed her eyes, pretending to gag. She didn't look like she was about to tell him anything.

"If you or your father ever need anything. Borrow a cup of sugar, anything. You know where to go. Come on Sherry, we better get these groceries in the house before those frozen dinners thaw."

Dwight sprinted from his stoop. "Here, let me help you."

Mrs. Hopper positively beamed upon him. "What a polite young man. Wait until I tell your father."

She led the way across the street. He fell back to keep pace with Sherry.

"You don't have to be such a suck-up," she said. "It's just my mom."

"Please, don't tell your mom. But I've locked myself out of the house."

"This way, kids, right on into the counter. That'll be fine. Can I get you a Coke? Would you like a Coke?"

"Tab, Mother. You know I only drink Tab."

The Hopper women's house was a mirror image of Dwight's father's house across the street, the same floor plan down to the foyer and living room, kitchen and garage and the back bedrooms down the spine of the rancher.

The TV was blaring inside, the loud dramatic voices of soap opera actresses. From the back bedroom, he could hear a radio going with pop music. Dwight wandered around the living room, noting the love seat and the lifeless still lifes of roses on the wallpaper.

"Make yourself right at home," Mrs. Hopper hollered from the kitchen.

Dwight had never seen such flawless features, she looked like she could have been modeled on anyone of the million or so magazines that seemed to be scattered everywhere, but the house was a mess. There were baskets of laundry and half-folded clothes set atop an ironing board.

"Here's your Coke." Mrs. Hopper came out with two glasses of cola. "Could you take this Tab to Her Highness?"

Sherry was lying on her bed, kicking her bare legs into the air. She had the hi-fi on full blast, some AM station. Dwight handed over the drink, which she sipped suspiciously.

"I was afraid you got them mixed up," she said.

He looked out the window, at a backyard much like his own. He could see the mountain he had climbed this morning peeping over a splintered redwood fence.

"What's the name of that mountain?"

"What mountain?"

"Over there." he paused. "I climbed up it today."

"What for?"

He let the frilly girl curtain fall. "I don't know. I wanted to see what was up there. A lot of rocks and cactus and stuff. I thought I might see a coyote or something."

"I had a cat. Mr. Mittens. He got eaten by a coyote."

"Actually, I went up there for a smoke."

"You don't look like someone who would smoke."

"What type do I look like?"

"I don't know. But not that type." Sherry sat up on her bed and brought her knees to her dimpled chin. She took a long draw on her Tab. "Besides, nobody goes up to Lover's Leap except at dark. My boyfriend took me once, but then we broke up. Do you want to see his picture?"

She produced a framed snapshot from under her pink pillow, a yearbook portrait of a blond, squared-jawed behemoth in shoulder pads and numbered jersey. "His name is Steve, was Steve." She sighed dramatically.

Dwight knew Steve already, the kind of guy who paid no attention to someone like Dwight unless he was going to pick on him, rabbit-punch his bicep or grab-ass him in the john between classes.

"So, like are you living here for the summer?"

"Something like that. Just a few weeks, I guess." He finished his Coke. "Well, guess I better get back to the house. My Dad's coming home for lunch."

"Oh, Dwight," Mrs. Hopper called from her kitchen. "Here, I made extra." She handed him two parfait glasses of Jell-O, green lime and red cherry. "For you and your father."

"Hang on. She bent back into the refrigerator. Dwight couldn't help but gaze longingly at her backside. She came up with a can of pressurized whipped cream and squirted the top of each parfait glass, but got carried away with the hiss of white foamy cream and squirted some on his wrist.

"Oops," she grinned and with a perfectly manicured finger with a red fingernail scooped the splotch of cream from his forearm and stuck her finger in her mouth.

"Say hey to your dad for me. Tell him he has a very well-mannered son, and that we should be more like neighbors. Can you tell him all that?"

Dazed, Dwight met his dad at the driveway with the desserts in either hand. "What the—"

"Neighbors." Dwight jerked his head over his shoulder, motioning across the street where the two blondes waved from the bay window.

His father gave him a long side-look, whether of admiration or cunning Dwight couldn't tell. "We better be polite. You know how women are."

They smiled weakly and raised their glasses of gelatin and cream to the California sun, a gallant toast to the damsels who had rescued Dwight in his distress.

—

That night after their Chinese take-out (Dwight tried to use chopsticks, but failed. They wound up popping the sweet-and-sour pork in their mouths like hushpuppies or popcorn), Dwight suggested seeing a movie.

"Why not. Heck, this is Hollywood. They make the movies here," his father said. "Did I tell you I once saw Ernest Borgnine picking up his dry cleaning? Of course, he can afford it, but you wouldn't think a movie star like Ernest Borgnine would have to pick up his shirts, but that just goes to show, in America, you're just a working stiff, however you make your money. Something to remember, son."

Dwight wanted to see *Easy Rider*, because he'd heard that there was a girl in it riding a motorcycle topless.

"What's it about?"

Dwight shrugged. "Bikers, I guess?"

"Looks more like hippies to me." Dad frowned at the ad with Peter Fonda with his long sideburns and his star-spangled Harley. "I'm not sure your mother would approve. Hey here's a new cowboy flick. *The Wild Bunch*. And it's got Ernest Borgnine in it."

They drove the Corvair out into the California night, stars out, the lights of L.A. shining, and found the drive-in where the Peckinpah feature started after dark. Dwight's dad gave him a dollar and he went and got the popcorn, the Cokes and a candy bar. They sat in the cramped car with the speaker clamped to the half-way rolled-down window.

The movie started, and the children were playing with the scorpions when the Wild Bunch came riding in, dressed in World War I uniforms with puttees and campaign hats instead of chaps and Stetsons. This wasn't like any Western Dwight had seen. It was too modern, cars and machine guns, and guys didn't just fall over *kerplunk* and kick up their heels when they got shot. Bodies exploded in red slow motion, like fireworks set off in a slaughterhouse.

His father's mouth fell open, slack-jawed. He watched, popping the kernels of corn down his throat, then suddenly he started to gag.

He started banging the dash; finally he got out of the Corvair, like he was going to throw up against the side. Fortunately, this wasn't a movie theatre; no one seemed to be paying attention to the man flailing by the small car in the lot full of automobiles.

"Are you O.K.?" Dwight checked.

His father's face seemed ghastly in the glow of the movie reflected off the screen. The gunfire was getting louder in the hundreds of speakers spread over the acre of cars. Dwight pounded his dad's back harder and harder, like he was going to beat him to death, but his dad kept getting greener. Then his father, half-conscious, grabbed his hands, wrapping Dwight's arms around his chest, making Dwight squeeze and squeeze until the offending kernel came up and he spit it into the dark gravel.

Embarrassed, they got back in the Corvair and drank the last of their diluted soft drinks.

"Thanks, son. That was a real lifesaver."

But he still looked ghastly green despite the Technicolor glow and gore from the massive screen.

"You weren't going to die, were you?"

"Oh, no, I just couldn't breathe for a bit," his father laughed weakly.

Dwight felt better. Knowing his father, if the man willed holding his breath until he was beyond blue in the face, it was his dad who could be that disciplined.

Let's go, William Holden said.

Why not, said Warren Oates, and the four movie stars, including google-eyed Ernest Borgnine went back into the village and killed everybody and got killed themselves.

They kept watching the bloodbath in living Technicolor that just went on forever. Finally it was over, and they drove out of the lot.

"Well, that wasn't John Wayne, was it?" Dad cleared his throat like he still had a kernel or two caught somewhere.

Dwight felt sick himself, and worried he wasn't going to be able to sleep that night without bad dreams.

"I like Westerns where you know who the bad guys are and who the good guys are. Tom Mix, now there was a cowboy."

"Who's Tom Mix?"

"King of the cowboys, when I was a kid."

They rode a little longer into the night. "Next time, I pick out the movie, O.K.?"

"But you did."

"Hmm. O.K., next time. John Wayne."

Dad pulled over to a curb market, put the car in park. "You want to drive home?"

"Me? Drive? Home?"

He was having a hard time computing. His father was volunteering to let Dwight drive—Dwight, who still was a few weeks away from a legal license, though he had his learner's permit with him, which didn't seem very legal in California. Yet his father trusted him.

But beyond the excitement anytime he was allowed behind the wheel of a car, there was a doubt, then a brief disappointment. Did his father mean home as in Carolina or California? The sudden brief hope flared in his mind. That instead of turning off at the next intersection and cruising down to the suburbs, his father would let Dwight take the freeway out to the desert, over the mountains across the Great Plains, into trees again, over the river, back through the mountains, all the way to the Tar Heel state, and pulling into the driveway of the house. *Our house, where you, me and my mother, your wife, used to live.*

"Sure," Dwight said. Though he wasn't sure about anything this close to sixteen.

"That's right, check your mirrors, side and rearview, before you pull out," his father patiently explained, while Dwight adjusted the seat forward to compensate for the two or three inches his dad's legs had on him.

———

The Jell-O was only the start with Mrs. Hopper. In the days to follow, the happy divorcee would show up on their doorstep with her wonderfully manicured hands bound in oven mitts bearing a piping hot dish of tuna noodle, beef Stroganoff, Swiss steak, or her favorite, five-can casserole. "You know, you pull the first five cans of soup and vegetables out of your cupboard and mix it all together." It all tasted vaguely the same, nondescript bits of meat and flaccid vegetables bound with a paste of cream of mushroom or celery or something soup.

One evening after a filling dinner of Marla Hopper's self-proclaimed world famous chow mein, Dwight sat on the stoop and watched the swallows dart across the California sky, nabbing their own dinner.

Across the street, Sherry Hopper came outside with a baton. Dwight waved but she pretended not to see him. She slowly twirled the silver baton, flashing in the last light, hurling it into the air, and catching it behind her slender back, practicing her careful choreography for Steve Fuller and the football team next fall. Dwight watched and felt a hollow ache that he wouldn't be here for the season, watching from the stands. And as the darkness descended in the west over toward the ocean, the baton flew higher in the air, and the last light glowed red on the mountain that Sherry had called Lover's Leap. The place was probably named after two Indians, hand in hand, who had plunged over the side, or perhaps just simply the place to park your father's car and stretch out with the girl of your dreams. The leap of imagination he could not quite physically imagine but longed for in the sultry shape of Sherry Hopper. In his more excitable daydreams, the blonde who deflowered him was either Sherry or her mother, sometimes simultaneously. He had imprinted on his mind the downy hairs on Sherry's forearms, the constellation of freckles across her perfect pixie nose.

And as he watched her, she suddenly launched herself across the yard, and cartwheeled, once, twice, three times, her legs and arms spread in perfect symmetry like she had created herself within an invisible wheel that turned effortlessly and suddenly she was standing on her driveway, her arms crossed again, her hip cocked out, one foot planted, with the baton spinning in her hand, thinking seriously of whatever it is that is in a woman's thoughts.

He was startled by the sharp intake of breath behind him. His father was standing there, watching the same spectacle of girl flesh. "Boy," he said.

Dwight looked over his shoulder and up at his father's own transfixed face, slack- jawed, breath noisily rattling out of his flared nostrils, the same goofy, gaping look he held on his own face.

Horrified, Dwight realized maybe his dad was thinking the same terrible thoughts Dwight was. Never mind Mom back in North Carolina, maybe he had those ideas about Marla Hopper, and then came the even more shocking thought, maybe he liked looking at Sherry as well.

And in that stark moment, their minds and motives naked, they turned quickly away from each other. "Here, you better take their dish back." Actually, three days' worth of casserole dishes, stacked one on top of the other.

He crossed the street with trepidation, careful not to drop Mrs. Hopper's glassware, the parfait glasses stacked perilously atop two ceramic casserole dishes with matching lids shaped like nesting hens.

"My dad asked me to bring these back to your mom."

"Yeah," Sherry said, as she plunked down into the grass. He could not get over how graceful her movements were, how her legs moved.

"So," she said, nodding toward the neighborhood's mountain. "You still smoking?"

"Sometimes," he said. He wasn't sure of the proper protocol—was he given permission to sit too, even with casserole dishes? "When I feel like it."

"Aren't you afraid of getting cancer or something?"

He was afraid to admit his throat did feel raw when he smoked more than one cigarette a day or when he climbed to the top of the mountain. But his dad said that might be just the smog that gave him those dry coughs every morning.

"Naw," he lied.

Sherry plucked at an invisible hair between her blonde eyebrows. "I see you sometimes climbing up that mountain."

Dwight brightened. "You want to come or something?"

Sherry wrinkled her nose. "You mean walk? Don't you have a car?"

"My dad does. He let me drive it the other night back from the movie."

"I've got a learner's permit," Sherry said. "She lets me drive her to the grocery store sometimes. God, it's so lame around here. All my friends are off, going to cool places, and I'm stuck with Miss Fancypants."

Dwight couldn't imagine a better fate than hanging out with the pair of Hopper women. He noticed Sherry's toenails were painted a rainbow of purple and green. She couldn't help but be beautiful.

He dreamed of driving Sherry out on a date. He saw himself with his one hand on the wheel, his right arm thrown around Sherry's bare shoulders as she sat thigh to thigh with him. They would drive up to Lover's Leap. He had imagined this so many times in his mind. They would lie down in the front seat. She would lift her dress. But he could go no further in his mind than this. He had read about sex, flipping through racy paperbacks at the drugstore, but he'd never gotten a real good look at a girl. He almost wished it wouldn't be dark; he was curious about how all this would look in the light. He wasn't even very sure about kissing. He wondered how the man and woman didn't bang their noses together, or was there a protocol to necking where the man leaned left, the girl right and the lips met in the middle.

"What movie?"

"What?" Dwight came back to reality.

"What movie did you see?"

"*The Wild Bunch.* Really bloody. Everybody dies in the end."

"Gross," Sherry frowned, and then sighed.

"Sherry, your show is on. *Beverly Hillbillies*." Mrs. Hopper called out the door.

"Oh, God, mother," Sherry hissed.

"Do you really like *The Beverly Hillbillies*?"

"God, no. That's her favorite show, just because she thinks Jethro is a hunk. I like *Laugh-In*."

Then across the street, his father hollered out the front door. "Dwight. Telephone."

"Jeez, Dad."

"Come on, Son, this is long distance."

"Shit," he said, hoping to impress her.

"Tell me about it," said Sherry.

"Uh, I guess I better go."

"See ya."

He went slowly and sullenly across the street, hoping his slouch would impress the girl behind him, not wanting to hear the woman ahead of him.

"Hurry up, this is long distance. It ain't free." Dad held the door open for him.

The phone dangled from the wall. He hauled it up by its twisted cord, put it to his mouth.

"Dwight, honey, how are you?"

He couldn't believe what he was hearing. It was his mother on the other end, but something had happened to her voice. Her syllables were suddenly slowed down, like the operator had taped her voice and then slowed it down, sweetly Southern, countrified, like the thick batter on a piece of country-fried steak.

"Yeah," he said, not daring to speak more than monosyllables, lest he lapse into that same terrible accent. Mrs. Hopper had picked up on it right away. Sherry too, probably. He was doomed. He sounded barefoot and inbred.

She asked about the weather, everyone always talked about the weather in Southern California, like it was remarkable. "Not like it is here, I'm sure. Are the mountains like the mountains here?"

"No, but I climbed one the other day. There's a mountain back of the house."

"I bet it wasn't like our mountains," she said, pinning him to a strange allegiance with that word "our." He would never be free of family.

"It's too bad you couldn't see your Pop and Gram this summer. Did you get your grandmother's letter? Did you write back?"

"Yes, ma'am," he mumbled.

"What? Speak up, Son."

"Yes, ma'am," he mumbled louder. "Look, Dad needs me. I got to go.

"I love you, honey."

"Thank you," he said awkwardly. "Dad says this is expensive, I better go."

"With the money your father says he's making out there, he can afford it, sweetie."

Where did all this *sweetie* and *honey* come from, all this affection?

He hung up.

———

It turned out Sherry Hopper liked an audience. She had noticed Dwight eyeing her choreography as she practiced her intended move this fall from a mere drum majorette to a varsity cheerleader and a contender for homecoming court. Now they took turns each evening, sitting in each other's yard. Dwight dreamily watched her lithe, tanned body cartwheel and leap through the California dusk, until she tired and sat down beside him, her small breasts heaving with the effort, a glow of perspiration about her freckled nose.

He picked a blade of grass and held it between his thumbs and blew a sharp high note, muting its shape with a flicker of his hands.

"What's that?"

"Rabbit. You can call them out of the woods and kill 'em that way. My grandfather taught me to do that. It's a Southern thing."

"It must be." She wrinkled her nose. She didn't say it, but Dwight could tell she thought it was a hick thing.

He had better put Pop in a better light for her. "My grandfather walked out the way west with a friend and a cow."

"Why'd he do that?"

"He'd never been to California. He wanted to see the sights. Same as me."

Dwight couldn't just talk like Pop. He had to wing this on his own. He knew all their exploits up to a certain point. By his grandfather's geography, they never made it out of the American desert or over the Sierra Nevada. After that, Dwight was in unknown territory. But he saw it in his mind's eye. If he looked at the freckles on her face too long he got flustered, but if he stared off into the brown air just over her right ear, it was like he would see it all on a movie screen. He could hear the announcer's voice on a soundtrack:

When last we saw our heroes. . . .

They were stick figures on the horizon, a strange trio, two boys and a skinny cow. The cow was giving milk and they sat on either side of her and pointed the teats at their mouths. They milked her dry each morning into bladder sacks and slung these over her haunches. Under the sun and the slow miles, the milk churned into a soft cheese, and they dipped their fingers into the sour-smelling curd. Genghis Khan and his hordes of Mongols did the same, crossing the steppes of Asia. And Mongolia made the American West look like paradise. Talk about bleak. Mongolia is so barren.

"Maybe when we make it to California, we could just keep going, swim the Pacific and visit Mongolia," Wylie suggested.

"There's no need to be mouthy with me, son."

"High adventure, huh." Wylie got in the last word.

The sun fooled them, hanging most of the day straight overhead, then ducking behind sudden steep cliffs to bring on cold nights where scorpions skittered underfoot and the stars flickered piteously above. Navigating by the moon, hiding from the day's heat under great rocks, they roamed deeper into the canyon country. They passed walls of sheer red stone and limestone and basalt that towered overhead as they went deeper into the great gorges carved by ancient storms and long-dried seas.

They were so far down in the earth, the sky was only a white crack overhead, and the glinting light and the deep shadows of the cliffs played tricks on the eyes. Wylie thought he saw giant skeletons, embedded in the canyon walls, great whales, and long-tailed lizards with claws and massive jaws, the bony outlines of mysterious birds, fish and fowl and other creatures that had walked and swam and flown over these parts a million years ago. There were carvings of ancient hunters and strange, horned beasts a hundred feet high, but how did anyone get up there to make those petroglyphs? And still they kept winding deeper through the stone maze, the canyons that kept cutting back on themselves. They looked to be going so far back in time, they could turn the corner and meet up with Methuselah himself, some bearded guy old as dirt.

"Dwight, didn't you say this was a short cut?"

Dwight didn't have a chance to answer. The cliff reached out with an arm and clapped a stony hand on his mouth. Eyes opened in the red rocks on either side, and a host of squat, stout men stepped out of the canyon walls where they had been hiding the whole time. Their skin was copper, the color of the rocks. Boys and beast were surrounded by the tribe, pointing lances and aiming arrows at their pathetically white skins.

"*Hakomi?*" came a cry from the canyon wall.

The war party parted again, and out of a cleft in the canyon walked a woman in white-fringed buckskin. Her hair was braided into dark pinwheels on either side of her head. Her face was painted blue like she had been holding her breath a long time. And white powdered tears ran over her high cheekbones. When she walked, tiny seashells sounded on the fringe of her skirt. Wylie wondered where she had gotten those cowrie shells, living so far away from the sea.

"*Hakomi?*" She repeated her words, giving Wylie and Dwight to understand she was asking just who they thought they were, apparently trespassing in this particular canyon.

"Can you show us the way out?" Dwight asked.

"*Ha Namatucham.*" She motioned them to follow.

The woman led them and the warriors through a series of forks in the maze of the sandstone canyons until they came to a square, cut like a quarry into the stone. On all the cliffs facing the square, houses had been carved in the rocks as high up as you could see. Women and children scampered up and down the cliffs using carved hand holds and ladders.

"Well, I believe we're here." Dwight nudged Wylie. "Where ever here is."

The woman knelt in the dust and pulled both Dwight and Wylie down by their threadbare sleeves. *"Haliksa'i."* And with her forefinger, she began to draw in the sand the history of her tribe and what the future might hold.

"Let me see if I've got this straight," Dwight said. Along with his built-in compass orientation, Dwight Sparks prided himself on an intuitive understanding of animal tracks and languages of lost Indian tribes.

As Dwight was able to decipher the cryptic drawings and emphatic gestures, the lady's name was She-Who-Walks-With-Lightning. *"Pinu u Hochichvi,"* she shyly smiled and covered her maidenly mouth, then she drew a figure of a woman walking beneath zig-zag bolts from a cloud. She was in charge of thunderstorms, evidently, but hadn't been doing too well with the job. To Wylie, it looked like it hadn't rained in these parts in maybe a century or so.

She pointed at them, *"Pahana,"* the long lost white brothers who had been prophesied to come with *"Poko"*—she pointed at the cow—and then swept her hands at all the gathered people who began to cheer. Evidently the Pahana boys and Poko were here to save them.

"Near as I can tell, her ancestors have told a story for the dire times when the people would wither and nearly die, until a goddess with horns comes with a bell out of the canyons to save the people with her milk."

"Dwight, this better not be just another story you're making up," Wylie said under his breath, then louder for the Canyon People to hear. "Ain't nobody butchering my cow, but if all y'all want is a little milk, Ivy would gladly oblige."

English and Indian are easily understood when translated by hunger pangs. They all ran off to their little cliff houses and came out with clay pots. Dried up and small and shriveled, this tribe who called themselves the First People looked like they were at their last. Just a breath away from returning to the dust themselves, they hardly had the spit in their mouths to swallow let alone make words, but each waited in turn.

Wylie began squirting out a little milk from Ivy's first teat, then the next, and so on. Funny thing was the more he pumped, the more she gave. Magic milk; he must have milked for a full day, filling up every pot in the Rock City.

"*PAHANA wikvaya POKO, kuwanlelenta,*" the Lightning Lady proclaimed, which Dwight was given to translate as "Thanks, boys. You just saved us all. . . .

⁓

"You're making this up, right?"

"No, honest to God, my grandfather told me this. He had a friend named Dwight Sparks, who I was really named for, and they walked with a cow all the way across country."

"Wait a minute. Cowboys don't come from the mountains. Those are hillbillies."

"They were boys and they had a cow. If you think about it technically that makes them cowboys."

Dwight hadn't counted on interruptions. What if she didn't believe him? Everything depended on her believing him. "Don't you want to hear about how Dwight Sparks and Wylie got through the secret tunnel at the bottom of the Grand Canyon?"

"Yeah," she said warily.

Dwight didn't know how long he could make the tale continue to make any kind of sense. Any second she was going to butt in, but he learned to go slow. The slower you went, the more Southern he sounded, the better the story sounded. Slow stories are more credible than the hurried half-blurted tale. Enunciate. His mother was right. Anything you said slowly and firmly enough sounds like the honest-to-goodness truth.

⁓

. . . After the white strangers from the East and the four-legged Earth Mother had saved the Rock City people, there was a great celebration in the square. The Lightning Lady blessed them, dipping a green pine bough in a large bowl of water, both commodities hard to come by in that country, wood and water, and sprinkled their heads. The water fell on their faces, fresh and young. And Wylie recollected the last time he had seen rain.

He would never complain or gripe about getting caught out in a shower up on his father's upper pasture, or heading down the road a ways from the schoolhouse or the church service. In fact, he would never complain again in his life if he ever made it back home.

"Walk straight ahead. Follow not your eyes nor your ears, nor even what you may smell or touch, but follow after your heart. Walk in wonder," the Lightning Lady intoned solemnly, or words to that effect, according to Dwight Sparks.

And they began to walk, surrounded on either side by tribesmen in strange dress and tall masks that covered their heads and shoulders. They wore the likenesses of horned deities and beaked demons, spirits of animals and of mountains and of clouds that rode the desert sky. And all of them were waving branches of pine, until it felt like a gentle wind in that hot, small, enclosed place. The procession took them to an opening in the canyon floor, a hand-dug pit peering down into darkness.

Here, Dwight Sparks balked. "Look, last time I went down a hole, there were a bunch of dead Indians about took my scalp off. And you're still limping. I say we bolt and say adios to this gang."

"I don't think they mean us any harm," Wylie argued. "These folks know their ways around. I mean I reckon they been here about as long as the rocks."

"Excuse me, ma'am," Dwight asked the Lightning Lady. "You're sure this here hole is the best way to get to California?"

"Pisivayu." She pointed west and made a wavy motion with her hands.

"Pacific?"

"Pisivayu," she nodded, then pointed downward again. *"Nutungktatoka."*

"I reckon that either means, 'The path leads the diligent man to the heart of his desire,' or 'Here's the shortcut.'"

So the cow went down first, thanks to a huge windlass made with a tripod of piñon. Ivy was hoisted up off her painted hooves and none too happy, was moved mooing over the big hole. Slowly they lowered her down, her garlanded horns, tied with feathers and shells and bits of bone the last you could see, and her bellowing down below from the darkness.

"Much obliged. I think we can slide on down by ourselves." Wylie closed his eyes and, hand over hand, lowered himself into the darkness.

The hole reverberated with the stamp of the Indian feet in fringed buckskin and the rhythmic, guttural chanting like the earth's own song. It was pitch-black down below, but surprisingly cool and dry. No shivery sensation. They looked up toward the square of daylight above.

Up above, they could see the silhouette of the Lightning Lady, her headdress, like a giant ziggurat framed in the square portal, the passage between the reality of the above world and the womb from whence the People had come, First Man and First Woman.

Then she said something in her own strange tongue that was starting to make sense to even Wylie's bad ears, and what he heard clearly was an incantation: "Fear nothing in front of your eyes. Fear only what is in your mind."

Then like lightning from above came two fireballs. They jumped to the sides as sparks bounced across the rock floor. They had dropped two torches to light their way.

No telling how long they walked. They had pouches of dried corn; not the yellow or white corn, but maize in red and purple and gold kernels, ground into fine powder. Pour a little onto your tongue and the corn flour blossomed into bits of bread ground between the teeth, tasty and filling. Between the magic maize and Ivy's milk, they stopped and ate often, and sometimes they slept. And still the torches burned on."

"I'm about to burn up."

Dwight and Sherry lay together in her backyard in the dry heat. She had spread out a blanket for sunbathing and put on her bikini. Dwight had his cut-off blue jeans and he slipped off his T-shirt. He was embarrassed about his pale skin, never mind that his biceps weren't very big, the hair was splotchy on his thin chest, and his collarbones jutted out.

As a blonde, Sherry didn't tan so much as bleach. Her hair turned whiter and the golden down on her arms became like snow. The freckles on her nose were the only pigmentation that took the sun and her face grew more speckled as the summer worn on, though Dwight knew better than to tell her this. He understood you always had to be telling stories to girls.

"It's not fair. Angela Del Marco has that wop blood in her. Olive skin and all that."

"Blondes have more fun," Dwight argued.

To dump such a sun nymph as Sherry, this Steve guy must not be that on the ball, even for a varsity quarterback. Dwight outlined all the ways that Steve was stupid and Sherry was truly beautiful, and he could see no reason that once Sherry returned to campus with her new suntan and new attitude, why Steve would see the error of his ways. Steve had fumbled his chance at the prettiest girl in school. Fumbled right at the goal line, stupid jock. What Dwight really wanted to do was pick up the ball that Steve had fumbled and run, open-field running, dodging tackles, scoring. He badly wanted to score. But football seemed a funny way to talk about what was really on his mind.

He rolled over on his side and lit one of his father's cigarettes. Sherry Hopper's mother didn't mind, in fact, she had offered him one of her mentholated woman's smokes last week when he was over, returning the parfait and casserole dishes. But he declined. He didn't like smoking in front of adults. It was something he liked doing only on the sly.

After two weeks of smoking, he had gotten to the point where he didn't automatically gag each time he inhaled. He wanted desperately to be able to light a cigarette for Sherry, but she would only take a little puff at a time, then say, "Gross."

While the Byrds sang *Turn, Turn, Turn* on the transistor radio, the sun rose high overhead and polarized in front of his cheap sunglasses. He could feel every bit of sweat drain out of him. They baked themselves into parchment, bones left under the desert sky. If he craned his head forward, scraping his chin into his chest, he could see the mountain rising between his toes. He'd climbed it before. But what if one day, no, one night, he drove Sherry up in her mother's cool convertible and they lay together under the stars? They timed themselves, a half-hour on their backs, a half-hour on their bellies. And when Dwight got bored about talking about Steve, to fill the silence, he would continue his tale about of two boys and a cow making their way to California.

"Why," she said sleepily. He couldn't tell if her eyes were open or shut under the sunglasses.

"Why what?"

"Why would they walk all that way with a cow?"

"That's not the point."

"So what is the point?"

"If you're going to be that way, I won't tell you what happened next. I'm thirsty," he said. He'd talked so long his lips were parched and his throat was scratchy.

Of course, he had an ulterior motive for getting up. Sherry had untied the back of her bikini top. She didn't want a white streak across her back when she wore her gown to the fall formal, when Steve came to his senses and dumped Angela Del Marco for her, his truest fan and love. Maybe she would forget that her top was undone and suddenly leap up and he would see Sherry in all her glory.

She didn't budge. "There's lemonade in the fridge. Help yourself. Be a pal and bring me a glass."

His head swam when he got up and staggered out of the sun into the shade. He bounced for a second against the sliding door, leaving the sweaty imprint of his body against the glass. He looked back but Sherry had not seemed to notice his clumsiness. He got the door open and stepped into the cool linoleum of the kitchen, the air-conditioning that made him shiver.

At the refrigerator, he stood in the cold of the open door, bathing in the yellow arctic light, looking at the strangeness of the food they ate, yogurt, pimientos, pitted olives, cocktail onions, low-fat milk. He rummaged through the cabinets until he found drinking glasses, and poured tall glasses of lemonade Mrs. Hopper had made from cans of concentrate. Nothing was real in California. Everything was canned and processed and space age and cool.

The TV was turned up in the next room, and he could hear the breathy sounds of great exertion. He peered around the corner into the den. Mrs. Hopper was lying on the shag carpet with her legs in the air, kicking according to the instructions of a handsome muscleman on the TV. "That's it, ladies, keep pedaling. No coasting. It's all uphill."

It looked uncomfortable, her arms propping her hips in the air, her head turned to the side to watch the TV, her face flushed in distress.

She was pedaling a pretend bike upside down to rid herself of excess pounds. Turned upside down like this was not a woman's most attractive position. Gravity did strange things to the proportions of flesh. He'd never realized how wide her hips were. It looked like work just keeping the weight of her butt up in the air like that.

A girl's got to watch her figure, she had said even as she kept Whitman's Samplers in the kitchen.

Watching her figure, it occurred to him that Sherry would look exactly like her mother at this age. Her perfect girl's legs would turn to the consistency of the cottage cheese that women always seemed to be eating on their diets. Her calves would thicken, the ankles hold water.

Gawking, he felt vaguely guilty, and then got a hollow feeling in his solar plexus. She was pedaling fast as she could and somehow the hole in his heart was leaking. He thought of a giant balloon, a lightness expanding behind his ribs, pushing aside his heart.

⁓

"So what took you so long?"

"Uh." He tried to think of an answer, but she didn't wait, taking the glass from his clenched hand.

Sherry raised herself on the towel. He could almost see her breasts, or the tops of them, still cupped in the loosened bikini top. She held the glass to her forehead. "That feels good," then: "Could you rub some more oil on my back?"

He poured the white lotion onto his hands. He sniffed its coconut smell; he slathered it on her back, and rubbed it in, massaging her shoulders, her arms. It was laying on of hands, it was holy. He could do this for the rest of the day, the rest of his life.

"Umm," she said. "That feels nice. You're lots better than Steve."

He stopped suddenly at the name. Sherry stiffened under his hands, sensing her mistake.

"So tell me, those guys with the cow. They were walking underground under the mountain. What happened next, not that I believe you?"

He smiled. He followed the sound of his own voice, the story weaving out of his mind and mouth, around all sorts of blind corners. He didn't know what would happen until he said it out loud . . .

———

Dad had worked most of the time that Dwight was in California, the computer kept crashing, and being the troubleshooter, he had to go in to find and kill the bugs. Dad apologized almost daily. "I'll make it up to you. Swear, Son."

Which didn't really bother Dwight. It gave him time to hang out with Sherry Hopper, helping out. He even volunteered to mow their lawn. He worked on their lawn mower, took the rotary blade off with a ratchet wrench, then filed a new edge. He wanted the grass to be perfect for Sherry's cartwheels. When her hands touched down, he wanted it to feel like cotton or clouds or something soft, for her perfect rotations as she improved her pep, and summoned her school spirit.

But his father was acting strange now. Every time he came home, he and Dwight would look at each other, their mouths full, chewing, swallowing, expectant.

"I was thinking, doesn't seem right to come all the way out here and not see the Pacific, don't you think?" Dad suggested one evening.

In the middle of this desert and the watered lawns of the housing subdivision and the dry scrub hills, Dwight had almost forgotten there was an ocean nearby. Check out the chicks, surfer babes, sand bunnies. California girls in bikinis. It was the best idea his father had ever had.

Saturday afternoon, they drove out of the suburbs across the freeway and through the Southern California sunshine. Through the windshield, Dwight peered through the haze and looked for a sign of the sea, that first sighting of the water as they wound through the brown hills and down the freeway coast.

Dwight had no swim trunks, only the cut-off blue jeans with the long white fringe he combed out on his white thighs. He had had to explain to his mother that nobody his age wore blue jean shorts with hems. Dwight's bangs were getting longer, and he kept running his hand through his hair, and pulling it back from his eyes, and combing it every other second; this was the longest hair he'd had. His mother kept watch on his collar, and cried foul if the curls ever went below or over his ears. She kept brushing his hair back behind his ears; he kept trying to get it to cover his ears, which he decided were his ugliest feature.

They pulled into a sandy parking lot.

"You better keep those shoes on till we get to the beach," his father warned as they walked down a rocky hill. No dunes here on this part of the coastline, only great black cliffs where the mighty waves of the Pacific crashed and sprayed salted foam.

They spread white bath towels on the gravely strand, on what little shoreline there was in the cove. Dwight had been hoping for surfers or girls in bikinis, but this looked wild and deserted. The kind of place that people visited only to drown. There was a pile of beer cans near the sea grass, and the burnt embers and charred driftwood from a recent bonfire.

"Here we are." His father sat in his baggy Bermuda shorts, already showing sweat rings under his white T-shirt.

They watched the ocean come crashing into the cliff with the same sense of wonder and duty that they watched the map of the Ponderosa burn through the TV screen and the Cartwright clan come riding through for their close-ups in the opening credits of *Bonanza*.

"Last one in . . ." His father rose and started running very slowly, his arms held high, a very funny, un-athletic gait. Dwight dashed past him and into the waves. He dove in headfirst and came up, shaking his hair full of salt water. Whoa, the Pacific was cold, not nearly as tropical as he'd expected. He felt his penis shrink into his scrotum, toward the warmth of the groin.

"Man, oh man, that's cold."

His father floated, craning his head straight out of the water, like a tortoise sticking his head out of the shell. Meanwhile his big toes floated up at the other end like little white buoys. His hands made a little flippery motion, all that was needed to keep him buoyant in the water. Dwight felt himself sinking like a stone anytime he wasn't frantically kicking or dogpaddling.

"Relax," Dad said. "Just breathe easy, be still."

Dwight dipped his head back, and let the Pacific cover his ears. His good hearing worked underwater: he could hear the strange surge, the siren song of mermaids and mermen, whales way off the coast in their musical soundings, the sound of waves rubbing a continent.

He banged into his father's ribs and then a wave slapped the back of his head. Suddenly they were in the surf, and the waves were tumbling him like dice. He saw his father headed toward shore, his white thin legs and his narrow back gleaming in the waves, like some exotic bird. He did a little dance, hopping on one foot, banging the side of his head to discharge the ocean water from his ear canal.

Dwight came out dripping, salt water running from his nose, his throat burning. He sat on the towel next to his dad, and they watched the water that had nearly drowned the pair of them.

"Remember when you buried me in the sand?"

"How old was I then?"

"Maybe three. You were a cute kid. You couldn't get enough of the waves. Your mother thought you were going to drown. But you'd go toddling off into the surf, and the next wave would bounce you on your head. I laughed. Your mother screamed. *Gary, go get your son before he drowns himself.* Then you'd pop up after the wave pushed you to shore, just grinning and clapping your hands. I've never seen you so happy."

This was embarrassing, the conversational equivalent of getting out his baby pictures, like Gram always wanted when she and Pop came down for a visit, followed by an encore of his old report cards. It's a wonder they hadn't bronzed his first successful poop in toilet training.

But what was more embarrassing was his father's partial nakedness, when he sat there with his shirt off. There was a hollow in his chest, like someone had punched him hard like a cartoon character, with a big *oomph* that dented his ribcage and it never popped out after the punch. In the hollow was a thatch of gray hair, and below that his belly poked out in a paunch over the Bermuda shorts. Skinny arms and scrawny legs. The hair or what was left in a little crest on his head waved in the wind.

This was his father, his future, almost more than Dwight could bear.

"So what happened to your ring? Your wedding ring," he blurted out.

"I don't wear jewelry at the beach. Too easy to lose." His father shook his head, but Dwight couldn't see his eyes. He kept squinting into the sun, the salt in his lashes, the glare across the endless waves, the golden stream of everything. He wasn't going to admit any more than that.

"I'm going for a walk," Dwight jumped up. "What's around that bend?"

"Beach, I reckon. Maybe Mexico. Depends on how far you go." His father got up cross-legged and brushed off the seat of his shorts.

They headed toward the bend and around the jutting cliff, the water crashing in their ears. The wind whipped sand against their calves. The surf was loud, a bigger booming caught and amplified in the crescent beach that swung between the rock points at either end of the cove.

"Here's where Burt Lancaster and Deborah Kerr made out in the surf in *From Here to Eternity.*"

"Really?" Dwight blinked at a blank patch of sand, looking for scuffmarks of passionate elbows and flippering feet. He remembered the scene from the movie, the smooch in the surf.

"Could be. Sand and water. Put a couple there, it would work."

His father was a terrible liar. Dwight always knew when he was making up stuff, like the wedding ring.

They kept walking ahead and watching the waves come up, saw the foam frolic around their ankles then run sliding back out into the ocean, over and over, the constant crashing that mimicked the human heartbeat. Dwight had read about evolution in science class, how the first fish crawled up on the shore and begat a reptile over time, which grew lungs instead of gills and became a hairy mammal that climbed a tree, then climbed down and as a man walked around about a million years later. Dwight really didn't believe that he came from slime in the sea—he was more than that.

Still, he had memories of walking long ago with his hand in a younger man's hand, stumbling along at hip level. "What's that? What's that?" His father with fewer lines in his face then and more hair, but still always asking questions. "What's that? Dwight?"

But Dwight never felt he had the right answer for his dad. Dwight desperately wanted to get to the future when he would be his own man, and not just his father's son.

But walking into the prism of light off the Pacific Ocean, the constant roar of the water, Dwight soon forgot any arguments he had running with his father. His adolescent anxieties relaxed their grip on his growing limbs. He felt free as the sand squinched between his toes and the sun lightened his hair and darkened his skin. It felt like they could walk this way forever, all the way into the future, maybe down into Mexico and along the South American shoreline. If they kept going and never stopped they would sooner or later reach the Carolinas. He wondered how Wylie had felt when he'd first glimpsed what he'd come so far to see.

⌣

. . . The torches the Lightning Lady had given them for the journey slowly burned out, smoldering piñon wood that smelled like Christmas at first, then like charcoal and then like nothing. They wound further down into the earth, following the plunging passageway. With no sun or stars, no night or day to mark their time, they had no way to know how long they walked, maybe days, maybe hours, maybe a week.

"You know we're going down in a circle?"

"I'm just following the tunnel. Feel how hot it is? Reckon we're right under Death Valley."

"Or Texas since you're taking us in one big circle."

Wylie took the lead, and felt his way by hand through the strange tunnel. The opening seemed too small, but as he pressed forward, the walls seemed to open out and permit passage, and looking behind, he could swear they narrowed again. It seemed almost alive as if they were walking through the arteries of some slaughtered giant. But they were not the first to come this way. He couldn't see clearly but he felt his hands fitting into the distinctive handprints in the wall. Others had felt their way blindly along this underworld way.

Presently, a brilliant light shone ahead. Blinded, they made their way toward it. The hole was widening and they could hear the sound of great water. Wylie turned to his friend, and gasped. Dwight and Ivy's faces glowed with a golden luminescence, both the boy and the cow bathed in bronze, their limbs flickering like fire. Then a wave of salt water came crashing through the hole and in the next instant, they were spitting and spewing the sea from their mouths and noses. Ivy shook her horned head and bellowed.

They sloshed out of the opening and into the surf of the mighty Pacific Ocean. Overhead wheeled a flock of gulls that dove toward the waves. The westering sun was extinguishing itself, red and burning on the horizon where the water met the sky. Maybe it had only been a trick, when he saw his best friend and his cow turn to golden idols looking back into the long cave. Wylie ground his fist into the sockets of his stinging eyes. Everything gleamed so in that rich light of California. . . .

They rounded the rocky point and the beach ahead was full of bathers. Dwight and his dad kept walking, and perhaps the sun glancing off the crashing waves blinded them in the beginning, but it took a while for Dwight to register that the sunbathers here couldn't all be wearing beige bikinis, but in fact weren't wearing any swimsuits, weren't wearing anything at all, were technically naked, butt-naked.

His mother had warned him about hippies and their anything-goes attitude, but now his Dad had led him straight into a flock of these strange birds, all very much in the buff. There were fat ones and skinny ones, their hair was long, but the men seemed to have beards, then there were also the more distinguishing features of the anatomy. They walked by two guys lying side by side, their dicks like little birds peeping out of the nests between their legs. In the surf, he could see women floating, their breasts like buoys. Little children ran around, oblivious with their pee-pees and little clefts.

Dwight was self conscious that they were wearing clothes, the only ones who were. But even if they were to shed Bermudas and cut-off blue jean, their sickly white Southern white skin would still mark them as shameful squares.

"Uh, maybe we best turn around. I think we've seen the sights here," his father said, his voice up high in his nose as when he got perturbed.

Sometimes it seemed more civilized to keep your clothes on, to keep your thoughts to yourself, to not let everything hang out, to not rap out your resentments, but simply to keep walking, making your way back to the car, and back to the house.

———

It was the last item on Dwight's list, and true to his word, his dad took everybody to Disneyland the Sunday before he had to fly home.

They piled into the Corvair, Mrs. Hopper up front with her sunglasses and her perfume filling the interior, Dwight and Sherry in the cramped backseat. When Dwight reached across the vinyl seat and took her hand, Sherry did not flinch or turn away, but squeezed his hand gently then let go. It was hopeless. Her heart was set on Quarterback Steve, who even now was probably throwing footballs somewhere on a gridiron, practicing for the fall season. She had perfected her perky cartwheels just for him. And Dwight would be flying back to Carolina next week, back to his boring real life where he would be riding his bike again rather than driving.

His father had let Dwight drive around the neighborhood a few times, up to the convenience store, but not the freeway. Traffic was too wild. Dwight was terrified of trying to merge at sixty miles per hour into the river of Olds and Buicks, fearsome Fords, the little fish of a Corvair trying not to get eaten alive, crunched in the hungry metal grilles of those sharks.

At Disneyland, they parked in a distant lot, and got out and locked the car. They always locked the car now in California.

His father smiled behind his shades. "A5. We're orange, row 52. Can you remember that for me? Marla?"

And Mrs. Hopper in her bare-backed, polka-dot sundress, inspired by Marilyn Monroe, shot a white smile back across the roof of the Corvair. "I'm not that good with numbers. You can remember for me. Orange, just like my dress."

Dwight felt a twinge. This was his mother's job when they were all together. She remembered where they parked, held the number in her head for her father, who had other more manly things to worry about, like the traffic, or making sure no one pasted a bumper sticker on his car while he was inside their overpriced theme park. Once while they waited in the overheated car, he spent an hour scraping off with a penknife the I LOVED GHOST TOWN bumper sticker some stupid employee had plastered on their unsuspecting car.

They took a tram with other families. They weren't a real family, even though his father acted as if they were all together, even at the ticket booths.

"No, now, Marla put that purse away, this is my and Dwight's treat for you ladies. All those Jell-O and casseroles you've sent over. You've been fattening us up for the kill." Dad patted his belly, which did seem after this summer to be somewhat spreading.

"You all are such Southern gentlemen," Marla Hopper positively cooed.

They pushed through the thicket of turnstiles and beneath a fabricated Gothic arch that led into the Magic Kingdom, Main Street, and the castle ahead.

"O.K., you kids know what you want to do now. Here are your tickets. We'll meet out by the moat here, oh say, noon-ish, and grab a bite to eat."

His father was interested in the future, the General Electric Carousel of Progress. They had computer demonstrations, right up his alley. Arm in arm, Dwight's dad and Sherry's mom walked toward Tomorrowland.

"So what do you want to do first?" Sherry asked, already acting bored.

Dwight had never really watched the Mickey Mouse Club growing up, since the TV station didn't quite make it over the sultry Southern airwaves to his house, but he generally liked the Disney movies he'd seen, not the cartoons, but the action adventures like Swiss Family Robinson who had their own tree-house here. But his favorite was Tom Sawyer Island, full of rocks and bluffs and caves and woods, which seemed remotely familiar like Pop's farm.

Sherry wasn't impressed but kept to the artificial path. What if there were snakes out there? She actually seemed afraid. Dwight didn't know what to think. Would the Disney folks allow snakes to slither around the theme park? Or would the Mouse banish all sorts of creatures?

Sherry seemed to like all the rides that appealed to little kids. Mr. Frog's Wild Ride, the Dumbo Flying Carousel, "It's a Small World After All." The annoying song rang through his ears, and he could not shake it from his head.

Dwight wanted to try the Matterhorn next. They stood in line for half an hour to ride the zipping roller coaster. Sherry screamed and the cart slung them together, her soft body against his hard elbow.

"That's nothing. I'll show you the real secret place," Sherry said.

They circled back to Cinderella's castle with its gleaming parapets. Sherry took his hand slyly and pulled him into an alcove just inside the plastic portico. Tucked behind a stone column was a small red door with a sign, NO GUESTS BEYOND THIS POINT. She looked over her shoulder, and tried the door. It was open; they crept down a staircase, not stone and mortar, but gleaming white metal, with steel treads and fluorescent lighting. They were out of the land of enchantment and into an industrial complex.

"They say these tunnels go everywhere underneath the Magic Kingdom. There's probably an entrance on that stupid island," Sherry said.

They went down to the end of the stairs and looked down a long hall. In the distance, he could hear voices. Sherry poked her head around the side, then ducked back. "Omigawd," she clapped her hand to her mouth. "You won't believe it."

Dwight slipped past Sherry's warm body and craned his neck around the corner. It was Mickey Mouse in his natty tuxedo, or at least most of him. Mickey's head, with the frozen grin, the shiny black ears, the wide empty eyes, lay on a metal chair. The movie-star Mouse was actually a small man with a pocked face, balding, sharing a cigarette with a sweaty and slouching Cinderella.

But the secret vice of cartoon characters, that wasn't the worst thing. Like a blurred afterimage on his retina, Dwight saw a sign on the wall behind the headless Mickey and the slutty Cinderella. It was the yellow-and-black tri-petaled insignia of the Emergency Management Agency, the same sign Dwight had gone to school with forever. Underneath the Cinderella Castle were nuclear bomb shelters. In case of a Soviet attack, missiles raining down on the Magic Kingdom, Mickey and Minnie and Goofy had orders to come out and lead all their guests to safety beneath Adventureland.

"Hey! You kids!" the Mouse man screamed.

Giggling and shrieking they fled up the steps as fast as they could go, the enraged rodent screaming at them. They didn't stop until they were safe above ground again in the alcove of the Magic Castle. *Oh shit, oh man, oh shit,* Dwight kept saying with each gasp of air. Sherry was laughing hysterically. Dwight couldn't believe it.

Then Sherry did an even more unbelievable thing. She kissed him. And kept kissing him. Her tongue pushed past his lips and wormed warmly into his mouth. Dwight had heard about French kissing, but he never dreamed it would actually happen to him. They necked in the shadow of the castle, until Mrs. Hopper found them there.

"Kids, we've been looking all over for you. Where in the world have you been? We were about to call security."

"Sorry, Mrs. Hopper," Dwight mumbled while Sherry sighed.

Shamefaced, Dwight emerged from the fantasy shadows into the sunlight of reality. His dad was at the end of the Disney drawbridge, blushing as well at Dwight's indiscretion, he thought, until Dwight looked closer and saw the faint imprint of a lipstick kiss upon his father's face.

POST CARD

Most evenings now, the news was more than an old man could bear.

The dour anchorman scowling behind his heavy horn-rimmed glasses, jowls quivering indignantly, his thin black tie dangling beneath his dewlaps like an exclamation point, he recited the latest bulletins of hippies and yippies, riots and uprisings. Wrack and ruin, Last Days, everything hurried to its end, just as the preacher insisted each Sunday.

For the first time ever as a yellow-dog Democrat, he was pondering if he ought not to vote for the other candidate, not following habit but fear. What if this fellow was a fellow traveler like some said, code for Communist? Those people come to power, no telling what they'd do to an old-time tobacco farmer.

He could not hear much these last days. His fingers fiddled with the hearing aids nesting in the hairy whorls of his ears—mechanical little birds who never whispered but constantly cawed like black crows in his head. Nor did it help that the insects sang an unmerciful pitch in the grasses growing on the upper pasture this season.

Rather than try to catch the latest calamity on the television, he went out on the porch to sit a spell and let an old man's dinner die down. Something about her dumplings or that second helping of sliced cucumbers sat heavy in his belly.

He settled into the chair, like he weighed as much as a mountain, though in fact he had lost weight over the winter. The old woman would pinch his sides in bed. *Law, we need to fatten you up.*

The creak of his rocker hardly stirred the humid air. Try as he might, a fretwork of worry across his sweating forehead, he could not remember it so hot, not here in these hills, mercury shooting out the rusted thermometer like his own blood pressure.

He pulled the postcard from the bib of his overalls along with his smokes. Carried now more than two weeks, its corners blunted from rubbing against denim, the card was slightly curved from the heat of his body, warping itself around his old breast. He lit a cigarette and read the note on the back once again.

He could not recall the exact timbre of his only grandson's voice. Wylie wasn't even sure he know what the boy would look like now, if he came sauntering down the road and across the bridge. But he could see him clearly from years ago, a squirt in sneakers and shorts racing around the yard, playing with the pop-gun Wylie had carved for him. How the young'un loved that bridge, hours spent lying on the side, watching the water pass underneath, dropping apples from that old tree into the stream, borne away to the river.

That old apple tree was gone now like the little boy. Even as Wylie had yanked the chainsaw to life, he winced at the pain the boy would feel, that hole in his childhood when the rotted tree fell. Across the years came that same look on his daughter's face when he tore down her playhouse atop the barnyard rock, that hard season he thought he needed the kindling.

He caught himself staring off into the middle distance, more of a habit of his, as of late. He studied the card in his hand, the postcard he passed around proudly at church, to all his pals when they stood out amid the trucks, smoking cigarettes after the sermon, waiting on the womenfolk to get caught up on the gossip before each old couple headed home to a chicken dinner.

The front of the card showed fireworks exploding over a castle from a place in California called Disneyland. Wylie had heard the name, of course. He and Dwight Sparks in their rambles with the cow so long ago may have walked right through the place without knowing it.

On the back, he reread what his grandson had written, *Dear Grandparents,* (how formal, it made Wylie proud. Like saying "sir," the boy knew his manners.) *California is pretty cool, especially here at Disneyland. I'm sorry*

I couldn't see you this summer. Take care. Hope everything is fine and that you're feeling well. Your grandson, Dwight.

Wylie didn't remember the climate being so cool in California; actually it was mighty warm mostly what he remembered in the southern parts, but then the world and even the weather had changed in the intervening years. These days, he noticed more chill in the mountain mornings, winters seemed more bothersome, though he seemed to recollect much more snow from his boyhood. Perhaps they had traded cold for snow.

The weatherman kept saying they imported the cold weather from Canada, Arctic air whooshing across the country. Evidently there was nothing out there to stop it from coming all the way down from Canada nowadays, after they cut down all the trees in Michigan. And hot weather came up from the Caribbean, fiercer heat than he recollected. In his memory, everything was milder. He didn't have to stoke the fire so high in the stove to take the morning chill off. He did not sweat so profusely come August. It had been bad down in the Piedmont where his daughter insisted on living with his only grandson. The heat wasn't just hot, but humid. Air seemed to stick to your skin, to every liver spot. Sit on a man's chest until he could scarcely breathe. He found himself panting, his mouth hanging open and all the spit drying out between his teeth.

You sound like an old man.

He shook his head stiffly, trying to take his mind off his ailments. He tried to recall all the stories he told the boy. It had been a game between them. He could tell the boy was resisting all belief, scared to death he would get his leg pulled somehow, but Wylie could win him over, watch those eyes of his get wide as coffee saucers.

Now, he might have stretched the truth, here and again, but only in the interests of keeping the tale interesting. How easy it is to bore a little boy. He remembered how grown-ups seemed so full of blah, blah, blah, before they said anything that would perk up your ears. The secret was to leave off all that blather and bother that anybody with sense would figure out sooner or later. Get to the good stuff and quick.

And that fact remained that he and Dwight Sparks and a milk-cow named Ivy had set off walking one day from Beaverdam and walked clear cross country.

Walking in itself is not something you pay much mind to, but in itself it becomes work when that's all you do hour after hour, day after day, weeks on end. Even if you stop, why then you're in the middle of nowhere, with half a country to go and half behind you, so a body has no choice but put the next foot forward and keep on keeping on.

So walking becomes a wonder, a body wondering how far can it go. Can a man walk around the world? Probably only if he were Jesus, so he could walk across the Pacific, before he got to China, and then on the other side of Europe, he'd have to get his sandals wet again, strolling over the Atlantic. But Jesus never went that far, but hung around the Holy Land in his time.

But a man could walk clear across a continent. He and Dwight Sparks had proved that as boys, and a cow, too. Took longer than they thought, but they saw the country up close, step by step. It was so long ago, but he still could bring to mind sharp as ever certain trees and rocks they had seen, a sudden waterfall plummeting through a canyon, then abruptly stopping like God's hand had turned off a faucet upstairs. He remembered too a kettle of hawks, the sky full of a thousand soaring, circling birds of prey caught up in a feathered funnel.

Other parts were hazy to him, like how Kansas seemed to bleed into Colorado, and how only Dwight seemed to know their whereabouts in this ultimate flatness, straight and level.

Sometimes he still felt the same strange feelings he had had on the journey, like a hole had opened up in his chest. Sensations he swore he would never forget as long as he lived, and he suspected into eternity. That was what it felt like, timeless.

Walking, you lose track of things. It can be a wonderful diversion. One day they had walked through a field of green grass that grew about knee high and spread out before them nearly forever, it seemed. The grasses brushed their legs as they walked and felt good, like massage or feathers. The sun warm enough, perfectly dry, no dew to soak through their boots. Dwight Sparks, having a slightly longer stride than Wylie, had taken the point, and went about three and half foot to Wylie's every three. So by mid morning, he was a little ahead; an hour later, a little more; and soon by mid-afternoon, Dwight had pulled pretty far ahead. But the walk was so pleasant and Wylie lost track of all time or miles and just walked through the high grass, at peace with himself.

Then he saw Dwight on the horizon, about half his body about to go over the slight curve of the land, which wasn't perfectly flat after all, and Wylie felt a slight twinge of fear go through him, the first unpleasant thought he had all day. *He's going to leave me behind.* But then, his buddy turned on the horizon and looked back, waved his arm in greeting. Wylie returned the salute. They were out of voice range anyway. He waved him on into the west. He would catch up when Dwight stopped to make camp.

Those nights, he remembered lying on his back on the plains, looking up at the stars. One thing could be said for a lack of trees. He had not realized how closed in he had been, how comfortably cradled by Buckeye Bald on one hand, the Frozenhead's peak on the other. His little room in his little house deep in the holler. The world feels so large some days, it feels comforting to come home and just close the door at the end of the road.

Out in the open, he slept sound, even though bears and panthers and lions and wolves probably circled their fires at night. Dwight and Wylie sprawled like babes in a crib, mouths hung wide open. The cow, too, dozing on her feet. Some desperado could have walked right in and tipped her over, tied them up, made off with whatever they had, which was an old gun that you couldn't trust to shoot straight.

They had seen some people on the way, remote homesteads they came across on the plains, following old fence lines past long wheat fields, and stopped at the farmhouses. Here lived men who didn't say much, and women who kept their eyes to the ground, but still brought them plates of food, as good Christian people. The land changed, but the folks remained friendly along the way. You could tell by looking at a house as to your likely reception. Those lots with rundown looking mules or skinny cows, you kept passing by, these were folks too poor to be asking for a place to stay, or too mean-spirited to offer. Not that Wylie and Dwight had been freeloaders the whole way. They had chopped their share of wood along the way, and when the trees gave out in the west, there were other chores folks were happy for them to do. They sheared a sheep, butchered a hog, cut hay, snapped beans, strung barbed wire, dug a well, hauled sunbaked bricks to the little casa a Mexican man was making in the desert.

Then rested up some and a little less hungry, they bid their hosts good-bye and started walking again. The cow following after, without any bidding now. Headed always westward, California here we come.

There were times he got tired, like he couldn't take another step. He felt so numb, the blood refusing to travel out to his toes or fingertips. Wylie would sit down on a rock or the hard ground itself, his head in his hands, wondering why he'd come out here in the middle of nowhere. He could be back home, and he would think of all the things he missed. Though it wasn't really his family, their faces were growing dimmer in his mind, but he was homesick sometimes for rhododendron blooms or granite balds or Beaverdam Creek falling through hemlocks.

Sometimes up in the Rockies, they came across a path or a glade or a stream or something that reminded him of home, and he wondered if somehow Dwight hadn't been leading them in some big circle and unbeknownst to him, they had suddenly come back to Carolina. Then he looked again and realized that, no, they didn't have aspens growing in the Appalachians, and that elk over there on the other side of the stream wasn't like the cows back home. And the peaks were little too tall and pointed compared to the softly sloping shouldered mountains he was used to in Beaverdam.

As they made their way over the high passes, they saw the rocks torn away by slides, where the wind and ancient water fashioned the red rock into fantastic forms, like castles and minarets and pagodas that they had seen only in books.

He remembered the last leg, walking downhill, and along a rocky shoreline, water in waves he had never seen before, white-bearded, slapping at the shore. He dipped a handful to his mouth then spit it out. Salt, all right. Ocean it was. And the sun was burning out on the horizon, an orange ball falling, like a spark into a boiling cauldron, and then it flashed green, extinguished, and suddenly day was done and it was night.

They built a fire on the shore from driftwood, branches from distant trees, gnarled by the surf, waterlogged now, dried into twisted little forms. They piled these up on the beach and warmed themselves against the fire, listening to the surf that kept rushing in and slapping at the rocks, then falling back, retreating only to surge ahead again.

And he glanced up at the sky, the same stars that had raced with them across the continent. He spied Orion now, the hunter in the sky with his dog, higher up the seven Pleiades, only six of which he could ever count. Cassiopeia, Castor and Pollux, all them Greek stories. But Wylie liked to recast the stars into his own tales. He saw the shapes of two boys walking, staffs in their hands, and a cow following after them. You could see anything you wanted in the stars, and you could reach up and wipe them away with your hand and start all over. It made no difference in the universe. Stars were up there asking to be looked at by anybody for a million years.

So this is it, isn't it?

He didn't feel sad about this fact, only a little wiser. It felt almost like a prayer, more than a question, but he felt at peace. He didn't buck the idea like his mind balked against all the bits and bridles the Baptist preacher and Sunday school teacher seem to want to rein him in with.

"Well," said Dwight, warming his hands before the fire.

Wylie looked at his friend's profile, where the firelight played, and thought *Who was this stranger?* Dwight's face wasn't as fresh, but looked older, lined even, the bones had changed and hardened and grown behind the skin that was now weathered and tougher. The scar in his forehead from that terrible wound that nearly took him out in Kansas, the hair showed prematurely gray, and he was only a teenager.

By the light of the fire by the sea, he sat with his chin up on his knees, the way a little boy sits, huddled for warmth. Except the knees showed through a hole in either pants leg, worn white and smooth and then through, and his chin was rough with whiskers. It occurred to Wylie that his friend looked different, had grown into a man when he wasn't looking. The clothes that flopped around them on the way out west now seemed clownish and small.

"Well," said Dwight Sparks.

And they had been together so long, they didn't really have to talk much anymore.

"Yep," said Wylie, knowing exactly what his partner was thinking. He even knew the slow brains of the cow, trying to find something to eat amid the pile of seaweed they had hauled up for her.

"We've come a ways. You about ready?"

"Any time now."

And at first light they threw sand over the last embers of the fire, and turned their backs on the sea and started for home.

The way back had more adventures, and retracing their footsteps, he saw the country up close not for the first time, but savored it the second time. He looked more closely at the mountains of the west, the different types of trees and the wild animals that have long since disappeared. They saw a pair of bald eagles plummeting to earth, mating in midair, shrieking over the treetops. They saw a graveyard of buffalo skulls scattered under a bluff, and Ivy tugged at her halter, like maybe she remembered that calf, half buffalo, half heifer, that she'd carried, then lost way back on the High Plains. They saw old villages of adobe falling down into ruins, the broken potsherds all around, a life abandoned long ago.

They saw a man hanged in a small town in Kansas who had done something bad to a little girl, but it gave no one satisfaction to see a body dangling, a sack of blood and shit, by a rope around his broken neck, his dirty face. He didn't tell anyone about that scene, since it didn't seem to serve any purpose except justice, he supposed.

On the way back, the world seemed more settled. Farther east they went, they were met by more farms, more towns, more schoolhouses, and church steeples and fences. Fewer guns or gallows or cow towns. They saw airplanes dusting crops, they saw banks, and cars traveling dirt roads of new towns. The country seemed more settled. More folks had moved into the wide open spaces.

Heading home, he enjoyed the walk back in a different way. There wasn't the edge of danger over what lay over the horizon. He knew what lay ahead, knew he would not pass this way again.

So it went, walking into the sun by day, watching your shadows shrink toward you by noon, then stretch out before you in the long afternoons. Then at night, another fire, and only the stars and a cow for company.

He could feel fatigue pulling at his eyelids. He hadn't realized he was so tired. Every bone in his body argued with its neighbor. Toes not on speaking terms with each other. His feet yelled *unfair* almost every step of the last week. He was so tired. Wylie figured he could lay down here and sleep a century or so, and still be behind in his rest.

"What was your favorite part?" Dwight Sparks asked.

"Probably, the ocean."

All the way back, they replayed all their adventures and compared notes, burnished the exploits they planned to tell once back.

"I can't say the Pacific was what I expected."

"It went on for as far as you could see. How big do you want?"

"I thought it was going to be, well, bigger."

"It's the biggest ocean in the world. You don't get any bigger than the Pacific Ocean."

"I know. I know. I just thought it'd look bigger."

"It was plenty big and you know it."

Amazing how the miles would pass by as they argued for the sport of it.

"I think we seen it all. Deserts, plains, bayou or two, flat land, straight up mountains, prairie and salt flats, glaciers and geysers."

"Jungle," Dwight said. "We ain't seen the jungle."

"There ain't no jungle in North America."

Wylie liked to remind Dwight, that while he had the built-in compass, Wylie had actually gotten an *A* on the geography test the last time they were at the schoolhouse.

"I know that," Dwight protested. "We need to head down to Panama or South America and see us some jungle on our next trip. We could get us a new cow even, maybe a herd or two and head down to Argentina. I read where they have gauchos down there, fellows don't call themselves cowboys, and they don't have lassos; they use these bolos. Rocks with ropes wound on. Send them flying over the Pampas grass. We could quit this cowboy stuff and be real gauchos on the next go round."

"We ain't Argentines. We're Americans."

"Butch Cassidy and the Sundance Kid went down there to rob the trains and banks down there. They were good Americans."

"It ain't our place down there."

"We built the Panama Canal didn't we? We got every bit of business down there as in Beaverdam."

"I ain't going," Wylie said.

"Come on, you old cuss. It'll be fun. It'll be like starting out west all over again. Except it will be real south this time. You go so far south the seasons get all turned around, and you get summer at Christmas and snow in July down there. We've got to see that."

"Nope," Wylie just shook his head. The only thing he had been looking for in days was a particular shape of the mountains of home. He crossed a whole land, and back again, knowing where his home was now and would be to the end of his days. No more roaming for Wylie Rominger.

—

The old man looked at the postcard again in his hands and came back to his own age again, the creaking knees in a slowly moving rocker. There was a tingle up his arm, a tightness in his chest. Definitely that second helping of the sliced cucumbers. Gas, he guessed, but he'd had this sensation lately, this growing hollowness inside that no food could fill. An engulfing emptiness. Oh well.

He pushed himself out of the chair; his tough old arms trembling slightly and nearly slipped.

He took a few logs from the apple tree inside. Still green and wouldn't burn. Winter wasn't far off, he knew, despite the heat. The old tree with its green apples was nothing but a stump. He would burn it as kindling all winter. And soon there would be nothing left of the tree his grandson had so grandly romped beneath so many summers past. All the heat of summer and the memories of the time spent with an inquisitive young lad just going out into a new world was held in that freshly felled wood. He would warm himself by that fire when the winds were howling their lonesome voices down the flue of his chimney, whipping around the house, calling his name out of the cold and back to the time Wylie would remember being warm.

LAST LESSONS

His sophomore year in college, Dwight wrote and published his first and last short story. That year he had turned nineteen, finally moved out of his mother's house and into the dorm on campus, learned to question everything his father had ever said, believing that he simply knew better and more than his old man. He was legal to drink beer, old enough to be drafted for a war that had fortunately ended, finally coming into his own. That year he felt in control of his desires, his destiny, wised up to the world—until he discovered that he couldn't tell a story right to save his or anyone else's life.

Dwight had signed up for creative writing, an English department elective taught by a former journalist who had penned exactly one political novel while serving in the Washington press corps. As a sophomore, Dwight was the youngest in the class of mostly seniors, mostly women, owl-faced feminists with studious glasses and no bras for their small breasts. He noticed they wrote a lot about sex in graphic detail, and weren't afraid to read angry obscenities out loud in class. Every Thursday afternoon in the seminar, he suffered the blood rushing to his face and elsewhere.

Shyly, he turned in his story, more of a sketch really, a stream-of-consciousness monologue influenced by Faulkner, whom he was reading in his Literature of the South survey (jokingly called Grit Lit by the appreciative but Yankee-born adjunct instructor). Dwight created an old man, based somewhat on his grandfather, but more on himself, or at least an older, wrinkled and wiser version. His protagonist had no name other than the Farmer, an existential Everyman who engaged in ongoing philosophical arguments with a Scarecrow in his field.

Between the man of flesh and the man of straw there can be no truce. Their battlefield was an acre of fallow bottomland the Farmer forever tilled unfruitfully beneath his rusty, trusty Massey-Ferguson. At field's edge, the sinister scarecrow issued silent scornful challenge.

It went on from there, on and on. Like the proprietor of Yoknapatawpha County, Dwight fashioned paragraphs with impossibly long sentences, loaded with fancy words he found in a thesaurus and lots of italics to indicate the Farmer's despairing frame of mind while the Scarecrow intoned baleful prophecies and jeremiads against an absurd universe. Plowing back and forth in his own ruts, the Farmer jousted with the straw man, slowly going mad with the philosophical implications of it all. In a furious rage, he turned his tractor, meaning to mow down the Scarecrow, but instead, tragically, the tractor tipped on the uneven ground and crushed the poor Farmer. The story ended with turning tires and crows circling over the still-standing Scarecrow.

In the workshop, the owlish women debated the true meaning of the black birds, and decided the Scarecrow seemed more fleshed-out as a sympathetic character than the old man. The journalist circled Dwight's more glaring grammatical errors and judged the piece "a promising beginning." Cleaning up a few commas, he promptly submitted his misunderstood masterpiece to *The Jester*, the college literary magazine.

To his amazement, his piece was published the following month in the fall issue.

On that miraculous day, he walked through the golden leaves that fell from the elms on the Quad, secretly knowing he'd finally found his path in life. In his trembling hands, he held his future. He read his name and then went through the pages filled with his creation. He read each word slowly, silently. They hadn't changed a thing, even the typos, adding a few of their own. By the time he reached his dorm, he was no longer reading to himself, but out loud to whoever would listen. In his hall, he knocked at the doors of his friends, sitting on their unmade beds, and read the story from room to room.

"Author! Author!" applauded Darcy, his perpetually stoic and often stoned roommate. Darcy was a junior and an art major who painted great black and brooding canvases after the manner of Motherwell and Malevich.

Darcy stuck his kite-high head out in the hall and hollered, "Gentlemen, we are in the presence of true genius, a cause for celebration. Drinks are on Dwight tonight."

The hall's inhabitants filed across the parking lot with Dwight leading the profane processional. They packed themselves into the bench seats of Darcy's late model Olds, and cruised to the nearest watering hole.

The Safari Room was a dimly lit, darkly paneled, and sadly ambient lounge located in a strip mall just off campus. The head of a mangy water buffalo mounted over the jukebox watched with glassy indifference the no-neck jocks muscling to the bar while frat boys and sorority girls in golf shirts and cuffed khakis shagged to beach music on the sticky floor.

Wednesday was Hump Night, halfway through the week and a cause for celebration with half-price draft beers. Crowded into the corner of a banquette, Dwight beamed all evening with triumph. Golden hops and heady foam flowed like nectar from the chilled glass pitcher.

"Champagne for my real friends. Real pain for my sham friends," Darcy led the toast.

"But this is beer."

"Don't be so literal, Martin. We're drinking. You're buying."

They drank to each other's genius, clinking their mugs harder and harder. They drank to Darcy's future retrospective in the Museum of Modern Art. They raised their glasses to Vijaj's theorem of quantum orgasmicosmocology, which would relegate Einstein's relativity to a mere footnote in the history of physics. They saluted St. Perry, the foul-mouthed divinity major who would certainly become the first Baptist Pope. Hailed Phelps, the Poli-Sci guy whose highest ambition was to head the Republican National Committee and work for Ronald Reagan when he ran for president someday. And of course, there was Dwight Martin, heir apparent to Hemingway and a shoo-in for the next Nobel in Sweden.

Around midnight and their fifth pitcher, feeling at peace with all the world, Dwight gazed into the glass eyes of the water buffalo and saw reflected there a mystical insight into the secret of the universe. Amid the laughter of his friends and the music from the jukebox, with the magazine that was his first claim to fame rolled in his back pocket, his mind swimming in a bleary torrent of euphoria, Dwight Martin believed that he would never die, that not only his words, but his consciousness, his deepest thoughts (this very insight he was having) would live forever. The core of him, that which was the essence of "Dwight," would never be extinguished but would forever float out there, a bubble on the great waves of the ocean, a spark borne on the solar winds that filled the cosmos.

"Pay up, author." Darcy elbowed him and the goofy grin fell off his face, as he spilled beer into his lap. Brilliant insight faded to alcoholic blackout, and that was the last Dwight remembered of the best night of his life.

———

His next coherent and conscious moment. A desk lamp glared in his face and Darcy was shaking his shoulder, a scared look on his artistic, acned face. "Hey man, are you alive? You got a phone call."

Dwight lifted his throbbing skull and understood they had somehow been transported from the booth in the Safari Room to their bunks in the dorm room. Darcy persisted in poking him.

"Phone, man. Says he's your dad."

Dwight was still half drunk and only half dressed. One sock, no pants, his shirt stubbornly hanging from one wrist where he pulled it over his head. He staggered toward the pay phone at the end of the hall and after a few grabs retrieved the dangling receiver from the end of the twisted cord.

"Dwight? You there?"

His father's voice on the other end made him stand straight up and square his shoulders. "Yes, sir."

"I know it's late, son, but your mother asked me to call. I have something to tell you."

Dwight dropped the phone from his sweaty palms, then batted at it, bouncing off the wall. "Dwight!" his father's voice swinging through the air.

"Sorry. I'm here."

"Your grandfather. . . ."

Dwight didn't want to listen to the impossible news his father was delivering. Instead, he pressed his fingertips against the painted cinder block of the wall, then his palm. He began to push with all his strength as if he could push the block out of its mortared position and create a port-hole to the outside air. He desperately needed to breathe, but there was no air in this hallway, no air in his tight throat.

"Dwight?"

"Yes, I'm here." And he was, still standing there with the black receiver screwed into his drunken ear.

"I'm sorry son. I know what he meant to you. I'll see you when I get there."

Dwight hung up the phone, and tracing his fingertips along the concrete wall for balance, returned to his room. Darcy whispered in the dark. "That was your dad? Everything all right?"

"No, it's my grandfather." Dwight toppled into bed and passed out again.

He was dreaming, that was all. In his Psy 101, they had covered the chapter on dreams and dream interpretation, and the footnote that excessive alcohol intake inhibited the Rapid Eye Movement stage of sleep that was prerequisite to a proper dream state. The filmstrips of private fantasy and sexual longing skipped on the sprockets of the brain. Dizzy with alcohol, his dreams staggered from synapse to synapse, firing off loose memories like firecrackers, small pops of light and electricity in the storm of his cranium. Images of cows and buffalo grazed across the gray matter of his mind, pulling up cuds of cerebellum. Their hooves trampled over broken pop-guns, his final exams, the bones of dead Indians, the bare breasts of women, all the electrical archetypes. He could not tell a story straight even in his own sleep.

His mouth fell open and the air wheezed in and out of his lungs, scratchy with cigarette smoke. Just before first light, he began to snore, an offbeat ragged rhythm that cut through the air like a hacksaw through plywood.

Darcy got up, cursing his hangover and his roommate and went off to his studio class to sling black paint on a primed canvas to suit his dark mood. But before he left, he threw a pillow over Dwight's head.

The faint light over the trees to the east turned into day. The dew on the grass on the quad burned away as the sun climbed over the chapel. The first classes began, people ran late to class, with cups of coffee and doughnuts, cutting across the quad instead of following the sidewalks around, so that there were ruts worn in the grass at the diagonals, like the cow paths Dwight had seen on his grandfather's farm, the stupid, stubborn herd mentality of cows and coeds. The biology students were already sequestered in their labs, cultivating in Petri dishes their ambitions for med schools and six-figure incomes. The accountants were crunching the numbers in their calculators. English majors sat through Shakespeare seminars, plotting their revenge when they got to law school.

Classes changed. People went to labs and library and lunch.

Dwight stirred at last. It was one o'clock. His cheek was puddled in drool on the bare mattress where the fitted bed sheet had slipped the corner. He had lost all of his spit and his tongue cracked in his desert of a mouth. The feather pillow Darcy had plopped on his head weighed about a ton on his pounding brain.

But he felt even worse when he remembered the phone call that was no dream, and his father's voice. His ears, no longer numb, echoed with what his old man had been saying. "Dwight. . . . your grandfather. He's dead."

Dwight pulled himself from bed and sprayed himself down in the shower, dug through dirty clothes in his dresser. He had been postponing his weekly trip to the washing machines in the basement of the dorm. He sniffed at a sweatshirt emblazoned with the school mascot, a Demon Deacon, a contradiction in terms he had never quite fathomed, something like a Baptist Sonofabitch, Bitching Baptist. It didn't smell too bad as he worked his swelling head through the neck hole, wrestling inside the black fleece, lint, until his hands found the sleeves and he got it on backwards at first, then righted it. The only clean pants he could find were a pair of denim overalls in the back of his dresser drawer, a student's privileged appropriation of working class apparel.

In the closet, his Sunday suit he never wore to any church or social occasion hung in a filmy plastic sheath. He lay the suit on his unmade bed and threw a white shirt and tie, dress shoes, dirty socks, spare underwear on top, rolled it into a bundle. He may have dropped a sock or two down the stairs and across the parking lot, but he was already running late. He piled his mourner's wardrobe into the Vega hatchback.

Heading out of town, he gunned the engine, but a Chevrolet Vega, Detroit's awkward answer to the Japanese economy cars, had all the pick-up of a sewing machine. At fifty-five miles per hour and above, the frame of the badly machined car vibrated, threatening to unloose every bolt and rivet.

He drove west along U.S. 421, the old Thunder Road that moonshiners once raced out of the mountains with their Mason jars of illicit liquor crated in the back of cars, down to the dry counties and thirsty sinners. The road shot through tobacco and corn fields across muddy Piedmont rivers into bare woods and rolling hills, red clay banks, white churches and falling barns. The four-lane narrowed to two winding lanes. Still speeding, he ran up on a barely creeping flatbed truck with a cow in the back. Dwight rode the rube's bumper, the cow's flicking tail and bony haunches staring him in the face.

If he didn't find room to pass, he would have to drive to Boone and beyond with this view of a bovine backside. Every time he speeded up, trying to pass, the truck sped up as well. He couldn't see the farmer's face in the side mirror, only a tanned, wiry arm hanging out the open window. Then came the final indignity, the tail suddenly lifted and straightened, the back legs splayed to cascade a green stream. The shit showered the asphalt and splattered across his windshield.

Dwight hit his horn and swung out into the other lane, but his horn was lost in the louder scream of a semi hauling down the slope toward him. He swerved too hard back across his lane and the shoulder caught his right front tire. He hit the brakes and fought the shimmying Vega to a standstill off the pavement and onto the gravel as the dust settled.

The flatbed with the cow had disappeared, while the semi that had nearly creamed him was halfway to Raleigh by now, but the Vega's cheap car horn wouldn't shut up. He jumped out of the car and opened the hood, burning his hand on the radiator before he finally found the source of the terrible sound and yanked the wire. In the sudden silence, he could hear his heart's frantic drumming, and then his stomach heaving. He swallowed hard, then turned his head and vomited, a gush of bile and beer and guilt.

—

He drove slower, the tires pulling strangely since his detour into the ditch, through Boone and toward Tennessee, then the familiar turn-off, pointing the way to Beaverdam. The road began to climb into a series of switchbacks across the face of the mountain toward the gap, and then into the corkscrew descent on the other side into the cove. He met little traffic, until he rounded the last rock overhang and saw the familiar farm spread like a postcard before him. Every last car and truck belonging to Beaverdam looked to be parked in Pop's front yard.

He drove across the still-creaking bridge and parked near the woodshed. The porch was crowded with strangers, weathered men he remembered from his grandfather's church. They were smoking, their faces the color of the ashes they tapped off their cigarettes. They nodded curtly to him, but no one stopped him from going inside. Another crush of people in the parlor, old crones who slowly parted as he edged sideways through the whispers. "It's him." "Wylie's Grandson." "Poor thing." "Looks just like him." "Law, I thought it was Wylie from fifty years ago."

And then he was face to face with his grandmother. Her face in ruins. She hugged him hard, that inescapable odor of perfume and sour old lady. And he felt her soft breasts against him and her body shaking so, and he patted her humped back.

"Dwight, you're here. We were worried." It was his mom, and Dwight was terrified to see her face red and swollen, as well. "Oh, Dwight. He's gone." She hugged him, but didn't let go, sobbing silently on his thin shoulder.

Dwight didn't know what to say, what to do. He wished his grandfather were here. He would know the right thing to say to lighten their load. Dwight glanced at the chair where the old man had sat in front of the TV, the impression of his hindquarters still evident on the vinyl cushion, but the chair was empty.

The family pressed through the crowded house. The kitchen counters were lined with food, dishes covered with tinfoil, platters, more stuff than a body could eat in a week. Plates of food appeared almost by magic on the table as they sat down. Women whom Dwight did not know hovered like silent angels, calling him "honey" and "sugar."

"That's right, honey, you need to eat now. Keep your strength up, sugar."

Dwight pushed the plate away. "What happened? Dad called, but . . . I don't . . . how?" He needed to know, but couldn't make the words come out.

In a low monotone, his mother explained: "Daddy, Pop, your grandfather, he . . ." She halted, overcome with tears for a time, but slowly the story was told: Pop was sitting by the fire, couldn't sleep, said it was something he ate. He had eaten two helpings of sauerkraut and pickled pig, his favorite dish, but his overindulgence came back to haunt him at bedtime. He drank a glass of water and bicarbonate Gram mixed for him. Said he would sit up a while longer. She went on to bed. She saw the glow of the fire under the partially closed door, the TV turned down low. And then she awoke in the middle of the night, and knew something was wrong. "Wylie?" she called and called again, the fear creeping in her voice. She went barefooted into the unusually cold room. The fire had died in the stove. He was still sitting there, watching the TV, its screen a field of static hissing in the corner. By the blue flickering light, she could see his eyes were open but empty.

"It's my fault," Gram wailed. "The pork was bad. I should have known."

"Now Mama, don't say such a thing." Dwight's mom grabbed her mother's hand, then the two women fell together and fell apart.

Dwight could bear no more. He rushed to the bathroom, bolting the door. At first he thought he might be sick. He doubled over the toilet, heaving but nothing came up except a sour smell from the commode. Then he tried from the other end, he unhooked his overalls and sat a spell, straining to empty the dark guilt coursing through his knotted gut but he could manage no movement. His grandfather had probably done the very same the night before, wondering what his body was doing to him, feeling faint, perched atop the cold sweating porcelain. Dwight stood and flushed away.

He went to the sink and ran the tap to wash his hands, his face. He covered his hand to his mouth and nose and smelled the beer still on his breath. Dwight didn't think he'd remembered to bring his toothbrush in his frantic race from his dorm room. He opened the cabinet. There were the worn toothbrushes of old folks who soaked their fake teeth in glasses each night rather than brushing the few molars left in their old heads. He found a bottle of mouthwash on the glass shelf. He gargled and spit.

Closing the cabinet door, he was startled by what he saw or what he thought for a second he saw in the mirror. Dark rings under his eyes, the eyelid drooping over his left eye, the genetic wink of his maternal inheritance. It was his grandfather's face trapped in his own. He turned his head to the side, warily eying himself in the glass, to see if the ghost would show himself again. He frowned at his fear, his self-pity.

Stupid to think his story had caused an old man's heart to suddenly stop a hundred miles away, that just killing off a cardboard character he had not properly named or made recognizably human would have such dire consequences in real life. Death was not just philosophical, not just a convenient ending to a sophomoric story published in some student magazine.

What were you thinking?

He slipped from the bathroom and made his way again through the gaggle of women in the parlor, their soft hands lighting on his shoulders like doves, cooing their soft condolences. "Sorry. So sorry. Anything we can do . . . "

He pressed through the silent men on the porch, who mercifully parted without a word or an intrusive touch. Out at his car, he fetched the rolled-up, creased and beer-stained copy of *The Jester* with his joke of a story. From the glove compartment, he took a pack of bent cigarettes.

He didn't return to the house, but felt the eyes of the smoking men follow him across the yard, past the woodshed to the barnyard. He swung open the metal gate on its squeaking hinges, made sure to close it behind him, even though there was no livestock to worry about getting out. What had happened to all the animals? He remembered the cow, of course, a pig in the pen to be fattened up for slaughter, the cluck of chickens in the henhouse with its wooden ramp leading like a drawbridge into the castle. There was a drayhorse at one time. He remembered Pop driving a sledge with the blinkered horse up the mountain to cut a cord of firewood. Now bits of old harness hung rotting from the walls of the barn.

He went down the long aisle where the stable doors were closed with latches of gray wood. Bits of hay, dried dung, the smell of tobacco in the rafters. The odor of aged piss, that put him vaguely in mind of zoos and circuses, as close as he came now to the beasts that gave him milk and eggs and cheese and the meat he ate every day.

The metal milk can he remembered his grandfather filling lay rusted in the corner, catching rainwater that leaked through the shingled roof. What had became of the old cow he had so feared as a child, that descendant of the mythic bovine his grandfather had walked cross-country in all the tales? The only traces left were hoof marks cut into the trampled dirt.

Behind the barn, out of sight of the porch and the house, he lit a cigarette to calm his nerves. He sat on a gray-lichened rock that served as the northern cornerstone for the barn, leaned against the weathered boards. Smoke stung his eyes as he flipped through the magazine. His mouth twisted around the cigarette as he read with growing contempt and shame what he had written. He had presumed to know so much, who had realized so little. He tossed his cigarette and snuffed it out under his heel.

Pinching the corner of the magazine by the fingertips, he let the pages hang open. He flicked the wheel of his plastic lighter. The flame caught along the bottom edge of the page and crept into the ink.

He flung the flaming magazine away into the sere grass. The red embers ran along the dried stalks like fuses, and the flames headed toward the barn. Suddenly afraid, he leaped up and stomped out the smoldering blaze. He had done enough damage with what he had written, no need for arson.

The ruined magazine lay open. His byline was burned away. He raked dirt over it, a grave to his own vanity. The gesture felt forced and empty, the kind of crap you would read about an immature hero of a bad book, the kind of book he would likely write.

He knew it was only bad timing, knew that his story had no more power over his grandfather's fate than it could bring him back to life. No one in his family would ever read a word he had written. He swore that, even though he had a whole stack of *The Jester* fall issue under his bed in the dorm room, a paper monument to himself.

He studied the sagging barn, the color of rain and rock. It looked a hundred years old, but his grandfather had built it from fresh-sawn timber the year his mother was born. But his dad was right. It was nothing but an eyesore now, a memorial of hillbilly poverty, rusted tin roof, an RC Cola advertisement still legible on the side. Pull it down and start over before it collapsed in itself. Tear it down, tear it all down.

Dwight pushed against the barn with all of his might, just as last night answering the telephone in his drunken stupor he had tried to push through the dorm wall. Tensing his shoulders and arms and neck, his teeth clenched, he heard the creak and groan of the warped planks. It did no good. He flung himself at the wooden wall, slammed his fists, kicked his feet, until a single plank fell from its rusted nails onto the ground. He was sweating and trembling and breathing hard.

He stepped back, leaned over, his hands resting on his knees. He spit on the ground. Nothing did any good. Burning the story, pounding the barn, spitting. Nothing he did made a difference.

That night, he saw the remains of the deceased. That was exactly what the mortician said as they arrived at the funeral home in Boone. "Would you like to see the remains of the deceased," he said in a voice Dwight would forever understand as the definition of "unctuous."

How do you say, "No thanks," at a time like this? He followed the man's pin-striped back into a room marked with a placard WYLIE ROMINGER. The guest of honor was laid out at the other end in the open casket, highlighted by soft spotlights in the ceiling while inspirational music poured like syrup from an intercom.

He worried if he might faint or throw up at the casket's side, but no, it wasn't his grandfather laid out in the box, only some mortician's mannequin. The cheeks were too high, the mouth set too tight. And the hands were all wrong. He almost expected if he lifted the sleeve he would see the seam at the wrist where these toy models of human hands had been screwed in. The fingers were shriveled and small and plastic in appearance. And the eyes seemed clenched and not at all peaceful, like they might snap open, better yet wink at him, like this was all a bad joke.

The family was forced to sit on chintz sofas amid the flowers while neighbors from around the cove filed by to pay their respects. The university sent a wreath commemorating Wylie Rominger's twenty-five years of service on the campus custodial staff.

Dwight shook hands with perfect strangers, all the people in Pop's real life. "We know how much he meant to you. Salt of the earth. We're so sorry. He's in a better place." He heard over and over how popular and friendly a man Wylie was in his community, a man you could count on, who would drop everything and do anything for a sick or ailing neighbor. And how proud Wylie was of his grandson in college. Perfect strangers kept asking Dwight point-blank how he was doing in school. "Wylie always said you were the one with all the smarts in the family. Showed us every letter and postcard you ever sent. Why, I remember how he about talked a man's ears off about how early you were talking as a toddler."

Dwight quit listening after a while. He felt awful, like he owed all these people an apology. He never knew Wylie the way they did. He never would. That was what Death meant.

The body was back on morbid display Friday for the funeral, and the same faces at the visitation now packed the pews of Beaverdam's white-washed Baptist Church. He went up the aisle, escorting Gram while the unctuous undertaker had his mother's arm. They were the spectacle of the survivors; all the teary eyes in the place followed their shuffling steps along the blood-red carpet. Dwight saw new fans turning slowly over-head, circulating the still air but making no difference whatsoever to the terrible heat trapped inside his suit. Cold sweat dripped out of his armpits like melting icicles. He was afraid his grandmother would collapse at any moment. He deposited her in the front pew reserved for family, then let his mother slide in. Before he took his seat, he stole a dark look at the congregation.

Dwight was surprised how many folks came out, how sad they all looked. They were sad faces to begin with, rawboned, wens and warts, plain and the just plain ugly he always associated with country folk. But honest, not deceptive, no phonies like himself.

Dwight knew he should be feeling something, but what? Grief should set in instead of this peculiar numbness, like the Novocain the dentist once shot into his cheek. He had chewed the inside of his mouth raw for the sake of the rubbery sensation. He stared at the body in the box. He glanced over at his mom, his grandmother, their faces undone with run-ning makeup and tears they daubed away with wadded balls of tissue. He might as well get started. He blinked hard, fluttered his eyelids, willing the floodgates to open. He could hear the dry squeak of his own eyeballs. Nothing. Nothing at all.

Dwight understood he wasn't going to get to weep. This was grief itself, this gaping hole where his grandfather had always stood or some-times sat in that perpetual rocker, always spinning his wild stories, but now inexplicably, irreplaceably gone, like solid ground had given way, and the mountains themselves had collapsed. All those stories he told that Dwight was never quite sure whether to believe or disbelieve, about walk-ing all the way west with a cow, the old man saved the most unbelievable story for last. Sitting, not out on the porch during a summer visit, but up late at night in the dying autumn with an upset stomach, Pop would just up and leave, walk out of the world of the living, leaving behind only a wrinkled husk of himself to lay out in the box, while he headed for the strangest country of all.

The service began with prayers and hymns, all said and sung in the raw nasal twang of this country church that made him wince. Like tuning a radio and coming across the steel guitar jangle of country music, before he kept going to the more familiar rock 'n' roll station. Whoever said country was cool?

He heard the doors at the back of the church. A muffled cough. His father slid into the pew next to him. He nodded curtly at Dwight, mouthed, "I'm sorry." Then he stared straight ahead at the casket and the preacher and the kind words being said over the new owner of the casket.

Dwight was dumbfounded. Not only was his dad here and running late—the man who prized punctuality above all virtues—he was unkempt. Dwight stared at the side of his father's face, at the small scab at the sharp bend of his jawbone where his razor had missed a patch of west-coast stubble and left a red nick. His father was such a fastidious man. At work he never rolled his cuffs, nor loosened his tie or unbuttoned his collar. He abhorred scuffed shoes. He shined his shoes neatly every Friday on newspaper, lining up his brushes and tins of polish.

Now Dwight stared at the mistake on his father's face. He could reach over and flick away the red scab with his fingertip and make his father's face bleed that single red bubble of mortality. He giggled at the terrible thought, and he couldn't stop. He bent forward in the pew, gasping, holding his hands over his mouth, laughing louder. He could feel his father's and then his mother's hands running up and down his back, gently and then more frantically as his fit continued. He couldn't help himself.

Finally his father yanked him upright in the pew, flashed him the dark look that said: "What is your problem? Why can't you straighten up, grow up, fly right? Why are you such a disappointment?"

With his father's disapproval, Dwight could finally contain himself, get a grip as his giggling jag subsided.

On it went interminably, the droning eulogy, the twangy choir, all the tears and snuffling in the pews around him. It was a funeral after all, a pall on the church. He had not realized how many lives had been touched by this one man, not a shriveled thing in the box they were about to bury on the mountainside. They stood and mournfully sang Wylie's favorite hymns, tunes the old man was always humming to himself out on the porch. "Just As I Am." "The Old Rugged Cross."

Then it was over, the box hoisted on the broad shoulders of Pop's neighbors, in white shirts, bad ties, ill-fitting suits. Strong men, with limbs like the plow-horses and trees they cut, they staggered up the red-carpeted aisle, out the double doors under the weight of Wylie in the box and their unbearable grief.

They loaded their cargo into the hearse, the family fit into the limousine, and the congregation scattered across the gravel lot to their dusty sedans and pick-ups.

The cortege went less than a quarter-mile over a wooden bridge over Beaverdam Creek, bumping down a washed-out road. Cows lined the barbed-wire fence on either side. Dwight watched the stupid creatures watching the slow procession.

They parked in mud at the bottom of the hill, while the hearse went on ahead, bumping up the grade as far as was safe, then pulled to the side, angled, so the box wouldn't come flying out when the pallbearers opened the back. These were big men, but their brows glowed with sweat, their sleeves pulled high on their straining forearms as they carried Wylie Rominger uphill to his final rest.

Meanwhile, the mourners picked their way up the mountainside, planting feet and canes and walkers in the slick grass, following in single file a faint trail where cows had traversed the slope on the way to greener cuds. Halfway up, they entered the graveyard, the stones here arranged upright by design rather than scattered by nature, a half-acre square of pristine grass fenced off from the hungering herds.

At the graveside, everyone leaned at an angle. With nothing to hold onto, it took sheer will to stand on this piece of earth. He could hear the arthritic crack of old knees all about him. His mother had her arm crooked around her mother. His father had his right leg extended, his hands pressing on their backs, propping them up, making sure Gram or Mom didn't topple backwards. Dwight felt the uneven ground beneath his shoes. His leather soles slipped on the dewy grass. Every muscle strained in his inclined calves.

The shovels were speared into the mound of clay by the rectangular hole. The men wrestled the box over the pit. The wreath of flowers slipped down the lid of the sloping casket.

The preacher's slow words drifted over psalms written by a shepherd minding a flock in faraway hills in another time. *I will lift up mine eyes unto the hills.* Wylie's favorite Bible verse.

His eyes swept across the hills on the horizon. Over that ridge lay Tennessee and the way west. It was gorgeous up here. The blue mountains ringed the high pastures, cows quietly grazed in the sun, the farmhouses dotted along the quick and tumbling waters of Beaverdam Creek below. A few high white clouds swept their shadows over the mottled hillsides. The leaves of the timber had gone to gold and red in those tracts beside the evergreen hemlock, the thickets of laurel and rhododendron.

It was almost over when his eyes lighted on the row of markers, just above the open hole where they were going to plug Pop. He spied a tattered American flag waving before one marker, and then did a double-take when he thought he saw his name. He squinted harder at the stone, holding his breath, waiting for the *amens* to end, and as everyone headed gingerly downhill to the waiting cars, Dwight made his way uphill.

It was left to Dad to climb back up and fetch Dwight.

"Son, it's time to go to the house. Gram and your mom are waiting. We can come back after they finish the grave."

Dwight paid no mind; he was bent over the wrong grave, not even his own grandfather's, muttering to himself. "Look, it's true. It was all true. Like he said."

"Of course," his father replied in confusion. "You ready to go?"

But Dwight kept staring at the gravestone that carried part of his own name and much of his childhood, weeping at long last until he could no longer read the inscription DWIGHT SPARKS, BORN BEAVERDAM 1898. DIED IN AIR COMBAT, FRANCE, 1918.

DEADWOOD

They wandered the house after the mourners had left the condolences and casseroles. So much food it seemed they would never have to cook again, the kitchen table and the counters were crowded with fruit pies and cakes, green beans and squash, platters of pork and fried chicken.

Gram sat in the parlor, stunned, red-eyed, staring out the window. His mother was caught between kitchen and parlor, wringing her hands in a dishtowel, trying to clean up amid the chaos of her grief. His father sat on the edge of the sofa, going through a shoebox of yellowed papers between his feet, frowning at Pop's last will and testament.

Dwight stepped out into the autumn chill. He tried sitting on the porch swing, but the chains were rusty and creaked ominously. He could hear his weight pulling against the bolt in the ceiling over the porch, and he worried that the half-rotted and weathered contraption would break and send him flying out into the yard. The wind blew and the rocker at the end of the porch swayed.

Ghosts, Dwight scowled.

He stomped across the yard and kicked the stump of the apple tree, the dead roots reaching into a crumbly clay. Inside the woodshed, forgotten logs, a rusting maul, the iron wedges. He picked up the hammer, a hefty twenty-pounder. He tapped the wedge into the grain of the stump and then swung the hammer overhead, missed the wedge, and felt the sting vibrate through his hands. He spit into his hands—what for? He wasn't sure—although he'd seen this before in cartoons, the bulky strongman about to hit the strength meter at the carnival. He rubbed his palms against the smooth handle. He lifted the hammer overhead, and brought it down, this time hitting the wedge with a pleasant pealing ring, driving it halfway through the length of wood. He ripped the wood in half with his bare hands and felt better.

He began to cut the apple wood his grandfather had left behind, too old and sick to cut more kindling. Winter was coming on, and the fire was burning what little was left. It was something he could do for his Gram.

He worked up a sweat and unhooked the brass fasteners of his overalls, and slipped off his sweatshirt, then rehooked the galluses. Each time he swung the maul he made the iron wedge sing out, the wood cracking straight down the grain, then he stacked the splits in a corner. He swiped at his nose with his knuckles, and then rubbed grit in his eyes just to prove he wouldn't cry too easily.

He thought of Pop sitting in this very shed whittling a toy pop-gun when he was a boy throwing a hissy fit. How kind a man. What a shitty kid.

Dwight didn't see his father standing in the doorway, watching with a strange look that seemed almost like admiration. "Hey, John Henry."

"Who?

"John Henry, steel driving man."

"This is wood, not steel."

His father held out a folded piece of paper. "Here, this is yours."

Dwight leaned the hammer against the stump. He opened up the paper, an official looking statement from Pioneer Mutual Equities, a long list of figures. "What's this?"

"Evidently, your inheritance."

"You know I'm no good at math."

"No, you need to figure it out. You need to think about what you want to do with it all."

His dad leaned against the doorway and looked out into the dusk toward the house, his hands digging deep into his pockets, jiggling his loose change, his car keys, a habit of his for as long as Dwight could remember.

"Your grandfather was a man of surprises. I can't say that he and I were ever that close, but he knew how much I cared for your mother and you, so I suppose he tolerated me for that reason. I had no idea what to talk to him about, having never raised tobacco or milked cows or been much for the great outdoors, and he of course had no idea what I did for a living. But he must have been listening when I used to spout off about stocks and mutual funds. Rather than just talking I should have taken my own advice and invested like he did."

Dwight was aware he was getting sawdust and sweat all over the official looking document. He kept trying to hand the paper back, but his dad shook his head.

"No, you keep it. If I'm reading the will right, all that's yours upon graduation from college or the age of twenty-five, whichever comes first. But in your case, sport, it better be school."

Dwight wiped away sweat from his brow, and felt the tears welling in the dry sockets. The figures were all fuzzy now.

"It's your money, but for Godsakes, Son, don't go out and spend this all on something stupid. You don't need a new car. That Vega still has a lot of mileage left. This could be the down payment on a house or bankroll for a business, or maybe grad school. Not everybody gets this kind of leg up this early in adulthood," Dad was saying as Dwight kept staring at the piece of white paper.

In the dusky shed, in the shadow of the mountains, in the darkness of his grief, the bottom line figure of $15,013.97 flashed at him, a lifetime of nickels and dimes traded for all the tall tales he'd heard as a boy and secretly measured himself against.

WESTWARD, 2000

Dwight Martin never understood why travelers read novels in airports, noses pressed to the latest best-seller about serial killers or lawyers, while real life streamed about them in the terminal, a thousand and one stories on their way to different destinies and unforeseen fates. Dwight never tired of people-watching, wondering what their lives were really like.

He had sat in so many airports over the years, most of his career in corporate America had been spent in these anonymous concourses, identical from city to city, all abbreviated names on the arrival/departure boards. He could sometimes only keep track by checking the souvenir shops, what sports team was featured on the T-shirts, but now there were so many new franchises popping up, he had lost that frame of playful reference.

No one walked anymore. Everyone had to run breathless across concourses, down the moving sidewalks only to settle into another seat in another row by another gate waiting for another seat on another plane that was late, waiting always for his heart to quit his pounding, his breath to catch its gait.

The man beside him was pecking and mousing at his laptop, a man, much like himself, balding, chins, a pot belly, a wrinkled blazer, the wheeled portable suitcase beside him. Probably he had a last-minute report to fax back to the office, or a Powerpoint presentation to tweak for the client waiting tomorrow in some downtown citadel of blazing glass. Dwight stole a look and saw naked flesh, genitalia. The guy was surfing for porn, hot slut girls in all the familiar and acrobatic positions.

Dwight liked people-watching, but mostly only when they kept their clothes on. He liked guessing their stories, but the reality of their sad desires was all too depressing.

Dwight moved a few rows down. It would be another two-hour layover.

He could call home, if that would make any difference. His son Will would answer the phone in that flat monotone he had developed. Or Janet would have that snippy voice, wanting to know when he was getting home, outlining the latest disaster of appliance or appearance or arrears that would need his immediate attention.

In the beginning, he remembered coming home, happy to kiss his bride, lift their baby from his crib gurgling into the air, shaking the laughter out of him. Now whenever he raised his arms over his head, he heard something crack in his shoulders.

He needed a vacation but that would only mean going to the airport. He hated to fly, to travel. If only he could go somewhere new, different in his life.

It had been a bad trip. Hostile encounter, glum managers around a conference table with pastries on paper plates, as he went over the latest plan for motivation and morale improvement. He was in the people business, making their workers work harder, happier, making the price of their fully-vested stock go ever up.

He wrote a newsletter on motivation, trying to keep managers more focused on a bigger picture than the profit margins of their division. Technical writing. What his father would have been proud of, if he were still alive, while his mother acted accepting but not so secretly disappointed. He could hear her sighing, that eternally tired exhalation that punctuated all conversations when he called her retirement villa.

At least, Janet didn't bother to hide her disappointments after, what? Fifteen years next month. (He got out his index cards, jotted a reminder: don't forget anniversary, double check, what precious metal is 15th?)

How he used to come home ravenous with desire, the stewardesses (pardon, air staff now), those women with wings pinned over their breasts, offering pillows and drinks, who had always driven him wild. He would come through the door, and Janet was willing in those days, pressing her mouth against his. Then one thing leads to another, and then to nine months and then years spent cradling and caring for this new life and suddenly the little boy is grown into a sullen stranger who mopes about the house. He nods curtly when called, drawls his monosyllables, and spends most of his day plugged to a screen, whether TV or computer or video, a pallid-faced boy who shuns direct sunlight, the outdoors.

That was what awaited him when he returned home, still hours and another connection away.

For now, he could remain anonymous, outside of his life, watching the endless river of air travelers streaming across the concourse, harried businessmen, college students, young women, all different races, ages, all of humanity it seemed, trying to make their connecting flights to the next tarmac, the terra incognito of their lives. There goes a happy fellow, that's a real bastard there, someone he'd like to know at another time, a woman he could fall in love with. But as Dwight watched the crowd, he slowly had the unshakeable sensation that he was being watched as well.

Across the way through the swarm of passengers, Dwight found himself eyed by a strange trio, a pair of pioneer lads with their cow. Historic Photos of Appalachia was now on exhibit at a local museum, whatever city he was in now. It was a life-sized poster of two boys in straw hats, their arms draped over the bossed horns of a large cow. Dwight smiled. How long had it been since he'd seen a cow?

Oh, yes. Remember?

Worried about Will and the amount of quality time he spent with the boy, Dwight tried a father-son outing, a walk along in the new nature trail that ran through the wooded park near the suburb where they lived. The green leaves overhead, the twisting path around rocks and bushes, places to hide and play, pretending to be Indians or bandits or whatever boys liked to make believe in this new millennium. Will brought up the rear, hands in his pockets, this look of absolute, utter boredom written all over his changing face. The boy had been disappointed the park had no website he could click on for a virtual tour instead of this tedious stroll through unrewarding reality.

Dwight tried to point out things of interest. But he didn't know the names, the genus, what wisdom he could impart about this particular specimen, other than, "There's certainly a big tree."

He scouted the ground ahead, wondering what would happen if he found a fossil or an arrowhead like his grandfather had pulled from the dirt pile almost by magic so many years before. Did they even make ancient arrowheads anymore? Dwight wondered, or had the whole of the country been so excavated and rearranged and replanted and redesigned into facsimiles of the past, that no such authentic fossils or artifacts remained? Everything was in a museum somewhere or in the cyberspace the boy inhabited.

Then they were at the end of the park, the boundary. What was that smell? It was familiar, the mix of grass hay, piss and shit, a distant scent from across decades, the smell of Pop's farm.

But here at the back of an industrial park, what seemed impossible—a cow and her calf, grazing by the fence. And Will looked at him with something bordering on fear in the earnest blue eyes inherited from his mom. And Dwight felt that surge of love again for the both of them, wife and son, his family.

They watched the calf nuzzle under the mother, greedily seeking out the teat. The cow eyed them warily through the chain mesh.

"Go ahead, touch him, go ahead."

The boy wiggled his fingertips through the diamond spaces of the chain-link. The cow lowed and backed away, but not before the fingertips which had only known the hard mouse of a computer had connected with the warm brown fur, the velvety nap of the heifer.

———

"Flight 4088 now boarding."

Dwight shook off his memory and remembered where he was, where he was going, the ticket in his shirt pocket. Sighing, he stretched himself a last time in anticipation of having to squeeze into the aisle seat of an overbooked flight. He gathered his briefcase, his overnight bag and rolled his meager belongings, artifacts from his real life, toward the gate.

The boys and the cow watched from the photograph taken nearly a hundred years ago, staring into the future.

"Psst, psst."

"What?"

"Think we can move yet, Wylie?"

"The Camera Lady said to hold still."

"How long?"

"Guess until she says we can move."

"Don't smile now. Desperadoes don't smile."

"I ain't smiling? You?"

"Naw. Look brave now."

"Stop it, Dwight. You're going to make me laugh."

And the cow tossed her horned head. "You too, Ivy. Hold still. Lady's going to make us famous."

The cow mooed but did not move. The light captured them, looking westward, their faces full of wonder at what lay ahead.

END

ACKNOWLEDGMENTS

Though writing is largely a solitary art, no novel gets written without a host of help from early readers and supporters. I'd like to thank Lewis Buzbee, Virginia Weir, Ann Scott Knight, Nan Cuba, Faith Holsaert, and the tribe of the Warren Wilson College MFA Program, as well as the Asheville Area Arts Council for grant support, and the Virginia Center for the Creative Arts. Thanks also to Amy Rogers and Betsy Thorpe of Novello Festival Press for seeing this book through its birth. My deepest gratitude goes to my wife, Cynthia, for seeing me through twenty years of writing.

NOVELLO FESTIVAL PRESS

Novello Festival Press, under the auspices of the Public Library of Charlotte and Mecklenburg County and through the publication of books of literary excellence, enhances the awareness of the literary arts, helps discover and nurture new literary talent, celebrates the rich diversity of the human experience, and expands the opportunities for writers and readers from within our community and its surrounding geographic region.

THE PUBLIC LIBRARY OF CHARLOTTE AND MECKLENBURG COUNTY

For more than a century, the Public Library of Charlotte and Mecklenburg County has provided essential community service and outreach to the citizens of the Charlotte area. Today, it is one of the premier libraries in the country—named "Library of the Year" and "Library of the Future" in the 1990s—with 24 branches, 1.6 million volumes, 20,000 videos and DVDs, 9,000 maps and 8,000 compact discs. The Library also sponsors a number of community-based programs, from the award-winning Novello Festival of Reading, a celebration that accentuates the fun of reading and learning, to branch programs for young people and adults. The Library was a winner of the 2006 National Awards for Museum and Library Service, the nation's highest honor for libraries and museums that make their communities better places to live.

THE COLD MOUNTAIN FOUNDATION

The Public Library of Charlotte and Mecklenburg County and Novello Festival Press gratefully acknowledge the Cold Mountain Foundation for its generous sponsorship of the 2009 Novello Literary Award.

Established by Asheville writer Charles Frazier, the Cold Mountain Foundation is pleased to support the work of Novello Festival Press and its mission of giving a voice to Carolina writers.